reckless driver

reckless driver

Lisa Vice

A DUTTON BOOK

DUTTON
Published by the Penguin Group
Penguin Books USA Inc., 375 Hudson Street,
New York, New York 10014, U.S.A.
Penguin Books Ltd, 27 Wrights Lane,
London W8 5TZ, England
Penguin Books Australia Ltd, Ringwood,
Victoria, Australia
Penguin Books Canada Ltd, 10 Alcorn Avenue,
Toronto, Ontario, Canada M4V 3B2
Penguin Books (N.Z.) Ltd, 182–190 Wairau Road,
Auckland 10, New Zealand

Penguin Books Ltd, Registered Offices:
Harmondsworth, Middlesex, England

First published by Dutton, an imprint of Dutton Signet,
a division of Penguin Books USA Inc.
Distributed in Canada by McClelland & Stewart Inc.

First Printing, March, 1995
10   9   8   7   6   5   4   3   2   1

The author wishes to thank the Cummington Community of the Arts, Hunter College, and the Ludwig R. Vogelstein Foundation.

"The House of Blue Lights" received a 1992 PEN Syndicated Fiction Award.

Excerpts of this novel, in somewhat different form, have appeared in *Farmer's Market, The Bridge, Bluff City, Rohwedder, Welter, Plainswoman, The Time of Our Lives,* and *Word of Mouth 2.*

 REGISTERED TRADEMARK—MARCA REGISTRADA

Library of Congress Cataloging-in-Publication Data

Vice, Lisa
    Reckless driver / Lisa Vice.
        p. cm.
    ISBN 0-525-93863-X
    I. Title.
PS3572.I253R4 1995
813\.54–dc20   94-33579
                                                                                            CIP

Printed in the United States of America
Set in Sabon
Designed by Leonard Telesca

PUBLISHER'S NOTE

This is a work of fiction. Names, characters, places, and incidents either are the products of the author's imagination or are used fictitiously, and any resemblance to actual persons, living or dead, events, or locales is entirely coincidental.

This book is printed on acid-free paper.
∞

*for Martha
who believes
and for Zoe
who came back*

reckless driver

dandelions

I'm six going on seven and I hardly ever cry anymore, but Mommy says when I was a little baby, I cried so bad she had to stick me out in the coal shed. She says she couldn't hear herself think with all the racket I made, I was such a naughty baby. She says when I was born I had me a head of black hair and she figured the nurse was bringing her the wrong kid. But when I was two years old, my hair turned blonde and it's been blonde ever since. Just like Marilyn Monroe's is, Daddy says. He makes me sit on the arm of the davenport and cross my legs like Marilyn Monroe.

Mommy says when I was two years old I was such a handful she ended up going to the hospital to get her plumbing fixed so she'd never have to go through that again. She was in the hospital for almost two weeks but she acted like she was just going to the grocery store for a loaf of bread when she left. "I'll be right back," she told me, because otherwise I'd've had a fit. When she didn't come back, I had a fit anyhow. I cried and called her name and I didn't hardly sleep or eat. Daddy had to keep the screen doors locked because I kept trying to get out of the house and go up to the grocery store to get her.

When Mommy finally came home I acted like I didn't even know who she was. I kept whispering to Daddy, pointing at Mommy and asking him who that lady was. I wouldn't even give her a kiss or let her come near me. She says it made her pretty mad.

One day I was out back running around and Daddy said, "Lana, go pick some flowers for your mommy." I went and picked a big bunch of dandelions and handed them to her. She was sitting on a blanket under the cherry tree. After that, she says I remembered who she was.

lace curtains

Abbie's the oldest of us two kids. Exactly five years and thirty-two days older than me. But she's not the first baby Mommy had. Shirley Jean was Mommy's first little baby. She got her name from Shirley Temple. Shirley Jean slept in a bureau drawer with a blanket for a mattress. That was back when Daddy was in the war. Then Shirley Jean died and got buried in Massachusetts where Mommy was born. Mommy says they couldn't afford a decent gravestone. Just a metal marker that says BABY. After she buried Shirley Jean, Mommy moved to Indiana. That's when Abbie came along. Abbie got her name from Mamaw Franklin. But her middle name, Irene, is from a song.

Mommy says she wishes she never left home. She says Indiana is full of Holy Rollers and a bunch of people that think their shit don't stink. She used to wax her floors like the rest of them, but now she doesn't give a damn.

I try to tidy up the house for Mommy and I sweep the kitchen. But no one ever comes over to visit excepting Uncle Cleon. He comes over the first Sunday of the month. All he cares about is having himself a home-cooked meal since he's a bachelor living in a furnished room clear over in Kokomo.

I remember back when Mommy still tried and that time we did spring cleaning. We took down the lace curtains and washed them in hot sudsy water. The suds turned grey and the water smelled like the dusty curtains. I got to pull the wet lace and hook it over the nails on the wooden curtain stretchers so they'd dry in the right shape. We laid them on the grass to let the sun bleach them. They smelled so good out there in the hot sun with the cherry blossoms floating down over the grass like snow.

We opened the windows and polished the furniture with lemon polish. We put dust rags on the broom to get at all the cobwebs up on the ceiling. Abbie got to use the vacuum cleaner and when she vacuumed Daddy's chair she found a quarter and three dimes. I started crying since I wanted to have me some money too. Abbie said I was a spoiled brat. Mommy said, "Don't fight, you two."

I got to smear Bon Ami all over the windows, inside and out, and Mommy and Abbie came around after me and wiped it all off with old torn-up sheets that got so dirty we couldn't believe our eyes. Mommy sang "Zip-a-Dee-Do-Dah" and Abbie sang "Frère Jacques" and we got all the windows clean.

Now the curtains smell like dust and they're all ripped up from where my dog Gretchie gets her toenails caught in the lace when she jumps up to look out the window to see me coming down the sidewalk. Now the whole house is a mess but Mommy says she wouldn't be caught dead doing spring cleaning again as long as she lives.

chicken little

Abbie told me once that Mommy is what you call two-faced. When I was real little I used to think that meant I could sit on her lap and pull her skin down like a rubber mask to get a good look at her other face.

Mommy's sitting at the table now having a cigarette for dessert. I go over and try to sit on her lap but she says I can't on account of her and Abbie are getting ready to have a talk. Abbie's doing the supper dishes and Mommy's keeping her company. It's private, Abbie says.

"You're too big to be sitting on anybody's lap anyhow," Mommy says. "Nearly seven years old and too big for your own britches."

"I'll bet you're not too big for your old man's lap," Daddy says. He's sitting in his chair in the front room, slapping his legs.

"You asked for it," Mommy says.

When I sit on his lap, I feel like my head's about to fall right off. He's got one of them chairs that's a La-Z-Boy and it tips way back so we're kind of laying down when we sit in it. He squeezes me real tight up against his prickly whiskers. I feel like my head's about to fall right off and roll across the floor. Then my arms and my legs'll fall off too.

"Here's the church, here's the steeple. Open the door and look at all the people." I wiggle my fingers in Daddy's face.

"That's old Hairy Ass Truman." Daddy points at a picture in the newspaper of a guy with a hat on. "He used to be president. Before we got General Ike."

When Daddy starts rocking and jiggling his legs the way he does, the newspaper in front of us gets all shaky. I keep trying to

4

read what it says, but the words are too teensy for me to get a good look at. Anyhow, I can only read some words like the ones in *Chicken Little*. That's this book I took out from the library, but I never gave it back. I didn't mean to keep it. It ended up so overdue I was scared to bring it in. Miss Fippin—she's the librarian—never says a word about it when I go to get me some more books. She just asks me if I'm planning on reading up the whole library and I tell her yes.

I keep *Chicken Little* under my mattress. I can read it all by myself anytime I want to. The little chicken finds out the sky is falling. She tells all the other animals about it, the dog and the pig and the horse, but nobody listens to her.

Daddy says okeydoke. He's done with me sitting on his lap, so he pushes that doohickey on the side of his chair and lets me go.

pretty boy

Mommy says Neila Grimes is the biggest nib nose that ever lived. It's just our kind of luck she ended up on the other end of our party line so we can never say a peep without having to worry about the whole town of Windfall finding out about it the minute we hang up the phone.

When you pick up the phone and say hello, there's this click and then you hear Neila Grimes breathing. She never says a thing, just breathes. Every once in a while when she's listening in, her parakeet Buddy starts saying, "I'm a pretty boy" over and over again while you're trying to talk.

One time Mommy was right in the middle of telling Winona Flowers about how she was thinking she might try becoming a Nova Cosmetics Girl when Mommy said right out, "D'ya think that'd be a good idea, Neila?" Mommy said later on, old Neila Grimes didn't even change the way she was breathing.

Another time, Mommy got so sick and tired of the whole thing she hollered in her meanest voice, "If you don't get offa this party line right this minute, Neila Grimes, I'm going to come over to your house and wring your frigging bird's neck."

But Neila Grimes didn't hang up. She just acted like she hadn't heard what Mommy said. And that bird of hers kept on saying, "Pretty boy. I'm a pretty boy."

france

There aren't any pictures of me from back when I was a baby. When it came time to go pick them up, Mommy had just spent her last cent on the grocery bill and then she never did get around to getting them. She says if you've seen one baby, you've seen them all. There's a bunch of baby pictures of Abbie sucking her fingers the way she always did and there's a baby bracelet with little tiny beads that spell out Abbie's name but I don't have one of them either. All I have from when I was a baby is my teddy bear I got my first Christmas. He has patches on his hands and feet from where I chewed them off before I knew any better. In the summer, Mommy used to put on patches made from old sheets and in the winter she put on wool ones but she quit doing that a long time ago so my bear still has to keep the wool patches on no matter how hot out it gets.

I like to go up in the attic and look at all the old pictures. There's one of Mommy when she was a kid in her crocheted bathing suit with a big bow tied in her hair and there's a bunch of her and Auntie Thelma leaning up against some car showing off their legs.

Daddy was a GI in France and there's a picture we have of him and all these other guys dressed in uniforms. He's got a hat on and he's so young it's kind of hard to figure out which one is him. I always have to look at all the rows and rows of faces and touch each one till I pick him out. Once I find him, I can't figure out how come I didn't see him right away. He's got his hat tipped forward and he's staring right out at me.

I guess Daddy's what you call handsome. He's real tall and kind of skinny and when he smiles his green eyes sparkle like broken glass by the side of the road. His hair is the color of wet pennies. Mommy says when she first laid eyes on him, she thought she'd died and gone to heaven.

I know he was in France because he sings about it all the time. "There's a place in France where the women wear no pants and the men go around with their ding-dongs hanging down." He always holds himself like he's got to go pee when he sings that song. Mommy says, "Quit it, Floyd. Innocent eyes are watching." He just laughs and tries to give her a kiss.

Him and Mommy fight about France all the time, about how Daddy had a girlfriend over there named Marie. He was wishing he could marry her but then he had to marry Mommy. Abbie says she can remember clear back to when I was born and Daddy wanted to name me Marie. He claimed it was after some pinup girl he liked, but Mommy said she was going to name me Lana after one of her movie stars, Lana Turner. So then he tried to name me Lana Marie but Mommy got so worked up about it I ended up not even getting a real middle name.

Daddy always calls me Lana Marie when we dance together. We glide around the front room to that song he likes, "Stranger in Paradise." I stand on top of his stocking feet and put my head against his tummy and turn my face sideways. Daddy smells like cigarettes. His belt buckle scrapes into me and I can feel his zipper. I'm like one of them big rag dolls they have in the catalog, the kind you strap onto your feet and dance with. Daddy sings the words and my neck hurts and we dance.

The last time I was up in the attic looking through the box of pictures I found this one of a big hill covered with white crosses. When I asked Daddy about it he said, "Gimme that!" and snatched it away. There's this one picture of him when he was a little boy and he's got a dress on. He says that's because Mamaw Franklin wanted to have a girl so bad she thought she could turn him into one. It's a good thing the army got to him when it did. The army made a man out of a boy. He says it put hair on his chest.

"Suppertime," Mommy calls so I put the pictures away and go downstairs. I bring the picture of Daddy in his uniform with me so everybody can have a look at it.

"I'm real proud I served in World War Two," Daddy says.

"Yuck," Abbie says like she doesn't even hear him. She's staring down at her bowl of navy bean soup like she's hoping Daddy'll tip the table over the way he did that time he got mad about Mommy laughing. But tonight he just pounds his fist on the table so hard our spoons rattle.

"Look at me!" he hollers and everybody does. He's sitting there in his chair at the head of the table where he always sits. "I'm telling you. If it wasn't for me, Hitler'd still be alive and kicking. There wouldn't be food on this table. This world wouldn't be safe if it wasn't for fellows like me." He's got this look on his face like he's waiting for one of us to say something. But nobody says a word. Then he starts slapping the ketchup bottle so he can put some in his soup and we all start eating real slow like nothing's going on.

Hitler's this guy that stuck a whole bunch of people in some ovens over in Germany. I saw pictures of it in a magazine. At first I didn't even think it was people but Abbie said it was. "That's the whole reason we had the war," she said. "Hitler didn't like the way they went to church, so he tried to kill them all. The Americans changed all that."

I bet what Daddy did was he marched right up to Hitler's house in broad daylight and went right on in without even knocking. There was old Hitler sitting in his chair watching TV and drinking a beer. Daddy said, "Hitler, your goose is cooked." Then Daddy shot him just the way the Rifleman does the bad guys on TV.

9

down cellar

When me and Mommy do the washing, what we do first is we boil Daddy's hankies. We use that big black pot Mommy cooks green beans and potatoes in. We put it on the back burner and they boil and boil and then we take them down cellar to the washing machine.

It's pretty dark down cellar even though we have a light bulb. The walls and the floor are dusty old cobwebby cement. Sometimes when I lie in bed at night I get to thinking about how there's this guy down cellar hanging on the wall. It's like I can see him right through the floorboards. He's practically bare naked except for this cloth wrapped around him like a diaper. His wrists and his ankles are tied together and he just hangs there moaning. I told Mommy about it and she said I sure had a wild imagination. When I told her sometimes he comes up to my bed and grabs me she said she knew what I needed and made me take a big spoonful of milk of magnesia. It tastes just like chalk. When I think of that guy down cellar I act like I've got me a big whip and I go down there and whip him good just like Zorro would do. But I'd never really go down cellar by myself. Not in a million years. You couldn't pay me to.

The ceiling's so low, when she walks down the cellar stairs Mommy has to bend her head so she won't bump it. She's so tall even in her stocking feet she's almost tall as Daddy. It's always wet down cellar so that's why we have the sump pump sitting in this drain hole in the floor. When it rains a whole lot, it pumps all the water out of the cellar. That way when we have a flood, the house won't float away. A little frog lives in the water around the sump pump, but the soap from the washing machine always kills him eventually. Then another frog comes. Me and Mommy name all the frogs Freddy.

Mommy fills up the washing machine with the whites first while the water's still hot. Then we wash the darks in the same water to save on the utility bill. It doesn't really matter if the water's dirty already since the clothes are dark anyhow. The washing machine swishes around and Mommy sits on the cellar steps and watches it and smokes one of her cigarettes. She lets me blow out the matches. I love the way burnt matches smell.

"I used to help Grammy when I was a little girl like you," Mommy says. She fixes my ponytail that's come all loose. "I used to wear a big pink bow tied on top of my head. It was the style. Nobody wore ponytails like now."

I try to catch Freddy but Mommy gets mad.

"You want to electrocute yourself? Don't go messing with what you don't know. When I was a little kid I practically died messing around with what I had no business with."

"How come?"

"I was fooling around with this stick I had. Poking it in the ground and in the bushes. Then I poked it in a hole in this tree we had out back. Turned out it was a wild-beehive. Them bees took off after me so fast I didn't know what hit me. They were stinging me like crazy. On my eyes and my lips and between my fingers. Even up under my dress you-know-where. My brother Carl came out and started beating the bees offa me with his fists."

What happened was Grammy wrapped her all up in little strips of rags she soaked in water and baking soda. Mommy's face got so swelled up she couldn't hardly see. Then Grammy unwrapped her and smeared mud all over her. When that dried, she wrapped her up again in the baking soda rags.

"They figured I was going to kick the bucket. Or else end up blind," Mommy says. "For over a week I did nothing but lie there like a mummy. But here I am."

She blows smoke out the dark holes of her nose when she laughs. Then she gets up and starts feeding me the hankies through the wringer.

"Pay attention, now," she says. "Make sure you don't get your fingers caught. The wringer can grab ahold of your hand and pull your whole arm through till it's flat as a pancake if you're not careful."

When all the clothes've been washed and rinsed and put through the wringer we say good-bye to Freddy and take the clothes upstairs in a basket. I stand out by the rhubarb with the grass tickling my legs and help Mommy hang them up on the clothesline in the sun. The sheets flap in the breeze and the hankies are practically dry when I hand them to her.

shreida huckaby

S hreida Huckaby lives right smack dab in the middle of Windfall, up on Main Street next to the parking lot behind Purtlebaugh's Grocery Store. She lives in a great big white house with red shutters and white ruffled curtains in every one of her windows. Mommy says she married into money but it didn't do her one bit of good. She lives in that great big house with her fine china, linen tablecloths, and the prettiest cut glass you ever laid eyes on, but she's still the sorriest girl in town.

That's because she's been to Logansport. It happened right after her little girl Mayline was born. Mayline was a baby in diapers when Shreida started going through the change. That's when her husband Booth started carrying on with some lady from across the county line. It drove Shreida out of her mind. Mommy says the men in white coats had to come and take Shreida away. Mayline went off to live with Shreida's sister-in-law Caroline up in Indianapolis. Caroline just wants to do Shreida dirty since she got her hands on the Huckaby family money. She won't even get out of the car to say hello when she brings Mayline over to visit and she's always trying to fix it so Shreida can't see her own kid.

Shreida lives in that great big house with her daddy, Carlton Purkey. He's the one Mommy says you'd better cross the street to get away from if you see him coming towards you. He always walks around town with his hand in his pants playing with himself and spitting big gobs of chewing tobacco in the gutters. I can always tell when I'm walking uptown if he's been by already from the brown spit on the cement. He even spits in the water fountain in front of the pool hall so if you want to have a drink you have to go to the other water fountain clear down on the other end of West Jackson Street.

One thing about Shreida Huckaby is she's as pretty as a movie star. She's got what you call auburn hair and it kind of falls over her eye and she pushes it back with her hand. Daddy says Shreida's stacked like Marilyn Monroe and he draws curves in the air. Mommy says she's the spitting image of Lauren Bacall but looks can't help you if you're unlucky in love. I ought to know, she says.

Most of the time Shreida Huckaby walks around Windfall in her pink terry-cloth bedroom slippers and an old faded house-dress talking to herself and looking for her husband Booth. If you see her and say hello she just looks right through you. But on Sundays she gets herself all fixed up and goes to church and acts normal. She puts on a big white hat with a black ribbon around the brim, wears lipstick, and has on a black-and-white polka-dot dress and high heels.

One time she brought Mayline to church and I got to have a good look at her for myself. Mayline is as skinny as a rail and her hair's so blonde it's nearly white. You can see her pale pink scalp peeking right through. Her eyes are watery blue with thin white eyelashes and her eyebrows are practically invisible. She was carrying a little straw pocketbook she kept opening and closing with a loud snap all through the sermon. She stood out on the front steps afterwards in her pink lacy dress with about ten crinolines underneath while all the ladies fussed over her and asked her about what grade she was in and all. Her voice was all gravelly sounding like she had a bad cold. Abbie says that's on account of how many times old Shreida's hung her upside down out the window. Something like that's bound to have an effect on your voice box.

Abbie claims she saw it with her own two eyes one time when she was on her way uptown to get a coke. She said what happened was she heard this funny sound like a kitty cat crying and she looked all around and then she looked up and there was Shreida Huckaby dangling Mayline out the upstairs window of her house. Shreida had a dreamy look on her face like she'd just seen a pretty bird land on the telephone wire and she stuck her head out the window to get a better look at it. And there was

Mayline, her mommy hanging onto her by the ankles, crying something awful, her plaid skirt flapping around her head and her yellow cotton underpants out where the whole world could have a look. Mayline was crying and saying, "Please, Mama, please." And her face was bright red the way your tongue gets after you eat a sack of red hots.

Folks say Shreida doesn't mean no harm when she does that. Just every once in a while when Mayline's there to visit, Shreida can't help herself. Usually what happens is somebody'll give Gus Riley a call and he'll have to come uptown and pull Mayline back inside the house.

Shreida always acts like she just woke up from a dream, like she's got no idea what's been going on. It's all on account of how bad she took it when Booth ran off on her. Something like that can't be helped.

jitterbug

D addy got so mad tonight he stomped out to the shed and started playing his Tommy Dorsey record full blast. We didn't get to finish eating supper because he took the bowl of stewed tomatoes and flung it at the wall. Now we've got a big red stain on the wall over by where Mommy sits. Abbie says it'll never come out. I don't even get what it's all about. All I know is Mommy says she's giving him the silent treatment. She says they're heading for divorce number two if he don't watch his step.

I don't remember the first time they tried to get a divorce because I wasn't even born yet. Abbie can barely remember it since she was still in diapers. Mommy says what happened was Daddy got pretty mad and started chasing her around the backyard with a baseball bat. Abbie got so scared she snuck away walking barefoot down the railroad tracks to Mamaw Franklin's house. This was way back when Mamaw was still alive. Abbie sat on Mamaw's front porch and waited for her to get home from the canning factory and when she did, she gave Daddy a talking to, asking him what exactly he meant to do if he caught up to Mommy with that baseball bat. The two of them figured they'd better get a divorce but then later on they decided to give it another try. Then before they knew it, I came along. Mommy says having me was supposed to save their marriage, but it didn't work.

After Mommy and Abbie go off to deliver the Nova Cosmetics, Daddy calls me out to the shed and shows me how he can cook canned beans on the coal stove he's got out there and he gives me a taste. He says he might just move in out there and sleep on his army cot. After he eats, we do this dance together called the jitterbug. He likes to do that because he says it reminds him of back when all the GIs that didn't get sent home in boxes got to come home free as jaybirds. "I'll tell you one thing," he says. "This old world hasn't been the same since the day the troops stopped marching and started jitterbugging."

The shed's got a dirt floor and a workbench where Daddy keeps his toolbox and cans of nails and his paintbrushes and all. Once Daddy let me and Abbie use it as a playhouse. Abbie drew a line in the floor with a pointed stick to divvy it up down the middle so we'd each get half. Then Daddy changed his mind and told us to get out. Abbie says he's an Indian giver.

When Daddy's not around, me and Penny play Annie Annie Over, tossing a rubber ball back and forth over the shed roof. Penny Reeb is my next-door neighbor. She's also my best friend. Lonnie MacAbee and his little brother Butchie are our neighbors on the other side and Lonnie's in the same grade with me and Penny. When we play out in my yard, him and his brother just stand in their yard at the edge of the boundary line watching us. Their hair's so short and blonde they look bald. Mrs. MacAbee won't let them set one foot on our property since she's snubbing Mommy. They used to be friends when they both joined the Homemakers Coffee Hour Club. That was way back when Mommy tried everything. She even won a prize in this contest they had. What you had to do was make your own hat and Mommy made hers out of a bird cage she found in the attic. It even had a stuffed canary sitting inside on a swing. She won first prize and got to take home this plastic cake dish with a lid that's see-through so you can look in and see what kind of cake it is without even taking the lid off. Now Mommy calls Mrs. MacAbee a big fat sow. She says if I go over in their yard, she's liable to sit on me till I pop like a balloon.

the old rugged cross

W hen Daddy sits on the back porch whistling "The Old Rugged Cross," I run around in the wet grass catching lightning bugs so I can smear their lights on my cheeks and make my face glow in the dark.

He's trying to teach me how to whistle so I go and sit on his lap and he shows me how to pucker my lips and blow. I try to whistle the song and he sings it to help me remember the tune.

"I will cling to the old rugged cross. And someday I'll exchange it for a crown," he sings. I blow and blow but I can't hardly make a sound except for my lips puffing air.

Daddy can whistle so pretty it makes me feel like crying. He whistles the regular way just about any song you ask him to and he can whistle for a long time. He also whistles through his hands this special way that nobody else can. He puts his hands together like he's going to cup some water and he moves his fingers while he whistles through his thumbs and he makes all these different sounds and it sounds like some kind of bird.

safety sue

L ana! Psst. You awake?" I sit up in bed and there is Abbie leaning on her elbow watching me. The big full moon is shining in our window. Downstairs, Mommy and Daddy are making their animal sounds.

"You want a Safety Sue story?"

I say OK and I curl up in my covers and get ready to listen. Daddy is grunting. He sounds like he's caught in some kind of tunnel. Mommy is making screechy sounds.

"Once upon a time Safety Sue was walking around and she saw a girl sitting on a rock crying her eyes out. She stopped and touched the girl's head and the girl looked up at Safety Sue for a minute and then she started crying and crying again. Safety Sue sat down next to her on the rock and said, 'What's the matter, little girl? I'm Safety Sue, here to the rescue. So please tell me what's the matter so I can help you.'

"The girl stopped her crying and she sat there sort of hiccuping and sniffling and she thought about how she wished she had a hanky and Safety Sue knew that's what the girl was thinking so she reached right into the pocket of her dress and took out a white hanky with daisies on it and gave it to the girl and she blew her nose and wiped her tears and when she felt a little bit better she told Safety Sue how her mommy gave her permission to wear this pearl pin. It was shaped like a heart and it used to belong to her mamaw so it was real special. What happened was she stopped to look at the tiger lilies on her way to school and the pin dropped right off her dress and then when she was about to reach down to get it she saw this great big black spider with yellow spots on it and it had a little tiny red spot by its head. She

19

was scared that meant it was a black widow. There was her mamaw's pin right underneath where the spider was sitting in its web but she didn't dare try to reach in and get it and that's how come she was crying her eyes out.

"Safety Sue said, 'Show me where.' So they got up and went over to the tiger lilies and the girl pushed back the long leaves real careful and there was the spider and there was the pretty pearl pin shaped like a heart. Safety Sue said, 'Today's your lucky day 'cause I have some string and a safety pin.' Safety Sue took the string and the safety pin out of her pocket and tied the string to the safety pin and opened the pin up so it'd be like a fishhook. Then she dangled it down past the spider. The spider was sitting right smack dab in the middle of the web but it didn't even move an inch and after a couple of tries, Safety Sue hooked onto the heart pin and pulled it up. Then she put it back on the girl's dress.

"Remember what Safety Sue always says?" Abbie asks me.

"Always have a safety pin handy 'cause you never know when you're gonna need it," I say.

"Uh-huh."

"And never ever get yourself so scared you give up. Somebody'll always come along and have a real good idea."

"Right-a-roonie."

"That was a nice one," I tell Abbie. Abbie stands up on her bed and wraps her quilt around her till she's all covered up from head to toe like a cocoon. Then she flops down on her bed. Daddy is snoring. Mommy is sloshing water around in the bathroom. I hold my teddy bear and rock my head back and forth on my pillow. I think about the shell Uncle Cleon brought us back from Florida when he went down there to visit. It sounds like the ocean is inside of it when I put it up to my ear. It's pink and smooth and shiny inside. But on the outside it's got these twisty sharp little points.

paper dolls

S ay you were walking uptown and your underpants fell off. What would you do?" Mommy wants to know. She's sitting at the kitchen table drawing paper dolls. She draws a big bow in the little girl's curly hair and adds some lace to the hem of her dress. She takes a big sip of her coffee and when she puts her cup down there's a red lipstick print on the rim of the white cup. She picks up the scissors and starts cutting. Me and Abbie are on the floor playing with the paper dolls she's already made us. It's raining out so hard it's as dark as nighttime and the wind is rattling the windowpanes. Mommy says if it keeps up much longer, she'll go stir crazy. She's already counting the days till summer vacation's over and we go back to school.

"What would you do, Ab?"

"I dunno, Mommy. What'm I supposed to do?"

"Well. The way I see it, you've got yourself three choices. You can either reach down and pull 'em up. You can step right out of 'em and keep on walking. Or you can step out of 'em and reach down and put 'em in your pocketbook. So. What would you do?"

Abbie stares down at the paper doll in her hand. She looks worried like this is a test at school and she's going to get an *F.* "I dunno," she says.

Mommy takes a big puff of her cigarette. "Hell," she says. She lets out the smoke, aiming it up at the light bulb on the ceiling. She flicks her ash into the ashtray. "What I'd do is I'd step right out of 'em and keep on walking. Can't you just picture Old Neila Grimes coming uptown to get herself a quart of milk? I'd love to see the look on her face when she spies my drawers smack dab in the middle of the sidewalk."

windfall

According to Mommy, the worst thing that could happen to somebody is to wake up and find yourself living in a town like Windfall. She's getting out of here the first chance she gets. But at least Windfall's a whole lot better than Millersburg. That's this town over by Tipton. All they've got is one street that's a half circle off the highway. At one end there's a gas station that sells bait and it's got a bunch of old rusty cars out in back. At the other end there's the Church of God the Prophecy.

In Windfall, on West Jackson Street, there's Purtlebaugh's Grocery where we shop and then there's Kroger's at the other end. We never shop there because that's Brownie MacAbee's store and half the time Mrs. MacAbee's in there putting cans up on the shelves or else sitting in her lawn chair at the cash register hoping somebody'll come in and buy something. Everything in there costs a penny or two more than at Purtlebaugh's. In between, there's Belva's Beauty Room, which used to be up the street where the library's at now. Belva had so many customers she moved to a bigger place where you can look in the window and watch the ladies leaning back to get their hair washed in these pink sinks. After Belva rolls their hair up, the ladies sit under the big cone-shaped hair driers and read magazines. Belva's got a Coke machine and you can go in and get yourself an Orange Crush or whatever if you're thirsty when you're walking by. If she's not busy, she'll let you sit in one of her seats and have a look at the back of your head in her great big mirrors.

Daddy gets his hair cut once a month at Stubby's Barber Shop next to the pool hall where there's always some old guy smoking

22

a cigar, leaning over the green felt table with one eye shut, staring at the pool balls, or loafing around on the bench out front reading the paper.

If you get hungry, you can go to Jack's and have a jelly donut or a fried egg and at noontime you can get a hamburg or a tenderloin sandwich with pickles or a slice of black raspberry pie. Next to the post office where Mr. Connors works, there's Baker's Five and Ten. When you go in there, Mrs. Baker starts following you around the second you step inside. If you stop and pick up a coloring book or try to look through one of their kaleidoscopes, she'll say, "You wanna buy that?" And then she tells you how much it costs. They've got a shelf full of yarn and all these things you can embroider like bibs with little ducks on them or else ladies' hankies with pictures of flowers stamped in the corner, plus the hoops and all the different-colored threads. They've got every kind of candy there is: chocolate babies and red hots and root-beer barrels. Jawbreakers and candy cigarettes and paraffin bottles.

Mr. Baker's always standing in front of the cash register next to the candy, counting up how much money he's made so far. They aren't friendly at all, no matter what you buy or how many times you go in there, but next door at the post office, Mr. Connors—everybody, even his wife, calls him Connie—will talk your ear off if you let him. He plays this game acting like I'm a stranger even though I go in there every day. "Who've we got here?" he asks, leaning over the counter with our mail in his hand. "You got any ID?" He scratches his chin and looks all puzzled. "Ain't I seen you in one of them Wanted posters?" Usually Abbie's the only one that gets mail since she's the president of the Sal Mineo, Frankie Avalon, and Everly Brothers fan clubs plus she's got about a million pen pals.

There's always a bunch of boys hanging around waiting to stick pennies on the railroad tracks so the train can smush them flat when it goes by. The railroad tracks divide Windfall in half. On one side is Molly's Bakery where they've always got a bunch of dusty-looking decorated cakes in the window. Then there's Applegate's Drug Store. They have comic books and a gum-ball machine where if you get a spotted ball you win ten cents. One time I was in there and I got three spotted balls in a row. Mr.

Applegate came out from behind the soda fountain and banged the machine on the side and gave it a good shake. "You run along now," he said and wouldn't let me try for another. That really burnt me up.

There's the Bulldog Lanes that used to be a bowling alley but now it's shut down with a padlock on the door and the windows all soaped up. There's Myron's Feed and Seed where all the farmers go. And Syd's Tavern where you can't go in unless a grown-up is with you. Sometimes I get to sit on a stool and have a Coke while Daddy drinks himself a beer and Syd cracks open peanuts for me. If you keep on going you pass by Bisbee's Funeral Parlor and end up at the Backlash over by the reservoir.

If you have a boat, you can ride clear over to Blanketport. My next-door neighbor Penny Reeb's daddy has a boat and once in a while he takes the two of us out fishing in it, but all we ever catch is carp. Way back before it was the reservoir, it was Wildcat Creek and all the sewers used to run into it. When they first dug it out and it filled up with water, Lonnie MacAbee dove in head-first and came up with toilet paper on his head.

Mommy says only the Reebs would eat a dirty fish like carp with that many bones to pick out of it. The Reebs'll eat anything. Mr. Reeb brings home turtle eggs he finds in the woods and one time they even ate a great big turtle he caught. Mrs. Reeb boils up the dandelions they dig out of their backyard and she even fries the dandelion flowers after she dips them in egg and flour. I know because I get to go over there for supper once in a while and there's always something to eat I never heard of.

tarzan

Every single night after the supper dishes are done, Gus Riley's little girl Sharon comes out on the front porch of her house down the street from us to practice her tongue clicks. She can click her tongue so loud I can hear it even when I'm up in the closet in my room with the door shut tight. It sounds like a big loud clock going "tock."

Every single night—Mommy says you can set your watch to the sound of Gus Riley's car door slamming at five minutes to nine—Gus Riley goes out to his car and drives uptown so he can set off the curfew. The curfew's this siren he's got hooked to the top of the water tower over behind the post office. Mommy says you'd think Gus Riley'd never heard the war was over. She says it's like he's still expecting everybody to douse the lights for old time's sake.

When the curfew blows, that's a signal that means every kid in Windfall's supposed to get on home, or else Gus Riley'll pick you up and make a juvenile delinquent out of you.

After the curfew dies down, Gus Riley's son Gary comes out on the front porch and pounds his chest like Tarzan, bellowing and pounding till their dog Brandy howls like it's hurting her ears. Mommy gets so mad she slaps her dishrag on the table. "Half this town oughta be taken over to Logansport and locked up," she says. "And they can start with the marshal's family."

25

scrambled eggs

A fireman came in to school for Fire Protection Week and talked to us kids about how we could all be junior firemen. What he wanted us to do is go all over our houses and look for things that could start a fire.

What I did was look everywhere, even in the attic and cellar, for old newspapers and oily rags that were sitting around waiting to catch on fire. Then I took all the stuff I found out to the trash and checked it off my list. I had to look for extension cords with a whole bunch of things plugged into them and see if any of the wires were raggedy. Once we had a lamp that caught on fire when Mommy turned it on, but she already threw that out.

After all us kids brought in our lists with everything checked off, the fireman came back and gave us a test about how fires get started and what to do about it. I answered everything right so I got to have me a red fire hat and a badge that says I'M SMOKEY THE BEAR'S BEST FRIEND.

Daddy is always worrying about me catching on fire when I try to cook. I can never figure out if I catch on fire when I'm in the kitchen if I'm supposed to roll around on the linoleum or if I'm supposed to run outside and roll around on the ground. I know that running makes fire burn faster because fire needs oxygen to burn so I figure I'm supposed to roll around on the floor or else go and jump in the bathtub since water puts out fire too.

Sometimes I get to make breakfast for everybody. I make us scrambled eggs like Marvella showed me how to. Marvella's this real nice lady that takes me to church. I go over to her house all the time for a visit and she's teaching me how to cook. She gave

26

me my own cookbook called *Mary Tilden's Cookbook for Children* and there's a picture of Mary Tilden in the back. She's real pretty and she's got on a red-and-white-checked apron. In the back there's also this letter she wrote to all the kids reading her book. It says how cooking is a whole lot of fun. Mommy says she's just saying that to sell her stupid book.

Me and Marvella have made just about all the recipes in the book. We made scrambled eggs and salad dressing and brownies. She helped me fill out the diploma in the back of the book with my name and the date and all. It says I'm a superb cook. Superb means real good. But when I try to make stuff at home Daddy acts like I don't know a thing. He's always hollering at me to not ever try to turn the oven on by myself and I can't ever cook anything if I'm the only one home.

When I'm trying to make us the scrambled eggs, Daddy keeps coming over and pushing my sleeves back. I have on my blue quilted Christmas housecoat I got when I was six and the sleeves are already getting so short they're practically up to my elbows, but he's still scared they're going to catch on fire. He makes me stand so far away from the stove I can't hardly see the eggs turn from a yellow soupy mess to a nice thick custard the way they do.

"I'll divvy these up," Daddy says and he takes the pan right out of my hand. "The skillet's too damn hot for a little squirt like you," he says.

"Daddy's Precious Little Lana Banana," Abbie says. She starts staring at me the way she always does on account of she knows I hate having somebody look and look at me, but I ignore her because I'm the one that got to make breakfast and that's what really counts. Daddy divvies up the eggs and gives everybody some. But he gets the most. He says how my eggs taste real good. But Abbie claims she can make them better'n me.

Mommy never makes scrambled eggs. She only makes fried ones. We have fried eggs for supper every single Sunday night since we have our big meal for Sunday noon. I always get a great big headache as soon as I see that egg on my plate. Mommy fries eggs in bacon grease instead of oleo the way you're supposed to and she cooks them till the white part is all crispy and crunchy and the yellow part is dry as sawdust. She doesn't even try to do it the way Mary Tilden says to. Mommy breaks the yellow part on purpose. She says it's easier to flip them that way. I have to take tiny bites and swallow a giant mouthful of milk to wash it all down. I end up drinking about a gallon of milk just to get one egg down.

SOS

Daddy is a real cheapskate, Mommy says. He won't even let her have money to buy new underpants so half the time she ends up having to wear his and pin them around her waist with a safety pin. She lifted up her skirt to show me what she looks like with his thick white underpants pinned around her waist and I can't figure out what to do about it. She says she's doing all she can to make money selling her Nova Cosmetics, but whatever she makes she's planning on spending for Abbie to get new school clothes. I can get away with hand-me-downs, but Abbie's starting junior high so she's got to have special.

Daddy is even buying all the groceries now. He says Mommy lets money run through her fingers like water. He works real hard to earn a living, and he doesn't want her spending up all his hard-earned money. The first thing he did was go out and buy us a freezer he put out on the back porch. Now he shops at this special store where he buys us day-old Wonder bread and day-old cinnamon rolls with vanilla icing. He says it tastes good as fresh. Just heat it up in the oven first or make toast if you don't like it.

He's been doing all the cooking, making up these recipes to use up the fifty pounds of hamburg he got. His favorite one he learned how to make in the army. It's called SOS. That stands for shit on a shingle. What you do is you fry up some hamburg and onions then you throw in some flour and milk and stir it up good till it's nice and thick. That's the shit. The shingle is the toast you put it on.

Daddy bought a bunch of T-bone steaks just for him to have. He says he earned it and he's the man of the house. He keeps say-

29

ing how Mommy doesn't know shit about keeping house. He says she didn't know her ass from her elbow when he married her. She couldn't even boil water till he taught her how. Now he's going to teach her how to run a household right if it's the last thing he does. Mommy says she's getting rid of Daddy once and for all. Just wait and see.

running wild

I'm out in the back field, lying on my back in the tall yellow grass, watching the clouds move by. There's a hot slow wind fluttering through the grass and I can smell the manure from the pig farm down the road. The locusts are whirling around in the trees nearby, making their loud buzzing song. The back field didn't get mowed yet this summer and the grass is up to my waist in some places. When I lie down, nobody even knows where I'm at.

I hear Penny's back door slap shut. Then she's whistling like a mourning dove. That's our special signal. I stand up and wave so she'll know where to come find me.

The back field runs behind all the houses on our block. That means we don't have any houses right on the other side of the alley the way everybody else does. We all like it best that way. Daddy says it gives a fellow a feeling like he's not all hemmed in.

The field belongs to Mr. Porter, some guy that lives over by Blanketport. Everyone's always worried he'll sell the field and somebody'll wind up building out there, but he never even comes over to check on it. Mommy says Mr. Porter's just some old coot that never even has to leave his own front room unless he's walking into his kitchen to open his icebox. Folks that have money to burn can do whatever they want. The rest of us just have to wait and see what that'll be.

I hear the grass rustling before I see Penny. Then I smell Lifebuoy soap. Her mom is always making her get in the tub first thing in the morning and again at night. Penny says on account of germs. I only have to take a bath on Saturday night to save on the utility bill. "Hot water costs money," Daddy says if we let the faucet run for a second.

"Looky here at what I got." Penny is breathing like she's been running in a race. She kneels beside me and lifts up her shirt. A box of Diamond matches is tucked into the elastic waistband on her dungarees.

"Yikes strikes! How'd you get 'em?"

"They were right there in the cupboard over the sink. Shoved way in back. My mom probably forgot she even had them."

We sit cross-legged in the grass. Inside the box, all the wooden matches are lined up on top of each other. The tips are bright blue and each one's got a white spot on the end. There must be at least two hundred, maybe more. I'm so excited I feel like I swallowed a bumblebee.

"You go first," I say. "You found 'em."

Penny strikes the first match along the side. She pinches the very end of the matchstick and holds it up till the flame burns down close to her fingertips.

"Bombs over Tokyo," she says. That's my signal to stomp on it when she drops it.

I strike mine along the bottom of my shoe. I love the way a match smells and how it makes that hiss when it first lights up. When I move my fingers real fast through the flame, I can barely feel how hot it is. I hold on to the match as long as I can stand it.

Penny strikes two matches at the same time. I take two matches out and light them on hers so we have a match in each of our hands.

"Fire light, fire bright, fire burning day and night," Penny chants.

"Betcha I can hold on longer'n you," I say.

"Nuh-uh!"

"Uh-huh!"

The fire eats its way towards our fingers. Just when I'm about to drop mine, Penny drops hers.

I light another match and put it in my mouth, acting like I'm a fire-eater in the circus.

"You're crazy." Penny lights a match and pokes the flaming end into the dirt under the tangle of grass.

We keep striking two at a time, then three, then I light a handful all at once. I feel the way I do when I'm swinging higher and higher up towards the sky and then just at the right minute I let go and fly through the air.

The next thing I know, Penny's screaming bloody murder. A hot wind blows across the back of my neck. Flames rush like snakes slithering through the dry grass.

I grab Penny's hand, pulling her behind me towards the back of her house where her daddy keeps his minnow tank. We scoop water out with some old saucepans, careful not to catch any of the silvery fish that dart through the murky water. I spill half my water down the front of me running towards the field. When we pour it on, the fire kind of sizzles and steams, but it doesn't stop. I rush back for more. Penny is right behind me, crying so loud at first I don't even hear the fire engine, and then there it is, rushing down the alley, the bell clanging. The firemen jump down and start spraying water onto the fire. A big black cloud of smoke hangs over the field. Iggie Purtlebaugh's digging a trench along the edge of the alley, tossing the dirt onto the fire, smacking the flames with his shovel.

"Quit crying!" I shake Penny a little bit. "Quit it. If you don't, they'll know it was us." Penny's cheeks are smeared with tears and soot. She's kind of hiccuping and shaking like she's got the chills.

"Pen-ny! Penny Jean Reeb!" her mother calls from the kitchen window. "Get on in this house right this minute."

"Don't tell," I whisper. "Whatever you do, don't tell. Just act like all of a sudden it caught on fire. The way old oily rags'll bust into flames. Remember? Just don't let on."

The thing is, everybody knows what happened before the firemen even put out the last bit of fire because Mrs. MacAbee's standing in the alley telling anybody that'll listen how she saw the two of us run out of that field screaming to beat the band. "Them two little hellions running back and forth with them saucepans of water!" She grabbed her jiggly elbows and held her arms tight over her big belly. "If I wudn't so scared I'd lose my garage, I'da laughed my sides off."

* * *

33

Penny never gets hit because her parents claim that's how barbarians act. They don't believe in it. What they do is they give her a long talking to, then they ground her. When I sneak over to see how she's doing, she's laying on her bed, staring at the ceiling, crying softly. She can't come outside for two whole weeks no matter how hot out it gets. Not even if her sisters are going swimming or playing in the hose. "They might never let me play with you again," she whispers, crouching at the window with her face pressed to the screen. "And my daddy hasn't even found out yet. Who knows what he'll say."

"Penny! Who're you talking to?" I duck down when Mrs. Reeb starts cranking the window shut. "Lana Franklin, if that's you out there, you better get on home right this instant. I've had about enough of you."

That night when Daddy comes home from work he just stands out by the trash barrel in the alley smoking a cigarette and staring at the back field. When I step on the grass it makes a crunchy sound. He doesn't even ask me what happened. Before I can even tell him it was an accident he's smacking me on my behind and shaking me so hard it feels like my head's going to fall off and roll down the alley.

"What'm I raising here, some kind of py-ro-man-i-ac?" he says, smacking me with each word and pushing me in front of him towards the back door. He grabs me by the shoulders every once in a while to smack me real hard.

"That fire coulda burnt up half the houses in the neighborhood. Didn't I tell you to quit playing with fire? They got places for kids like you over at Logansport. Is that where you wanna end up?"

When we get inside, he's still real mad and his face is all red. A vein is popped up on his forehead and it looks like it's about to bust. He smacks me over and over again till I don't even feel it anymore. Mommy just sits at the table and shakes her head. When he's all done, she doesn't even say a word to me.

"She's running wild," Daddy says. Mommy just sits there with her legs crossed, bouncing one of her feet back and forth, smoking her cigarette, and shuffling her cards for solitaire.

I have to go to bed without any supper but I don't even care.

It's stupid meatloaf and potatoes anyhow. Abbie thinks the whole thing's pretty funny. She starts calling me a pyromaniac lunatic.

I lie on my bed on my tummy with my face in my pillow. My hair smells like burnt grass. I never got hit so hard in my whole life before. I have to keep reaching back and touching my rear end even though it hurts more to touch it. I just can't believe it so I keep touching it and touching it. It feels all hot and hard like I've got me a great big black and blue back there. I press on it till it hurts even more, then after a while it hurts so bad I don't really feel it anymore.

We drove over to Logansport one time and they've got this great big building behind a brick wall with a guard out front so the nutcases can't get out. Daddy's always saying how one of us kids'll end up there if we're not careful. I hope I'm not the one. I think about Penny. I try to figure out what I'll do for two weeks without her but I just can't picture it. Then I start wondering how I'll live if her mom won't ever let her play with me again.

I cry real quiet so they won't hear me downstairs. Daddy's scraping his knife across his plate and saying a bunch of stuff about how they have to hide the matches from me till I get old enough to know better. "What've we got here? She's seven years old and still don't know better. If we don't watch it, she's liable to burn the whole house down one of these days," he says.

After supper is over, Daddy makes me come with him to burn the trash.

"Fire's a powerful tool," he says, striking a match on the side of the trash barrel. "It can be man's friend and his enemy both."

A big grey newspaper ash floats up out of the trash barrel and glides down to the grass. The tiny red spark on the edge of it goes out before it hits the ground. I crush it with my toe anyhow.

The field is all shiny black and stinks like old wet trash. With the tall grass burnt down to the ground, the houses behind us seem a whole lot closer. I can see the Lackeys out in their back-yard playing horseshoes and Old Lady Winkler snapping beans on her back porch steps. There's not one single place left to hide.

cotton candy

Every July for a week the carnival comes to Windfall, and they close off West Jackson Street so no cars can drive through. I can tell it's starting when I wake up to the sound of the carnies hammering the concession stands together. When they're all done, I can look out my window and see the Ferris wheel rising up above the trees.

At the carnival, Abbie spends most of her money on the games. She wants to win one of them big blue stuffed bears or a statue of praying hands but all she ever ends up getting is them dumb colored-straw Chinese handcuffs you get your fingers stuck in. Or else she gets a Kewpie doll with its face made out of plastic so thin if you touch its nose it sinks into its face forever. Abbie will spend her money on just about anything. She'd buy a penny for fifty cents if you told her George Washington had looked at it. She's always sending away for stuff. Once she saved all her money up to buy one of them little dogs that sits in a teacup but Mommy wouldn't let her get it. She said she didn't care how little it was.

I always play Pick a Duck because you can't lose. The ducks float by on this stream of water and you just choose your duck. You can win a comb or a sheriff's badge or some jacks. That's the first game I play on Dime Day, which is the last day of the carnival when everything costs a dime. I pick a lucky pink one and the guy with an eagle tattoo on his arm hands me a toy watch with a baby-sized watch for my doll. Abbie's at the stand next to me tossing rings and trying to get hers over the one with the dollar bill taped to it. She winds up winning nothing.

"Pick a Duck is for babies," Abbie says. All around us people

I don't even know are pushing and shoving, waving hot dogs in the air. Ladies are yanking on their kids' hands and eating home-made Cracker Jack. A boy drops his ice cream cone and his mother slaps him on the side of his head. I leave Abbie trying to guess how many jelly beans are in a jar and snake my way through the crowd till I get to the bingo tent. All the ladies from the church I go to with Marvella are there and Marvella is standing up on a platform in the bingo tent calling out the numbers.

"It's the little Franklin girl, ain't it?" Viola Applegate asks, grabbing at my arm. Her fingers pinch me like a crawdaddy. She can't hardly ever remember who anybody is. Since her and Mr. Applegate run the drugstore, she claims she can't be expected to keep track of every kid that comes uptown for an ice cream soda. She smiles and pats the wooden folding chair that's empty beside her. "This here's a lucky spot."

Marvella gives me a bingo card and a handful of beans to use for markers. She won't take my dime. "It's on the house." She winks. "Don't forget to put your bean on the center square first."

Marvella reaches into this glass jar that has wooden markers with numbers printed on them. She reads the number then takes another one. All around me the ladies are muttering about which ones they've got but I don't have any. Viola Applegate keeps looking over to be sure I didn't miss any.

"I got bingo," Neila Grimes waves her hand at Marvella. "Yoo-hoo. Bingo over here." She points to a cut-glass candy dish from the shelf behind where Marvella's standing. If I won, I'd get Mommy one of them lacy bride dolls you put on your bed.

When I get tired of bingo, I get myself some cotton candy. I love the way it smells when the lady whirls the paper cone around and around and catches the pink web of spun sugar and it's warm when you first take a bite.

I save my last dime to ride the Ferris wheel one last time before the curfew blows. I love to be up high as the water tower, looking out over Windfall, seeing everything the way God does with the lights blinking below me and around me and the dark sky stretching far above my head. The wheel groans and lurches forward till it's completely loaded. My seat rocks back and forth, then we whoosh around and around.

I'm stuck at the top when I see Mommy standing on the railroad tracks with some guy that's got a straw hat on, the kind you win from tossing softballs through toilet seats. Mommy's eating a bright red candy apple. She's wearing the new dress she made, the one that's got what you call a full-gore skirt. It took her two weeks to figure out how to pin the pattern on and cut the pieces out so when she sewed the skirt together the black stripes in the cloth would look right when she was all done. They're waiting in line at the stand where you can take a turn and swing that big hammer to make the bell ring. Mommy has her hand on the guy's arm. I know it can't be Daddy because for one thing, he's too short. Mommy leans in close to him and says something in his ear and he laughs and takes his hat off and shakes his head like he can't believe what she said. You can always tell it's Daddy on account of his red hair, but this guy's hair is jet black.

I almost slide right out from under the safety bar as the Ferris wheel starts up and whooshes around and around and I'm up in the air and the lights are flashing and the bell rings and everybody's screaming and music is playing. I get this feeling kind of like somebody's sliding a knife in between my ribs and shaking it. Kind of like one of them pangs the ladies in Abbie's magazines get. When I come back down to earth, Mommy's not anywhere.

I find Abbie twirling at the end of one of the arms of the octopus. She's waving her arms, not even holding on for dear life the way I would. She has her mouth wide open, screaming her head off, but I can't figure out which scream is hers since the whole town is filled with everybody's voices screaming and laughing and crying.

hickory nuts

Leota Tupper is the one that owns the land across from us where the hickory nut trees are at. She rents out the field behind them to this farmer that plants corn. Every fall, she lets me and Penny gather up all the nuts we can eat so long as we fill up a sack for her. From the time the leaves start turning red till the snow comes, me and Penny run over there after school. We peel off the green husks and crack the shells open on the sidewalk with rocks, picking out the sweet meat inside. Uncle Cleon says eating hickory nuts is about as good as having a plate of fried squirrel. He always takes home a sack for himself when he's been over to visit.

Leota lives all by herself and her house is so old it's half haunted, everybody says. She never opens up the windows, even in the middle of the summer when it's so hot Lonnie MacAbee does his fried-egg experiment and the sidewalk in front of his house is covered with dried egg yolks from where he tried to fry eggs in the sun. Even when everybody's got their electric fans whirring all day and all night, Leota keeps her windows shut. The air inside is all thick with dust and it smells like wet newspapers and dirty old clothes and mothballs.

Every Christmas, Leota erases the names from the Christmas cards folks in town send her. What she does is she signs her own name on them and sends them back. She doesn't even care if she's sending you back the same one you sent her. She signs it *Leota Tupper* in her spidery handwriting and puts it in an envelope she makes out of red or green construction paper. She tucks the flap in to save a penny. Everybody says she's a miser. But she told me once she thinks it's a waste folks sending Christmas cards like it ain't good enough to holler "Merry Christmas" when they see you uptown. "It ain't good enough they send me a card, but I've got to send 'em one back or else they'll call me a snob," she says.

Leota Tupper has lived in Windfall her whole life and she's the oldest one at church. "When I was your age we took a horse-and-buggy ride over to Tipton," she tells me. "It took us all day. Would you like that?"

When she was my age, her house and my house across the street were the only ones on Carrigan Road except for Maudie and Iggie Purtlebaugh's. Iggie claims the Indians built his house, it's been here so long. The rest was just farmland and folks used horses to get where they had to go. Leota says how back in the old days when the town was just a feed store and a post office, folks acted different. They kept chickens in their backyards and weren't scared to get their hands dirty. Men used to drive horses up and down the back alley delivering coal and ice. Back then, the alley was kind of like a dirt road behind everybody's house. Now it's a grassy path that runs behind the houses towards town.

There isn't any alley on Leota's side, just cornfields behind all the houses as soon as the yards end. Leota Tupper's backyard has got a fence all around it with vines growing all over it so you can't see what's back there. I keep hoping someday she'll invite me out there but she never does. Me and Penny figure it's like in *The Secret Garden*. When Mr. Tupper died after his appendix busted, Leota quit going out there.

Not many folks in town get to go inside Leota's house. She even keeps the preacher standing on the front porch with his hat in his hands talking to her through the black screen. But just about every time I go over, she takes me inside for cookies and gunpowder tea. That's this special tea her sister Eveline sends her from Chicago. Penny says when I go in, I've got to pay close attention and keep my ears open in case I hear somebody in the attic crying. But there's just Leota with her twisted hands trying to get the cookie tin open, putting sugar cookies on a white paper doily, pouring tea into our blue china cups, and giving us each a lump of sugar. There's just her cat Tommy curled up under the stove snoring real loud.

mrs. zugel

I like school OK even though the teachers sometimes call me Abbie. That's just because they had my sister before me and they mix us up even though Abbie's got brown hair and Mommy's blue eyes and we don't look a thing alike. This year for second grade I have Mrs. Zugel. Mommy's going on dates with Mrs. Zugel's son Billy. He's a grown-up already because Mrs. Zugel is so old. He's what you call tall, dark, and handsome and Mommy says he's got bedroom eyes. Abbie says that means he's only got one thing on his mind. I asked her what was that but she just rolled her eyes and clicked her tongue at me. Whenever I look in the mirror to see my own eyes, the thing I can't get over is how when you look real close at your own eye in the mirror all you can see is it looking back at you. No matter what, that's what you see.

Billy Boy—that's what Mommy calls him—lives with Mrs. Zugel in this yellow house right near church. He's got this brother Bud that's not half as handsome as Billy is. Bud walks with a limp. Mommy went out on dates with Bud first but then when she met Billy Boy she fell for him hook, line, and sinker. Bud's a momma's boy. But Billy Boy's going places. "He's gonna be my ticket out of this hellhole," Mommy says.

Mrs. Zugel is a widow. She wears faded flower dresses and leans on this yardstick that she uses like a cane when she watches us out at recess. She also uses her yardstick to hit the bad kids with. One day she took Lonnie MacAbee out in the hallway and we could hear her smacking him good. He should've known better because she'd already taped his mouth shut with adhesive tape and made him sit in front of the room for the whole day. But he

41

always has to say cusswords. She was smacking him good, then it got real quiet out in the hall all of a sudden and when Mrs. Zugel came back in, she acted like she couldn't hardly lift her feet off the floor to walk up to her desk. At first I didn't know what it was, but then I saw she had two pieces of her yardstick, one in each hand. Lonnie MacAbee came in with tears all over his face. But he was smiling anyhow and looking all proud.

Now, Mrs. Zugel's got a brand-new yardstick that's bright yellow with black lines and numbers on it, not brown like her old one. But it doesn't look right. And nobody's half as scared of her as they used to be.

Mommy and her Billy Boy have a whole lot of fun together. She puts on her pretty dresses and her white high heels and the two of them go out dancing. They drive in his car out to some dead-end road in the middle of nowhere with just them and the cornfields and dance up a storm to the car radio. When she comes home she tries to act like nothing's going on. She told me and Abbie but I'm not supposed to tell anybody.

Once she came home with a big black and blue on her neck. She had to gob face powder on it and she was worried to death Daddy would see it. I don't think he noticed, though. If he did, I would've found out.

night-light

T he house is like a soft, aging animal turning over in its sleep, its bones settling with a thump as it curls around its own tail. The floorboards creak as if someone is sneaking through the rooms. Floyd tries to sleep with it, tries to measure his breath with the whispered snores of his children. But his head pounds, the pain probing relentlessly behind his right eye. Lana is beside him on the narrow bed, turned away from him, her face buried in her pillow. Out in the yard, a mourning dove calls. He eases off her bed, smooths the worn pink blanket over her shoulders, tucks it under her chin, and goes downstairs to the bathroom where he gulps down four aspirins at once, their bitterness lingering on the back of his tongue as he lathers his face and begins to scrape the razor across his cheeks.

He remembers during the night, Ruth waking him, her hand gripping his shoulder. "Floyd, you're gritting your damn teeth so hard you'll wake up the whole house." Afterwards, he lay on his side of the bed in the dark, unable to close his eyes, listening to the refrigerator hum in the kitchen. It was raining, the icy fingers of rain slapping against the windows. He thought of the water seeping into the already damp cellar—of how he needed to open the windows down there to let in some air but the last time he tried, he was pushing a screwdriver into the sill and it sank into the spongy wood and stopped. He was afraid to try again though he knew he had to do something about the mold growing on the walls, the sickening smell of it when he opened the cellar door. The storm window on the front of the house blew off last week. After the wind lifted it right off its hinges and it landed on the front yard with a crash, Floyd had only been able to pick up the shards of *glass and carry the broken frame to his shed with the promise of fixing it someday, even though he couldn't imagine building a new window. How would you fit the glass into the frame?*

All around him from the dark corners, the house seems to be calling him. All the things to be done. The floorboards in the kitchen splintered and caving in. Save me, the house seems to say when he takes a shower and the tiles rattle like loose teeth.

It was a bargain, this house, a handyman's special. The old woman who had owned it had been born there and when she died it went up for sale and stood for at least ten years before Floyd and Ruth came along. He was young then, but now he feels old. He lies in bed thinking of his life, the passing of days, each one just like the day before, until he is too old to go on.

The longing is heavy in his chest. He lies there trying to resist. Telling himself no. Telling himself he is weak willed, to keep a lid on it. There is only one thing he wants. He counts slowly backwards from a hundred, picturing each number floating above him in the dark. He stops at seventy-eight. Repeats the number again and again, the sound of it like a record caught in a scratch. Just this once, he argues with himself. No. Just this once and never again. He creeps up the stairs to where his daughters sleep. The older one wrapped from head to toe, shrouded in the quilt his mother pieced together from old wool coats and pants. The little one clutches a teddy bear, her face illuminated in the glow from the night-light beside her bed. She is afraid of the dark. Sometimes she wakes up screaming about boogeymen under her bed, how they reach up out of the dark and grab at her.

Floyd lifts the edge of the blanket and crawls in beside her. Pulls her close. Her ribs under his fingers make him think of a baby bird, all skin and bones and beating heart. He lets the familiar ache take over. Lets it flood his chest. His crotch. He tells himself she's too young to figure out what's going on. She's asleep anyhow. If she wakes up, he'll tell her she called him. That she'd had a bad dream. Had called him and he'd come up to comfort her. The calloused skin on his fingers, the dried scraps of skin around his nails, brushes her chest, trickles down to the waistband of her pajamas. His hand hesitates, as if about to catch something that could disappear any moment, then reaches quickly inside and touches her there.

the cat's meow

You let that bulldagger with the filthy neck talk you into cutting your hair off like hers?" Daddy slams his lunch bucket on the kitchen counter and stands in the middle of the kitchen looking at the back of Mommy's head. Her hair's all cut off nearly as short as his and her neck's been shaved. The skin looks white as a fish belly.

"She ain't a bulldagger. And she didn't talk me into a thing. I've got a mind of my own."

"The hell you do. And she's a bulldagger if I ever saw one. The minute I laid eyes on her I knew that."

"Go tell her husband Duane that."

"Duane? There ain't one bit of doubt in my mind who wears the pants in that household and it sure as hell ain't Duane."

Mommy gives Daddy a real dirty look. "It's my own damn head." She starts chopping the green beans like that's the end of it.

I'm setting the table for supper. Her favorite song, the one about twilight time that belongs to her and Billy Boy, comes on the radio. But Mommy doesn't sing along with me.

"I married me a woman whose hair I could run my fingers through."

"It's a hell of a lot easier to take care of. Just think of all the money I'll save on hair spray."

"Jesus H. Christ. Just because I try to save a buck here and there you don't have to throw it in my face." Daddy smacks Mommy on her behind and stomps into the front room.

Mommy moves into the middle of the kitchen and thumbs her nose in his direction. I want to ask her what a bulldagger is but she looks like she's about to have a conniption fit so I just keep arranging the forks on the table.

Ever since Winona Flowers and Mommy ended up such good friends, Daddy's been raising cain. Mommy says he's just jealous since nobody'd be his friend if you paid them.

Winona comes over nearly every day after us kids go off to school. Her husband Duane works the night shift and sleeps all day. She says she ain't got a thing better to do except hang around her own goddamned house with the blinds shut so she comes visiting. Winona Flowers cusses more than any lady I ever heard. She says she don't frigging care who the hell hears her, either. Let that shit-ass of a preacher Andrews get near me and I'll give him an earful to preach about, she says.

I can always tell when Winona Flowers has been over because Mommy forgets to start getting supper ready on time and when I get home from school, the ashtrays are all filled up with cigarette butts. Winona smokes the kind without a filter and hers are crushed out next to Mommy's filtered ones with red lipstick prints on the ends. There's always coffee-colored rings of sugar stuck on the tabletop from where Winona spills the sugar and slops her coffee over the side of the cup when she stirs it up. Mommy drinks her coffee black but Winona puts three sugars in hers and lots of milk.

Winona Flowers has got the messiest house I've ever seen and the brattiest kids in town. Abbie baby-sits when Winona and Mommy go out and I go over to help. Abbie says she wants to clean their house up good because it's not sanitary. In Home Ec, she learned about how a house is supposed to be germfree. But the real reason she wants to get it clean is because she's in love with Duane Flowers. He's the spitting image of Sal Mineo, one of the movie stars Abbie's got a fan club for. Abbie can't figure out what Duane's doing with Winona. When Duane gets a look at how his house could be all fixed up nice Abbie figures it'll dawn on him how he made a mistake marrying Winona and he'll get rid of her and marry Abbie instead. I told Abbie she can't get married because she's barely just turned thirteen. But it didn't make a bit of difference.

Even though me and Abbie clean Winona's house up, it looks like we were never there when we come back the next time. I don't think she even tries to keep it nice. She never washes the dishes. They just use them up, piling them in the sink and on the counter, even leaving them in the front room where they had snacks watching TV. Winona always calls Mommy to go out the second the last dish gets dirtied up.

Winona pays Abbie thirty-five cents an hour and Abbie gives me five cents of it. I do half the work, but she's the one that's to blame if anything goes wrong. Winona Flowers's kids run around the house screaming and hollering and trying to kill each other. Joyce is the oldest one. She's six years old, that's just two years younger than I'm going to be when I have my next birthday so she ought to know better, but last time she was in the kitchen juggling eggs while her sister Tammy was trying to get Little Duane to stick his head in the toilet and have a drink. It takes forever to get them to lie down and listen to a story but eventually they fall asleep, all of them with their clothes on, even their shoes. Winona never mentions a thing about it so I bet they always do that.

Winona took Mommy to get her hair cut last night while we were baby-sitting. They both got the same hairdo. It's the latest style called a DA since the back looks like a duck tail and the sides look like feathers. "DA stands for duck ass," Winona said.

Mommy puts the green beans in a pot on the stove and dries her hands. She lifts my hair away from my ear and bends down to whisper. "You wanna know a secret?" she asks. "Billy Boy thinks my hairdo is the cat's meow."

catching bees

I like to go out back and catch bees. What I do is I squat over the fat yellow dandelions and when a bee comes and lands on one, I put an empty jar over it and wait till the bee's ready to fly home. I watch its legs get all heavy with yellow pollen and then right when the bee's ready to take off, I slip me a saucer under the jar. The bee buzzes and whirls around and around but it's not going anywhere.

I figure catching bees is kind of like a dance you have to learn all the steps to by heart. You slip the saucer under the jar, turn it right side up, and when the bee flies down to the bottom, you slip a piece of wax paper over the hole then slide the saucer off. You have to put an elastic band around the rim to hold the paper down and poke some air holes so the bee can breathe. Sometimes I catch two bees at once. To do that, you have to wait for them both to land on the same dandelion and be ready to take off at the same time. You can't be in any hurry about it. You just have to wait.

By noontime, I've got jars of buzzing bees all lined up on top of the picnic table. Eventually they get tired of buzzing and try to crawl up the slippery glass but they just slide back down. When I'm all done, I take the jars to the shed where I put them on a shelf in the dark. When I'm ready to catch bees again, I empty the jars of dead bees out on the dirt floor and crush the crunchy bees with the toe of my shoe before I go out back to catch more.

I'm out back catching bees when Daddy comes out and says, "Get on over here and help me weed this garden." He's home from work in the daytime on account of it's his vacation but we can't afford to go anyplace. One time what we did was drive to

48

Massachusetts to visit Grammy and Grampy. Grampy's not Grammy's first husband. Mommy says she had better luck the second time around. They live in this trailer Grampy built out of wood. It's up on a hill with pine trees all around it and you have to go poop in an outhouse and take a bath in a lake. Grammy and Grampy both work at this dog-collar factory and we got to go there and they gave us a rhinestone dog collar for Gretchie to wear. She acts so proud every time I put it on her, like she's the queen of dogs. Gretchie's what you call a dash hound. Whenever anybody sees her they laugh and claim she looks like a hot dog with legs.

Daddy showed me how to pinch off the suckers between the stems of the tomatoes so they'll ripen up faster and it makes my fingers all green and sticky. Mommy's laying on an old quilt in her white short shorts and Abbie's beside her snipping the ends of her split ends with the nail scissors from her manicure set. Daddy stops to light his cigarette. I watch him look over at Mommy and give her a smile but she's facing the other direction so she doesn't see him. That's when old Hoostie Dean comes running up the alley all out of breath. He stands by our trash barrel hollering, "Finders keepers, losers weepers!" His voice sounds like an old rusty hinge. He's got a five-dollar bill he's holding in both hands like he's scared we might come and grab it away from him if he don't hang on tight. After a while, he grins and shows his rotten stubs of teeth.

It turns out he found it when he was poking around real careful through the MacAbees' trash barrel next door. It was in this old catalog they were throwing out. He always checks everybody's trash like he's going to find buried treasure. Whatever he finds that he wants, he puts in this little red wagon and pulls it around after him. Hoostie Dean's skin is grey like he's covered with coal dust and there are streaks of dirt down his neck like somebody drew a road map on him. Whenever I walk by him, I don't say hi or anything. Nobody does. It's not that we don't want to, it's just that he likes to be the only one that says stuff to you and only if he feels like it. If I said a word to him, he'd get real scared and run away with his arms wrapped around his head. I've seen him when the mean boys make him do that.

He's all kind of bent over, but I don't think he's that old.

Marvella told me he's always been thataway. Ever since he was a kid all he does is walk around looking at the ground to see if he can find anything worth picking up. In the afternoons, after he's gone through everybody's trash and filled up his wagon with what he wants to keep, he walks all around town looking to see if anybody dropped any money on the sidewalk or in the gutters. I've seen the guys that fix flat tires over at Mosbaugh's Garage toss pennies out on the sidewalk when they see Hoostie Dean coming. They do that so they can watch his face light up when he spies the money. Every time he gets up to the garage and sees the pennies sparkling in the sunlight the way they do, he acts like it's the first time he ever found any money laying there. He looks down at it, then he looks around him in every direction with a big grin on his face. He scoops it up real fast and stands there counting it over and over again, moving his lips like he's counting out loud, but he doesn't really say a thing.

claustrophobia

D addy's sleeping in the front room with his shoes off and his feet stink up the whole house. Mommy says having him home on vacation day and night like this is driving her right up the wall so her and Abbie went off riding around in the car. I wanted to go but Mommy said I had to stay home in case Daddy wakes up I can keep him company. But as soon as they take off, I run over to Marvella's.

Marvella's husband Vernon is watching TV in the front room, sitting in a corner of the davenport she calls Vernon's Spot. He's got the sound turned down, but he's staring right at what's on. He hardly ever moves or anything. He sits there with his elbow resting on the white lacy doily. Marvella's always teasing him about how he's like a piece of furniture and one of these days all she'll have to do is dust him off once in a while to keep him happy.

Marvella's house isn't like any other house I've ever been in. She's got a dining room that's supposed to be just for eating in, but nobody ever does. None of them ever even sits down to eat half the time because Vernon's got the ulcers and anyhow, her daughter Ruby won't eat a thing Marvella fixes. She only eats TV dinners and frozen turkey pot pies and cupcakes she buys from Molly's Bakery. Marvella lets her eat any old place she feels like since she's already fifteen and practically grown up anyhow.

Ruby sleeps in a room off the front room that was supposed to be the sunporch. Marvella told me Ruby can't sleep a wink if she can't see outdoors every time she opens her eyes. She's always been thataway. She's got to have windows all around her or else she gets what you call claustrophobia. That's when you feel like you're trapped in a closet and can't get any air. It's pretty cold in Ruby's room, but she piles on the blankets and turns her electric heater on high.

The funny thing is, Marvella's got this whole other house upstairs. What I mean is, there are three more rooms and each one of them's got furniture in it. One room is set up like a baby's room with a crib and a high chair and a potty chair with a yellow duck painted on the wood. There's the hobbyhorse Ruby used to ride on and a little white chest of bureau drawers with all Ruby's baby pajamas and dresses and bibs and diapers in it. One of the other two rooms is set up like a bedroom with the bed all made like any minute somebody's going to sleep in it and there are old clothes and stuff in the drawers and closets. It's a great big double bed with two pillows all covered with a pink chenille bedspread. Marvella says she keeps it ready for nights when Vernon gets to snoring so loud. If I could come and live with Marvella, this would be my room. I like to lie on this bed and pretend I'm waking up in the morning, looking out at the church across the street, and Marvella's down in the kitchen making biscuits. The ceiling is all smooth and painted white, not lumpy with plaster like at home and it's not all stained from rain leaking in either. The walls have pink and yellow flowers on them, not aluminum paper over the insulation like me and Abbie have to look at since Daddy started remodeling our room but never really finished it. At the end of the bed there's a bureau with a mirror that's so big I can see my whole self in it except for my feet.

There's one more room called the Junk Heap. It's got Ruby's baby carriage in it and Vernon's army uniform hanging on a hanger covered with plastic. There's a big glass fishbowl, a treadle sewing machine, and some beds that aren't set up. Marvella says you just never can tell what might come in handy. There's no sense getting rid of perfectly good things so long as you have the room to store it.

Marvella's always got pies and cakes and cookies all over the place and half the time everything's going stale. But Vernon's got the ulcers so he can never eat any of the goodies she bakes. He only eats bread he soaks in milk first. Mommy gets the ulcers too and one time she pooped blood. She was all scared about it. Doc Havey told her she had to give up cigarettes and coffee but she says she wouldn't know how to get through a day without her ten cups of coffee and her pack of weeds. Every winter, Mommy gets sick as a dog and the only way she can breathe is if she's under an oxygen tent in the hospital. She says if that's the only way she can get a vacation, she'll take it.

I'm running back home from Marvella's before the curfew blows and there's Shreida Huckaby walking real slow down Cass Street.

"Yoo-hoo. You see anybody out here that resembles my husband?" she says. I shake my head and keep on running and practically break my neck when I fall down sliding on the pawpaws that're all over the sidewalk. They smell just like rotten bananas and I fall smack dab on the cement sidewalk and smash up my hands. It feels like they're on fire and they're all red and I have these little bits of rocks in the scraped part. I stand there trying real hard not to cry. Shreida Huckaby doesn't even notice. She's too busy looking at the treetops like she's counting the leaves.

When I get home I show Daddy what happened to my hands. They're still killing me and they look all dirty with dried blood on them and he says he's got something to make it all better and we go in the bathroom and I figure he's going to get me a Band-Aid.

"It's right here," he says and unzips his pants and takes it out and makes me hold on to it. "You have to stop being such a great big bawl baby and help me walk my dog," he says and he gets all happy about it.

At first it's all squishy and then it starts to get big and Daddy tells me to hold on 'cause the dog's about to get away and he moves it back and forth and back and forth telling me to hold on tight then he pulls it away and wraps it up in his hanky and says to run along.

the withered hand

I've been going to Sunday school steady now for a whole year and only missed once last winter when I didn't have any clean socks to wear and was too scared to go. That's how come I got invited to the camp-out. I've never slept anywhere but home. Penny's going and she says don't be a fraidy cat. Mostly I'm scared I'll wet the bed. Mommy says you're not supposed to wet the bed after you start school, but I still do even though I already got promoted to third grade. If I don't quit it pretty soon she'll have to get me one of them electric sheets that wakes you up with a big shock the second you pee.

When we get to the camp-out, two army tents are set up in the park and a bunch of kids are running around playing kickball. Penny comes and shows me inside the tents. One's for Reverend Andrews and the boys and the other one's for Mrs. Andrews and us girls. Mrs. Andrews has a cot with a mattress on it and a pink fluffy blanket.

Reverend Andrews looks funny in his blue jeans and plaid flannel shirt. He's even got white tennis shoes on. He blows a silver whistle he's got hanging on a chain around his neck when he wants us to do stuff. We get to make an Indian campfire set up with the logs laid out like the points of a star. Reverend Andrews lights it, then he sharpens sticks for us to roast weenies and marshmallows on.

"You kids eat as much as you want," Mrs. Andrews says. "There's plenty. Don't nobody be bashful now." She puts a bag of potato chips on the picnic table and sets out the mustard and ketchup and relish. There's a big jug of grape Kool-Aid with ice cubes in it, but I don't drink any. I haven't had a thing to drink since a glass of milk with breakfast yesterday.

"There's the Big Dipper," Lonnie MacAbee says, pointing up at the sky with his flaming marshmallow. He starts drawing circles with his smoking stick.

"Praise the Lord," Mrs. Andrews says.

"In a little bit we'll put the fire out." Reverend Andrews stands up and nudges the logs towards the flames with his toe. "But before we do, let's light our sticks in the fire and testify. Let us each one thank the good Lord for our blessings."

"God is great, God is good, and we thank Him for our food." Lonnie MacAbee burps real loud then waves his flaming stick making red sparks sprinkle across the dark. The campfire pops and Lonnie starts laughing and snorting, swiping at his mouth with the back of his hand.

"Children. Be serious," Mrs. Andrews says. She's sitting on a lawn chair, her dress pulled tight and tucked under her knees. Her daughter Bobbie stands up and pokes the end of her stick in the fire. When it catches, she waves the flame in a figure eight. "I love my parents," she says. "I love you, Mommy and Daddy." Then she bursts into tears and runs to her mother. She's always crying like that. Mrs. Andrews pats her on the back and says, "There, there, sweetheart."

When it's my turn, Penny grabs my hand and whispers. Her lips are warm and soft up close to my ear. "Say something about Jesus."

"I'm glad Jesus loves us all the same," I say. I picture Jesus in his white robe walking on the water. I wonder if He's looking down from the sky now. When Penny stands up she says, "I love the Bible." You can tell Reverend Andrews is getting all happy. His bald head is kind of glowing and the firelight is flickering on his glasses. He takes them off and polishes them on his shirttail. When everybody's done, we have a prayer. Reverend Andrews goes on and on about how we have to serve the Lord and lead the sinners to church. He says how God is waiting to wash our sins away.

When we're all in our sleeping bags and Mrs. Andrews is in her nightgown with a pink hairnet tied around her head, she closes the flap to the tent and turns down the wick on her lantern. "I'm gonna tell you all a Bible story, then I want you to get to sleep," she says, laying down on her cot. First she tells us about how Jesus cured the man with the withered hand. How that hand was as dried up as a shrunken head at the carnival and how Jesus blessed it and made it good as new. Then she tells us about baby Moses in the bulrushes. "That was one lucky baby," she says. "Just think, if he hadn't've been saved who would've God had to tell the Ten Commandments to?

"Now go on to sleep. I don't want to hear a peep till morning."

In a minute, Mrs. Andrews is snoring so loud Penny gets the giggles then I start in and then the other girls do too, even Bobbie. The crickets are so loud there must be a million of them all scritch-scratching the way they do. I reach my hand out and Penny curls her fingers in mine. I start thinking of home. I can picture my teddy bear on my bed and Mommy and Abbie bending over the kitchen table cutting out cloth for one of their patterns. I can see Daddy in the front room with his feet up watching TV and Gretchie at the front window looking for me to come home.

In the tent, everyone's breathing deep and slow all around me, like they're whispering "hush hush hush." And though I thought I never would, I fall asleep and dream I am at the beach. Mommy and Daddy are burying me in sand. They scoop warm handfuls of sand over my arms and legs and belly, patting it over me till I'm buried up to my chin. They stop and look at each other, smiling all happy the way they used to do in the olden days. Then they start covering my face. Sand trickles down my nose and my throat and into my eyes and I can't push it away with my arms buried. Mommy pats and pats even though I'm choking and coughing. "We'll leave you an air hole," she says. "Relax, you little worrywart."

In the morning, Reverend Andrews keeps looking at his wristwatch and asking me if I'm sure my mother's coming. "It won't take much for us to drop you off," he says. Mrs. Andrews and Bobbie are already sitting in their station wagon. Everybody else has gone home.

Just then Mommy and Abbie drive up and when Abbie leans

forward so I can climb in the backseat, I can tell something's wrong. Mommy's drinking coffee from a paper cup and there's a box of sugar donuts on the dashboard. I don't even get to say how I didn't wet the bed. How when I woke up I couldn't hardly believe it and had to reach down to touch myself to be sure.

"We almost came back and slept with you," Mommy says. She's combing her hair with her fingers, looking at herself in the rearview mirror.

Abbie's got red marks on her face from the seat covers. "We had to sleep in the car," she says.

"How come?"

"When we got home after dropping you off, the old man had the doors all locked. Front and back. He had the venetian blinds shut so tight we couldn't even see him in there guzzling his damn beer," Mommy says. She's so mad she's biting the inside of her cheeks.

"We knocked on both doors. We even tapped on all the windows. But the old man wouldn't budge," Abbie says. When she says "the old man" her voice gets all hushed like she's saying a cussword.

"The old man'll open the door when this one comes knocking." Mommy points her thumb at me. "He never would've pulled that if she'd been with us to begin with."

Gretchie is on the front porch thumping her tail like crazy when we drive up. I figure she must've slept outdoors too. She jumps up and tries to lick my face when I tap on the front-room window.

"It's me. Lana." I tap again. Gretchie nuzzles my hand, whining. "Let us in." I tap till the windowpanes rattle and I hear his chair thump down. "Hold your horses," he says, peeking through the venetian blinds. When he opens the door, he acts all surprised. "Where in hell's name've you been? I was fixing to call the Missing Persons." He grabs me so tight I'm practically suffocating. Gretchie's barking and running around us in circles.

"You son of a bitch," Mommy says, pushing by us. "I'll get you for this."

"What?" he says. "What?" His eyes've got red streaks running through them and his hair's sticking up all over like some tramp's.

down the middle

T he old man came home from work same as usual, but when he tried to get in the back door, it was locked. Mommy had the front door locked too. On the front porch, his old cardboard army suitcase was packed. Mommy put in all his socks and underwear, his other set of work clothes, and his razor.

"It serves him right." Mommy thumbed her nose when he stood out there pounding on the door. In a few minutes, Gus Riley pulled up out front. Mommy said he had to come over to give the old man a summons. Once he handed it to the old man, that would be the end of all our troubles. Then the old man would be gone for good.

The three of us peeked out from behind the blinds in the front room and watched Gus Riley get out of his car and walk up the sidewalk.

"'Evening, Floyd," he said, looking down at the old man's feet. "I sure hate to be the one to do this. But it *is* my job." He handed the old man a piece of paper. The old man stared at it like he forgot how to read. Gus Riley kept turning to look over his shoulder at his house down the street like he wanted to be sure it was still there.

That night after the curfew went off, I thought about the old man and wondered where he was sleeping at and if he could hear the curfew blowing. He always makes us kids go to bed the second it dies down. But Mommy's letting us eat our baloney sandwiches in the front room and stay up late to watch *Gunsmoke*.

"It feels kind of funny in here without the old man," I say. Nobody sits in his empty chair.

"If you miss him so bad, I can fix that," Mommy says. "I can split this family right straight down the middle. You can be his. How's that sound?"

Abbie says, "Mom!" Like she's all shocked. But Mommy just flips the channel till she finds something she wants to look at.

canopy beds

One day there's a knock on the front door. Nobody hardly ever comes to the front door. Me and Abbie're in the front room in our pajamas, playing Catalog People. Abbie's always saying how she's too old for games like that, but she's playing the way she used to anyhow, sitting on the floor with me. We've got all the stuff we cut out spread all over the place. Canopy beds and washing machines and lawn mowers. Tables and chairs and smiling people in brand-new clothes. Everything's all spread out over the faded red front-room rug. When Abbie hears the knock, she freezes like a statue. Then she drops the scissors and runs upstairs.

Mommy comes to answer it. It's this guy I never saw before. He's some kind of giant. He must be at least seven feet tall, and he's got black wavy hair and a navy blue suit on. A wide blue-and-white-striped tie's knotted up under his white collar. When Mommy lets him in, his foot lands right on my baby in her crib. He's got on shiny black shoes with silver buckles kind of like what the pilgrims wore. Mommy gets all mad when I yell about him stepping on my baby. "Pick up your crap," she says.

"Won't you have a seat?" Mommy says to him all nicey nice and pours him a cup of coffee.

It turns out he's a lawyer. He told Mommy that maybe she ought to consider sending me and Abbie to foster homes till things settle down. Mommy says she just might have to do it. If she sends us away, she'll feel pretty bad about it but maybe it's the only thing to do till the old man starts forking over the child support.

For a long time, I couldn't hardly wait to go. I kept wondering what my new family was going to be like. I want one where everybody doesn't yell and scream their heads off all the time. I looked up *foster* in the dictionary and it said *nurture*. Then I looked that up and it said *promote the growth of* and *encourage* and something about nourishment. That's about food. I figure they feed you whatever you want in a foster home. *Promote*'s got to do with school. I didn't look up everything because it makes my head hurt to do that and anyhow, as soon as you look up one word in the dictionary, you have to look up another one. They never say it right out in a way you can get easy.

I tried not to act too happy while we were waiting to go to our foster home, but I couldn't help thinking about what it was going to be like. "Just don't get your hopes up too high," Abbie said when I told her my foster home was going to have canopy beds.

Before Mommy even decided what she was going to do with us, what happened was in the dead of night the old man showed up at the back door bawling his eyes out. "You're all I've got," he said. "You and the girls. You're all I've got." He was gasping, making these loud sounds like he was choking on his supper. "I'm sorry, Ruthie. Never again. Cross my heart."

Now the two of them're downstairs acting lovey-dovey, smacking their lips. "See," Abbie said. "What'd I tell you?"

heaven

I wonder how come God took practically the whole Dutra family, all six of them smashed up by a semi when they were out driving around in their Volkswagen. The old man said it served them right, buying one of them Kraut cars. Their white gravestones were all exactly the same, small and square like sugar cubes all lined up one after the other. Donnie and Dorcas. Danny and Denise and baby Diana. Plus Vilma, their mother. Their daddy was at work when it happened.

Denise was my same age and we both had Mrs. Zugel last year, in second grade. Denise sat behind me and spent the whole time poking me in the back then looking up at the ceiling when she got me to turn around. She didn't get promoted since she never even tried. I remember how her fingernails were chewed clear down till they were practically gone. Her brother Danny was one of the meanest boys on the playground. He once made LaDonna Clinton take a bite from a dried-up cow plop he snuck under the barbed wire to get from the farmer's field. He was kneeling on her chest telling her in this mean voice how if she didn't eat it he'd rip her dress clear off of her and throw it down the coal chute.

It's hard to picture the Dutras dead, laying in their coffins. It's hard to figure out what God wants them for up in heaven. Marvella says kids always go to heaven. Even ones that have never been baptized like me. She says Jesus loves children and she sings that "Jesus Loves Me" song. No matter what they do? I ask her. No matter what, she says. Children don't know any better so they always get the benefit of the doubt.

I don't think heaven can be such a great place if Danny

Dutra's up there but Marvella says being so close to God changes you. The worst person on earth, the person that's made a big mess out of his life by not being a good Christian, can become as sweet as honey in a place where everybody's loved.

I don't say anything about it to Marvella but sometimes I think God is like the guy that makes the cartoons. He's sitting up in the clouds getting a big kick out of watching us. He thinks it's funny what happens to us just like when everybody laughs when the Road Runner gets smashed or Bugs Bunny falls out a window headfirst.

the triumph of
esmerelda

I t's too cold to play outside and Abbie's over at Martha
Bisbee's house so I go in the attic. I'm kind of chilly so I
wrap up in Mommy's fur coat. She never wears it no matter
how cold it is out. It's out of spite, she says. I can remember the
day she got it. Me and Penny were out back jumping in a pile of
oak leaves when Mommy and the old man pulled up in the driveway. Penny never gets to save the leaves in her yard. The second
they start falling off, her and her sisters have to get out there and
rake them up so her daddy can burn them in the gutter. If Penny
wants to play in any leaves, she has to come over and play in
mine.

Mommy got out of the car wearing a long grey fur coat with
dark stripes in it and big furry buttons down the front. She
looked like a movie star. She had her black high heels on. When
she wears them, she's almost tall as the old man is. This was
when her hair was long and she had it twisted up behind her head
and she had her sparkly earrings on.

I ran over and pressed my face into the soft fur and looked up
at her. The old man had his chest pushed out and he was grinning, chewing on the earpiece of his glasses and looking at
Mommy. "Ain't she a living doll?" he asked.

Mommy's cheeks looked like powder sugar donuts. She bent
down and started combing the leaves out of my hair with her fingers. She's got these dark blue eyes that're so pretty sometimes
when we're in Tipton strangers stop her on the street to tell her

about it. "You're not from around here, are you?" they always ask.

I start looking at the pictures we keep in this box that our Thanksgiving turkey came in that time the old man got a turkey bonus instead of his usual ten dollars. He was pretty mad about it but we got to have turkey like everybody else instead of roast chicken the way we usually do. Mommy had to get up practically in the middle of the night to start cooking it.

We have a little book of snapshots of me and Abbie on this boat ride at the carnival uptown when we were little, sitting in a boat with matching sailor hats and sailor dresses on. Abbie is in front and I'm sitting behind her. The boats are floating on this tank that's kind of like a big plastic swimming pool. They're all chained up to this post in the middle. We each have a bell with a rope we can pull to ring it all we want. I'm ringing mine like crazy. We have steering wheels, but it doesn't matter which way we turn them. You can only go around and around in a circle no matter what direction you want to go in once the guy that operates the ride takes your ticket and pulls the lever. There's one of Grammy holding Shirley Jean. It's kind of blurry so I can't get a good look at her. She's bare naked except for a diaper. I don't get how come a baby has to die. That don't make any sense. I mean, the baby didn't even really get started living and then it's gone.

It starts raining and the rain sounds kind of like somebody's tapping on the roof and there's water dripping in a pan in the corner over where the mouse poison is at. Sometimes the light flickers and goes out so I have my flashlight handy in case. I have to be careful not to get a splinter from the old wood floor. The photographs are shoved every which way in the box like somebody was playing cards and had to quit. One of these days I'm going to arrange them in order. I'm going to get me one of them scrapbooks like Leota Tupper has with the black triangles glued onto the big grey pages to hold the corners down. There's me in my underpants holding up a stringer of catfish and me with my arms around Gretchie when she was just a little pup. There's me learning how to ride my bike with the old man holding on to the back and I've got my new jacket on, the one with pompons on the hood. That's back when I was five. Now I can ride with no hands but back then I was scared to death of him letting go. When he finally did he didn't even tell me because he knew if he did, I'd fall down just at the idea of riding by myself without anybody holding me steady. In Abbie's third-grade picture she's got her polka-dot dress on. I'm not going to keep my third-grade picture on account of I look so ugly. I hid it under my bed and when I brought it back in, Mrs. Hyatt couldn't believe Mommy wasn't going to buy them but I just told her we couldn't afford it. She didn't say anything about the way there was a dent in the pictures from my bedsprings. She's so old she can't hardly see a thing anyhow.

Sometimes what I do is I act like I'm looking at the photographs and I spread them all out but what I really do is I look at this little book the old man's got in his suitcase underneath his old army uniform. It's called *The Triumph of Esmerelda*. In it there's these pictures of this man and lady that take off all their clothes and act like they're dogs sniffing at each other. Then the lady, whose name is Esmerelda, lets the man comb the curly hair she's got between her legs. Mommy has hair like that too. She told me once if I wanted to see where the baby comes from just squat over a mirror and I'll see the little slit in my hoochy-ma-goochy but I never did that. What if somebody opened the door and caught me? I'm always scared somebody'll come in the attic and find me looking at *The Triumph of Esmerelda* so that's why when I look at it I keep it in between the pages of my *Little Lulu* comic and hold it up close to my face. Then if Abbie ever opens the door to come in or the old man or Mommy does, I'll just act like I'm reading my comic book and they'll never know the difference. When I look at the old man's book, I ache all over like I have a toothache in my bones.

sparky

J ust where the hell do you think you're going?" Mommy's laying on her bed with her chenille housecoat on smoking a cigarette and coughing like crazy. She just got out of the bathtub and the downstairs smells like bubble bath and the windows are all steamy.

"Over to Martha's," Abbie says. All Abbie ever wants to do now is get out of the house. Her and Martha Bisbee spend nearly every second putting on lipstick and makeup in Martha's room. Martha gets all the makeup she wants since her daddy's the undertaker. I don't say anything since I don't really have anyplace to go. I was just going to follow Abbie till she told me to get lost.

"It's snowing out," Mommy says. "Where's your sense? Just stay the hell indoors. I'm sick to death of the two of you crouping around. Every other day you're home sick from school."

Abbie stomps upstairs. When I get there, she's curling her eyelashes with this clampy thing she got from Baker's Five and Ten. Abbie hardly ever plays with me anymore. But since she can't go out, she agrees to play What Is It?

I get to be the one that lies in bed with the covers over my head. When Abbie puts something in my hand, I have to guess what it is. I love the part where I stick my hand out and open it up and wait to feel what Abbie'll put in it. Sometimes I can't hardly stand to keep my hand open. But Abbie makes me. She uncurls my fingers all the way and she brushes my palm up and down for a little while to make me wait even more. She finds all kinds of stuff for me to guess. Even if it turns out to be a marble she spit on, it still feels like an eyeball. She puts Sneezy, my hamster, in my hand. But I know it's him right away, he wiggles around so much.

Sneezy's got this little wheel he runs in like he's really trying to get somewhere. It moves around and around, but he stays in the same place. I don't think he even knows it.

Abbie puts a rubber spider in my hand so I quit playing. She says I'm a crybaby snot-nosed brat, but I don't even care. I hate spiders. I go downstairs and Mommy lets me wash the china dogs she collects. She keeps them on this knickknack shelf. She's got a Scotty dog and a beagle and even a poodle with real fur and a gold chain around his neck. She's got a collie dog like Lassie and an Irish setter that's pointing its paw straight out. She even has one she calls her mutt. It looks just like my first dog Sparky looked with pointy ears and a pink tongue.

Sparky was supposed to be everybody's dog but she liked me the best. When the old man tried to spank me, Sparky'd get mad and bark at him and act like she was about to bite his hand off. Then she really did try to bite the milkman once when he was bringing our milk up to the front porch. The old man said he was afraid she was turning mean.

Sparky had five puppies and one time when the puppies were big enough to run around out back, I came home from school and two of them were missing. I couldn't find them anywhere. Me and Abbie went all over the neighborhood all up and down the alley calling and calling. But there weren't any puppies anywhere. Then Abbie said we ought to go over to the farm and have a look. So we walked through the school yard to the fence and crawled under the barbed wire. Abbie had to help me so I wouldn't get all scratched up. We walked up and down the rows of corn and then we got to this pigpen and that's where I saw the puppies. They were both smushed flat in the mud. Abbie tried to hold her hand over my eyes but I looked anyway. She said the pigs must've trampled them. Poochie's head was all flat and her mouth was wide open. I saw her little tiny teeth. Spotty didn't even have a head at all.

Sparky's been dead a long time now. The old man shot her when I was off at Sunday school. For a long time I thought she'd run away. I looked all over for her and asked everybody about a million times if they'd seen her. Leota Tupper said she couldn't remember the last time she saw Sparky. Iggie Purtlebaugh said it seemed like just the other day she was over there chasing his cats up the maple trees the way she loved to do. Then Abbie told me. She said she heard Sparky crying so she looked out the window and there was the old man standing out in the backyard with that shotgun he keeps under his side of the bed. When he shot Sparky, she kind of jumped up in the air and then she laid down on her side in the grass. Afterwards, the old man put Sparky in his trunk and drove off.

slumgolium

The minute school lets out, I run across the frozen grass, down the back alley past our house. Mommy's car is in the driveway, but she's not home. She's in the hospital. She's got what you call pee-neumonia, the old man says.

"Whoa there, girl. Hold your horses," Iggie Purtlebaugh calls. "Where's the fire?" On his clothesline, pants and shirts hang stiff with ice. The bare tree branches look like fingers scratching the blue sky.

"C'mon in," Marvella says when I knock. "The door's open."

She has a frilly apron on and apples baking in the oven. The heat prickles my cheeks. With Marvella's soft arms around me, my nose gets pressed against her clean-clothes smell.

"I don't reckon you'd be hungry? Never in all my days met a living soul skinny as you. Skinny as you, but hungry as a horse." She unbuttons my coat, hangs it beside the door, and reties the sash on my dress. She pours Hershey's syrup into a glass of milk. "This'll get you started. Stir it up nice and good."

She's humming this song she taught us in Sunday school—the one about He's got the whole world in His hands. She spreads oleo on two slices of bread, sprinkles them with sugar, and presses one on the other with her freckled hand. She slices the sandwich into two triangles the way I like. Then she's over by the oven, pulling out a casserole. Marvella can never sit still. She's like some bee that's got to go and have a look at every dandelion in the yard.

"Jesus wept," she tells me. "That's the shortest sentence in the Bible. You know what that means don't you, sugar?"

"It means Jesus cried."

"Course it does. It means he cried. Do you know how come?"

"He was sad."

"Uh-huh."

"He was scared since he knew Pilate was going to kill him."

"Nobody can ever kill Jesus. He might've died but he rose up again the next day. Remember how we learned that in Sunday school? How Mary Magdalene goes to the tomb and that rock is rolled clear away and it's empty inside? Anyhow, Jesus didn't weep on account of he was scared. He wasn't the scaredy type. He wept because it about broke his heart to see what a mess folks were making of their lives. It about broke his heart. His is such a simple message. But half the people don't pay it any mind. Do you know what His message is?"

"Be good and do what your parents say."

"Well, you're right that that's in the Bible. But all Jesus ever asked us to do was love one another. That's it. Just love one another."

"And Jesus loves me?"

"Course he does." She sets the casserole on the countertop.

"How can you be sure?" I ask her.

"Because He says so. He loved children especially."

"No matter what? No matter what bad things they do? He never gets mad or anything?"

"No matter what. What could a sweet kid like you do to make Jesus mad?" she asks. She wipes the sugar off the edge of my mouth with her apron. Mommy told me once that God was always watching. That He was always looking down like a big nib nose that didn't miss a thing so don't think I could pull a fast one on Him. I don't know what I think. I keep mixing up which one is God and which one is Jesus. I mean I know which is which, but I'm not always sure which one is the one that's looking.

"This here's for you to take home," Marvella says. "It's tuna noodle. You like that?"

"We got leftovers from last night."

"Oh you do, do you? How's your Daddy holding up? He's sure got his hands full being mother and father both. Tell him I said take himself a break."

"Last night Daddy made up this recipe called slumgolium." When I say *Daddy,* the word sounds funny since I hardly ever say

71

it. To me, *Daddy* means a man walking up the sidewalk with a newspaper under his arm, whistling, his kids waving, and the dog running in circles around his feet. Not the old man, dancing to his cha-cha music, counting one-two-cha-cha-cha three-four-cha-cha-cha, grinning like crazy while hamburg and onions sizzle in the black iron skillet. "Cha-cha-cha," he sings and dumps in a can of beans, tasting, sprinkling brown sugar on, stirring, adding ketchup. "Easy as pie," he says. "I don't know what your mother's always griping about. I'd like to see *her* go work in a factory all day like I have to if she thinks *this* is hard work."

He stands so close I can smell the change in his pockets. "C'mere," he whispers. His face is all sad. His palms cup my cheeks so I have to turn towards him. That's when I see his pants unzipped, the thick brass zipper teeth are open, and the thing you pull like a little tongue is dangling at the bottom.

"The cat got your tongue?" Marvella says. She puts a baked apple in front of me. The whole kitchen smells like cinnamon.

gauze

I'm practicing being invisible. What I do is I see how still I can lie and if I have to move at all I only do a tiny bit so no one will even notice. I hold my arms and legs stiff, acting like they're made out of two-by-fours like the wood the old man made me my stilts out of so I could stand and wave at Mommy through the window when she was in the hospital. In her oxygen tent she looked like she was zippered into a plastic mattress cover. Now she's back home same as usual.

I try not to look at anyone or say anything and if someone tries to talk to me or calls my name I act like I don't hear them. If I have to talk, I whisper. My teacher Mrs. Hyatt says she's going to quit calling on me if I don't speak up and that'll show up as bad conduct on my report card and she wrote Mommy a note about it. Mommy says if I have something worth saying, I'll spit it out so just leave me alone.

At night, I lie in my bed and stare and stare into the dark. I act like I'm wrapping myself up in gauze. I wind and wind the thin spiderwebby cloth all around me, my chest and my shoulders, my arms and my legs and my face. I wind and wind till I'm all covered with gauze from head to toe.

santy claus

Every Christmas, what the old man likes to do is he likes to wait till a car is coming down the street and then he sneaks out the back door and throws the Christmas tree on the front porch and runs back inside.

"Did you see Santy Claus go by?" he asks. He points at the red lights disappearing down the road. "You just missed him," he says. Then I run and open the front door and there's the Christmas tree.

This Christmas everybody's all mad because Abbie got the old man a pair of socks and he had a fit about it and threw them right in her face. I got him this little wooden Goofy doll with his head on a spring and the old man acted like that was the best present he ever got and he put it on his chest of bureau drawers. Abbie won't talk to me even though I told her she could have all my chocolate stars. I even said I'd throw in my all-day sucker, but she won't even say a word.

Me and Abbie always get stockings filled with candy and nuts. We don't even have to eat dinner or supper on Christmas. We just eat our candy all day long.

The best Christmas we ever had when the old man brought home Gretchie. On Christmas Eve there was a knock at the front door.

"Who could that be? Santy Claus?" Mommy said.

Nobody hardly ever knocks on our front door, especially after dark, and we already had our Christmas tree put up with the lights on. I went to see who it was. The old man was standing on the porch with snow on his eyebrows and his cheeks all red. He just stood there like he was a stranger waiting for me to invite him in. Then I noticed something moving in the front of his coat. I peeped in and there was this brown puppy.

I was so happy I stood on my tiptoes and kissed the old man's cheek, which I almost never do if I can help it. I can still remember how his whiskers scraped my lips and the cold smell of his damp wool coat.

mouse poison

The old man is downstairs hollering and slamming the cupboard doors. "You think I don't know? You really think I'm too stupid to figure out what's going on behind my back?"

"Floyd, it's all in your head," Mommy says. Her high heels click across the kitchen floor. "I ain't doing a thing. And I'm not having any rendezvous with anybody on the sly."

"Shaking your tail all over town. I've seen you. Lipstick and perfume ain't all you're peddling."

"Quit it! You keep your hands offa me."

There's a slap and then the old man kind of growls like a dog.

"Don't you ever lay a hand on me again," she says.

The back door slams and then the old man's out in the shed with his Benny Goodman record on real loud.

"You want to play a new game?" Abbie whispers from her bed.

"Yeah."

"OK." She punches her pillow into a ball under her head and turns on her side to face me. "It's called The Old Man's Gone for Good. What you have to do is you have to think up a way to get rid of him once and for all. You give me a clue, and I'll figure out the story."

"What d'ya mean, a clue?"

"You know. How he dies. Say mouse poison or something."

"OK. Mouse poison."

Abbie sighs like she can't believe how dumb I am.

"How about ant poison, then?"

"All right. Ant poison." She cups her hands and stares into

76

them like she's a fortune-teller at the carnival reading her palms. "What happens is, Mommy's sprinkling ant poison around the kitchen up under the cupboards and on the countertops. The ants are real bad 'cause you were making a sugar sandwich one time and you spilt the sugar."

"How come I'm the one that has to spill the sugar?"

"Shh," she says. "She's sprinkling the white powder all over the place and then the telephone rings and she gets to talking to Winona Flowers and she forgets to wipe the ant poison up before she goes to bed. In the morning, the old man comes in and makes himself a sandwich to take in his lunch bucket to work. He sets his bread right on the countertop. He's such a tightwad worrying about the stupid utility bill he doesn't even turn on the light. So he doesn't even notice he's sticking his bread right in the middle of the ant poison."

"Then what?" I say.

Abbie giggles and falls back on her bed with her tongue out and her eyes rolled up in her head. "The end."

hello, brother

F loyd unlocks the blue wooden side door and lets himself
into the church the way he does every Saturday morning.
Usually he brings Lana along with him to help, but today
she was already gone when he got up. Despite the cool air, a fine
sweat breaks out on the back of his neck and beneath his nose.
He presses the back of his hand to his lips and leans against the
cinder-block wall. He tells himself to calm down and pictures the
tasks ahead of him. How he will take his supplies from the corner
cupboard in the kitchen, fill a tin bucket with hot water and am-
monia. The main thing, he tells himself, is to keep going forward,
step-by-step, one foot in front of the other. But lately he has begun to feel as if he is being yanked across a giant game board,
landing on the squares at random.

Something about a church kitchen, the sour smell of old
bread, stale coffee, cookies baked long ago, reminds him of his
mother. He lights a cigarette—he allows himself to smoke only
when he's in the kitchen—and takes the cash from the envelope
that was left for him. A little spending money, he thinks as he begins scrubbing at the fingerprints on the cupboards above the
sink. With his big hands clutching the damp rag, he tries to will
the memory of his mother: her blue veiled hat, her white gloves,
her white high heels, the ones trimmed with brown along the toe
and heel, scraping along the sidewalk on Sunday morning. Instead, the image of her shivering under the heavy wool quilt, even
though it was August, is all he can recall. He sees himself bending
over her. Weak, he thinks, I am so weak. As if he is watching the
whole thing in slow motion on a screen in front of him, Floyd
sees himself bend over his mother, feeding her tablespoons full of

crème de menthe. She'd been a teetotaler her whole life, proud she'd never touched a drop of liquor, convinced alcohol was the work of the devil. He'd told her it was medicine, wanting only to dull the pain, to hurry her on her way. He held the back of her head, her dry matted grey hair, as he spooned the green syrup into her shrunken mouth. Watching her waste away for months until her skull seemed ready to break through her skin, until her fingers were thin as wishbones, all the while knowing there was nothing the doctors could do, had made Floyd wonder just what kind of God would let a good woman like her suffer so long and hard. Especially after his father, who'd been as evil as the devil himself, had passed away in his sleep. They'd found him curled on his side, a smile on his face, as peaceful as a newborn baby.

Floyd crushes his cigarette out in the sink, then runs water over it to be sure it's out before he goes upstairs to the sanctuary. Because he likes being in an empty church, likes the feel of the space around him, the smell of floor wax and dust, he sits for a moment in a back pew. He is a large man—the dark red hair on his head wiry, sticking up in places where it is obvious he has tried to plaster it down—dressed in grey work pants and shirt, the uniform he wears even on weekends.

He dusts the honey-colored pews with his soft yellow rag. Runs it along the smooth rounded edges of the backs and seats. Turns the black cloth-covered hymnals right side up. Picks up the bulletins left behind, the dried wads of tissue, the red strips from packs of Life Savers, silver gum wrappers, a dime. He vacuums the red carpet that stretches down the aisle between the pews, whistling "The Old Rugged Cross" while he vacuums right up to the pulpit, which he polishes with his rag. He stands on the platform above the pews, looking out over the empty church, feeling a peace he's never found anywhere else. On Saturday, the church is his.

Lately memories have been coming to him, times he hasn't thought of in years. It's as if a row of doors has unlocked inside him and he can't do anything but wait and see what will roll out in front of him. Just like the generators on the conveyor belt where he works, they keep moving toward him. He can't stop them. As he stands at the pulpit, the dust motes streaming in the sunlight, he sees Ron Brown, his buddy back in the war, grinning *his crooked grin. The two of them had been as close as twins, both of them away from home for the first time, both with wives they barely knew writing them letters, and babies they'd never held already waiting to call them Dad.*

Ron is sitting in the front pew, telling Floyd that same dream he'd had the last night Floyd saw him. "All the churches take down their crosses," he says. He has his dress uniform on, his hat in his lap, but his big feet are bare. Ron never did like wearing shoes. He used to joke about how back home in Louisiana, in his town, nobody wore shoes. He claimed that having to wear shoes was ten times worse than eating army chow. "Us GIs all come home and there's neither hide nor hair of a cross. Nowhere to be found. The steeples on all the churches are bare where the crosses used to be at. All over the country, the religions start acting like they're one and the same. The Baptists and the Presbyterians, the Seventh-Day Adventists and the Methodists, even the Catholics, are all nodding and smiling at one another. It's like before the Tower of Babel when everybody spoke the same language and got along. The funny thing is, when you go to have a word with somebody, when you start to talking, colors come out of their mouths instead of words. And if you bend down to look in, you can see the sunlight shining right through their cheeks all red and green and blue just the way it shines through a stained-glass window."

Floyd remembers walking across a field, the parched grass rustling at his feet, the sun already baking his skin, burning right through his shirt. All around him the smoldering fires from the firebombs. He'd thought the whole world was ending right in front of his eyes, the flames streaking across the night sky, as he crouched down, his head in his hands the way he'd been taught to do. And he'd made it. Standing in the smoky dawn, he's sure he's alive, though he has a strong sense he's dreaming. He stumbles across the weedy field, headed in the direction where Ron fled, when there he is. Ron. The back of his head blown away, his face crawling with huge shiny blue-black flies.

Floyd stands at the altar wondering what to pray for, looking up at the stained-glass window of Mary Magdalene weeping at the open tomb. Sitting on a grey rock, her head bent, a handker-

chief at her eyes. Jesus is behind her in his white flowing robe, standing in the light. She hasn't yet turned to see him. Hasn't yet learned of the miracle. Floyd feels he is waiting just like Mary Magdalene. It would take a miracle, he thinks, straightening the red velvet cushions around the altar railing. It would take a miracle to get him out of this mess he calls his life.

Floyd takes a dust mop and whisks the soft tangle of yarn over the loincloth, over the gleaming thighs of the plaster form of Jesus hanging on the side wall. Jesus with his bloody crown of thorns, his palms open, bleeding. He remembers that time Ruth caught him praying in the dark, on his knees in the front room beside his chair. How she laughed and mocked him. "You damn fool. God could care less about you," she said.

The preacher on TV says Jesus is a friend to all. If only people would remember to turn to Him. He knows our deepest pain. He can hear our worst secrets and still be there to help us get back on the path to forgiveness of sin. Ruth had come into the room when Floyd was watching the show. "Did you ever think about how old Jesus must be getting mighty sick and tired of hearing everybody bitch and moan about their lives while he's up there hanging on that cross?"

Floyd doesn't know what to think. When he finishes his dusting, he sits down at the piano, picking out one of his mother's favorites, a tune he no longer knows the words to but that he heard her hum as far back as he can remember. He has an unlit cigarette—he figures God won't mind so long as he doesn't light it—jammed into the corner of his mouth, when he hears voices in the hallway. He's uncertain at first whether someone is actually there or whether he's hearing things. He looks down at his hands poised above the keyboard. Large soft hands like his father's, with freckles sprinkled like cinnamon across white bread. His hands feel like a pair of gloves someone dropped on the sidewalk. He stooped to pick them up. Now he carries them wherever he goes. But they do whatever they want. He has no say-so about the things his hands will do.

Three ladies, aprons tied over their dresses, come into the sanctuary with their arms full of flowers to decorate the altar. They stand with their mouths half open and eye him uneasily, like he's a thief who will snatch the flowers from their arms and rush with them down the aisle. Then, realizing who it is sitting at the piano, they smile nervously and say hello in their best Christian voices, as if they want to say, "Hello, brother." But the words are trapped in their throats. Their veiled eyes can't conceal how they feel about a man like Floyd Franklin. A man who cleans the church, but who rarely comes to worship on Sunday morning.

Floyd feels like they can see right into his life. They know how he will stop on his way home and spend the money he's earned, slapping it on the counter, exchanging it for the case of beer he carries out the door, the bottles rattling. They can see him in his chair in the front room, his shoes kicked off in the corner. They can smell his sweaty feet. Hear the empty bottles roll across the floor. They know his children crouch on their narrow beds, pillows wrapped around their heads. They are not surprised by Ruth stretched across the double bed, naked beneath her thin white nightgown, smoking in the dark. These ladies have eyes that have seen him in the dead of night, creeping up the stairs to his daughter's bed. They have seen his hands reaching up her soft thighs.

Floyd kneels on the rug, wrapping the cord around the vacuum cleaner. He feels like he has just been caught sneaking a dollar bill from the collection plate, caught sliding the crisp money into his front pocket, and there is nothing to do but pass the brass plate to the man beside him. Floyd kneels on the rug while the ladies bustle around him, their voices low, murmuring, like bees working the blossoms of a buckeye tree.

cleaning catfish

A bee's just like a kamikaze airplane and pilot all rolled up in one," the old man says, flicking a match into the grass and blowing smoke out of his nose. He runs his hand over his head, trying to smooth his hair back from his forehead. It still keeps standing up all over the place. He stands there staring across the yard at Mr. Reeb pushing his lawn mower up and down between his yard and ours, spitting grass clippings onto our side. Mr. Reeb's got an old white sailor hat pulled down to keep the sun out of his eyes. He keeps his eyes fixed on the grass like that's all that's worth looking at. Him and the old man quit talking to each other a long time ago. It really burns Mr. Reeb up the way we hardly ever cut our grass. The old man told him to mind his own damn business. It's my property, he said. I can grow hay if I feel like it.

I'm out back catching bees the way I like to do even though it drives Abbie nuts. She's always getting on me about how it's not normal. She says I'm too old to be doing stuff like that now that I'm nine. What will everybody say?

When I heard the old man's car pull up and the door slam, I knew it was him but I didn't even look up. I didn't even turn and wave at him the way he likes me to. I can never figure out if I'm supposed to be teed off at him the way Mommy and Abbie are. Mommy says she wishes he'd drop dead.

I kind of miss him sometimes, but I never let on. Mommy just got done telling me before she left how he has no business coming over and telling me his sob story and trying to get me on his side. They're having what you call a trial separation. That means after the old man cools off, they'll give their marriage another try or else they'll go to court.

I have a bee under a jar, so I'm holding my breath and waiting for the right minute to catch it. A bee's liable to sting you if you aren't paying attention.

"What d'ya say we go fishing?" The old man jiggles the change in his pockets. "Head over to White River and get us a mess of catfish." I can picture us driving down the road out in the country, all the windows down, a nice breeze cooling us off. Next to catching bees, I love fishing best. I lift up my jar and let the bee fly off.

The old man gets his shovel out of the shed and starts digging worms. The worms have made tunnels down deep where the ground is cool and damp. A bunch of pink worms wiggle in the dark dirt. One worm got cut in half by the shovel and the two broken pieces twist and jerk. When Iggie Purtlebaugh got his finger cut off in the meat grinder, what they did was they scooped his finger up out of the ground pork and Doc Havey sewed it back on. Iggie Purtlebaugh says it don't quite work the way it used to, but it's sure better than having no finger at all.

Me and the old man pull the worms out, dropping them into a tin can. He stops and rolls the sleeves of his grey work shirt up over his elbows. I remember back when I was real little I'd get him to make a muscle and then I'd hang on his arm like it was a chinning post. He lights another cigarette and shoves it into the side of his mouth, scrunching up his eye to keep the smoke out while he pats the dirt back into the hole.

When I go inside to leave a note, the old man sits in the car with the door open and one foot on the ground. He has his eyes on the rearview mirror. He's combing his hair and he looks like that guy on Abbie's favorite show, 77 Sunset Strip. She can never watch it when the old man's home on account of he's got to have Route 66 and they're both on at the same time.

The old man has the bamboo poles hooked up on my side of the car so I can hold on to them. I hang my head out the window as we drive. The air smells like ripe corn and manure. Most everybody thinks manure is a bad smell, but it's really kind of sweet.

* * *

84

"You keep your eye on them bobbers while I go set up the tent." The old man hangs an old army tarp on a rope between two trees. Twigs snap as he rustles through the brush, finding rocks to weigh down the sides and piling up dry oak leaves to make a cushion. He takes a beer out of the cooler he brought and drinks it down in a few gulps. Then he gets another one. I stare at the muddy water, at the bobbers floating there. Mommy and Abbie're probably home by now sitting at the kitchen table eating Kraft dinner. Suddenly I wish I was home with them.

My bobber bounces and tips over. The next nibble is a bit harder. The bobber twirls around then the fish takes the bait and swims with it, bending the end of my pole. The old man runs over hollering instructions. "Hold it tight now. Pull on it. Don't give him any slack." I can tell he's having all he can do not to grab the pole away from me and land that fish himself.

"Looky here. You got the granddaddy. It's a mighty big one." He steps on the tail of the catfish so I can poke the end of the stringer through its mouth and out the gill. I loop the tip through the silver ring and pull the stringer tight so the fish can't get loose. It's a big old catfish with whiskers sprouting from the sides of its mouth. It flaps its tail and opens and closes its gills, taking in air.

"They're biting now."

"Lemme finish getting the firewood. Then I'll fish with you." The stringer's hooked around this tree root and the fish I just caught is trying to swim away fast, like it's testing to see how far it can get.

The old man gets such a big bite his pole nearly falls into the river. I grab ahold of it just in time. He comes running over with a bottle of beer in his hand, beer all foaming out the top and down the sides. When he pulls his line in, a drop of water glistens on the empty hook.

"Boy, that was a close one," he says.

"I tried to get it."

"I know you did, sweetheart. No harm done."

He grabs me the way he likes to and kisses my forehead. His lips leave a wet place I wipe off with the back of my hand.

"Reverend Andrews says drinking and smoking are the both of them sins."

"Well, I'll say one thing. The Ten Commandments don't mention a thing about thou shalt not drink or smoke, now do they?"

"He oughta know. He's the preacher."

"The way I figure it. If it feels any good at all, old Reverend Andrews'd say it was a sin. Now you tell me. Why on earth'd God go and give us things that made us feel so good if we weren't supposed to have them?"

I can't think up any answer. One time the old man gave Abbie a bloody nose for no good reason. Mommy says when he gets to drinking, steer clear of him the same way you'd do if a mad dog was staggering down Carrigan Road. Just get out of his way.

I keep thinking how any minute Mommy and Abbie'll drive up. Mommy'll grab me by the arm and pull me into the car screaming the whole while at the old man about how he had no right to take me off like that. Every time a car comes along the road, I wait for it to stop, but it goes on over the bridge.

"What d'ya say we call it quits?" the old man says after we have six catfish at the end of the stringer, pulling each other back and forth. He pulls his line in and throws what's left of his worm in the water.

"Pretty soon it'll be so dark out you won't be able to see your nose in front of your face." He reaches over and pinches my nose between his thumb and finger. I used to really believe when he did that he had the tip of my nose in his hand. I'd cry till he put it back on.

"When I'm a grown-up, I'm going to invent me a bobber that's got a light bulb on it. Then I can fish all night if I want to."

The old man laughs. With his head back and his mouth wide open laughing, he looks like he's taking a big bite out of the sky.

I get to light the campfire even though the old man makes this royal big deal out of it like I'm still about five years old and about to burn up the whole place.

"Push your sleeves up," he says. I strike the match real quick down the side of the box and hold it to the newspaper he crumpled under the kindling.

"Step back now." I hold the match for a second longer, the heat of the flame creeping towards my fingers.

"Remember what to do if you catch on fire? Remember? What'd I tell you?"

"I know."

"What?"

"I already know." I say it all mean, wishing he'd leave me alone but once he gets started you can never hear the end of it.

"Roll on the ground till the fire's all out," I finally say, kicking some dirt into the fire.

"How come?"

"'Cause fire likes air and you've got to smother it."

"That's my girl. What'd you do if somebody else caught on fire? Say your old man was burning up? What would you do?"

"I'd get a blanket and wrap it around you real tight."

"What if I fought you? What if I was so scared, I just kept trying to run?"

"I'd trip you and knock you down and make you roll on the ground."

"Folks get mighty scared when something like that's going on. They're liable to do anything. You've got to take charge. Back in the army . . ."

"I know. I know." I can tell by the look on his face the way I said that is getting him all worked up. But he's already told me all this a hundred thousand times. Abbie says it's stuff like that that proves he's off his rocker.

To clean catfish, first you stomp on the catfish's tail so it can't flap around and get away. Then slice the head off right behind the gills, careful of the sharp fin on its back. Even when catfish're dead, they can still hurt you with that pointy fin of theirs.

The catfish keep moving their mouths after their heads get cut off. I guess it takes them a while to figure out they're dead. The old man slits them right down the belly and the guts spill out all at once. I can't figure out how they fit inside the belly the way they do since the guts look so much bigger than the empty place left behind. I pop the air sacs with the tip of the knife before I scrape the inside all clean and peel the skin off. Then comes the best part. I sprinkle the fish with salt and watch their tails curl up like they're swimming.

The old man rolls the fish in cornmeal and fries them in a

black iron skillet set over the fire. "It's mighty hard to be a good daddy. You got to understand how it is, Lana. The man of the house's the boss. He's the biggest and the strongest. But that don't mean it's easy."

Mommy always says when he starts in like this, it's the booze talking. He's full of hot air and he ain't got a lick of sense. I ask him how come somebody has to be the boss in the first place. "That's just Mother Nature." He scoops the fish out of the pan. "There's always a leader in any group. Otherwise we'd all still be living like cavemen. Look at Crooked Tail. There wasn't any daddy in that family, so he had to be the boss."

Crooked Tail was one of the puppies from Gretchie's last litter. We were supposed to get to keep him but at the last minute the old man sold him like he does all her puppies. Crooked Tail had a bump on his tail on account of it got stepped on when he was first born and this was supposed to make it so he wasn't worth any money but then this guy gave the old man a couple of bucks for him.

The old man keeps on talking but I'm thinking about the puppies and how cute they were and how sad I was when we had to sell them. My favorite thing to do was lie on the floor and let them run up and down me. One time I had on my new birthday blue orlon sweater and the puppies were licking my face and trying to jump up on my belly. They'd slip and slide on the linoleum trying to get a running start and then wiggle so bad wagging their tails they'd fall over. I was laughing so hard I was about to pee my pants and I didn't notice their little nails were making snags in my new sweater. The next thing I knew, the old man was yanking me up off the floor, making me step on the puppies. They yelped and ran back in their box to hide. He smacked me over and over again and hollered about didn't I know how to take care of anything and how Mommy'd spent his hard-earned money buying me that sweater and finally Abbie came in and said it's only a sweater. Don't you start in, he said and took his belt off and chased her all over the house.

The old man opens up another bottle of beer and drinks it down. I finish eating my fish without saying anything. I save the tails for last. They're so crunchy and good.

"We'll have to bury this fire before we go to sleep. Even when you think the fire's all out there could be just one live coal left. That's all it'd take to burn the whole woods up. So we'll do what Smokey the Bear says, okeydokey kiddoke?"

He rubs my hair then he puts his arm around me. His whiskers feel like sandpaper on my cheek. He tosses his beer bottle into the fire and the glass pops. *Hey Mabel, Black Label.* That little song starts going around in my head, over and over like on TV. *Hey Mabel, Black Label.*

"Yes siree. I reckon we'll have to bury this fire before we hit the sack." He opens up another beer and I scoot away from him. I was going to go get the shovel but as soon as I turn away from the fire it's so dark. I don't know where he put the flashlight or even if he remembered to take it out of the car.

"Take your mother. Now there's a fire'll never burn out." The old man starts laughing like he just told some real funny joke. Then he takes his glasses off and folds them up and puts them in his shirt pocket. I can see he's crying. I wrap my arms around my knees and stare at the fire. It reminds me of that time Lonnie MacAbee broke his arm falling off the slide during recess. We all just stood around looking at him laying in the dirt crying. Mrs. Zugel said not to touch him because we could make it worse and then the ambulance came.

In the morning, the old man is laying on his side snoring and the fire's all burnt down to red coals. The air smells like mud and fish, and robins are singing to each other up in the maple trees. The old man doesn't even move or anything. If he wasn't snoring up a storm I'd think he was dead.

The sun is a big orange ball coming up behind the haze. The locusts haven't started yet and it seems kind of funny not to hear them, like they're up in the leaves waiting for the leader to be the first one to start so they can all join in.

A muskrat comes swimming down the river real slow with its brown furry nose pointing up out of the water. I stand so still it doesn't even notice me. But if I wanted to, I could reach right out and touch it.

the meanest man alive

Mommy keeps telling us kids how once we hit eighteen we can move out on our own but for now she has to take the old man back and we all just have to make the best of it. "I just can't make ends meet," she says. "When I hit eighteen, I took off. You can too.

"I still remember the last night I spent at home. I was sleeping in bed with Auntie Thelma and Grammy came and got in bed with us on account of she was scared of my old man and she hoped when he came home drunk he'd just flop on the bed and not notice she wasn't in there. But when he finds her gone he comes right into our room and yanks her up out of the bed by her hair. A great big hunk of hair came right out of her head and she had to wear a hat for months till it grew back in. That's when I left. I'd had it up to here and I was old enough to get out.

"Let me tell you something. If you think you have it so bad, you've got no idea," Mommy says. "When I was a little girl we had hardly a thing. It was a depression going on. We couldn't have any candy and half the time me and Auntie Thelma went to bed with our bellies empty."

She said all she ever did back then was think about what she wanted to eat. She'd count bowls full of mashed potatoes and thick juicy steaks instead of sheep. I never did meet her real daddy. He died when he fell out of bed and whacked his head on the edge of his bedside table after having one too many. Mommy said that was the happiest day of her life.

Grampy came along after him. Grampy's what you call a happy drunk but her real daddy was a mean drunk. What she had to do when she was a kid was she had to walk all around town with a paper sack picking up cigarette butts she found in the gutters. She did that so her daddy could have a smoke. She'd bring them cigarette butts home and he'd make her and Auntie Thelma pull the paper off them and pick off the burnt part till there was a pile of tobacco for him to roll up into a cigarette. He couldn't afford to buy a pack of his own and anyhow cigarettes were hard to come by even if you did have two nickels to rub together to make a dime.

"If you think the old man's bad," Mommy says. "You ain't seen nothing. My old man was the meanest man alive. After he was done with his cigarette, you know what he did?" She doesn't even wait for me and Abbie to answer. She just goes on telling the story. "He made us stick our hands out so he could use them for ashtrays. It hurt like hell. And we weren't even allowed to cry."

nixon-kennedy debates

The old man put a KENNEDY FOR PRESIDENT bumper sticker on the back of his car. Mommy's got a NIXON NOW sticker on hers.

"Kennedy is about hope," he says. "He's the kind of guy that talks right to you. He's not afraid to look you in the eye. And he makes a whole lot of sense. He knows what this country needs. He's not all shifty-eyed like Nixon with his five-o'clock shadow."

"You're just like a mole following the smell of mole asses down a dark tunnel," Mommy says. "You can't see clear to vote for Nixon. Just you wait till election day. We'll see who's on the winning side in this house."

little red

Penny's daddy got them a dog. They named him Little Red since he's a beagle with red spots and soft floppy red ears. He doesn't get to be a regular dog, though. He's not supposed to be a pet or anything. Mr. Reeb says he's a working dog. He got him so he could take him out hunting rabbits and squirrels and stuff.

Poor Little Red has to stay outdoors chained up to his doghouse by the side of the garage no matter what. Even when it rains so hard the sump pump works night and day and it looks like his doghouse could float away. I bet even when we have a blizzard and Little Red howls from the cold, he still won't get to come in the house.

Every time I take Gretchie over there to visit, Little Red wags his tail so hard he falls down. When we walk away, he tries to follow us even though his collar chokes him. He yanks himself so hard he makes these loud gasping noises.

All day long, all he does is he pulls on his chain and runs around in circles. He's worn a circle of dirt in the grass and Mr. Reeb doesn't even care about his precious yard. But I don't see what's the use of having a dog if you don't want to love it.

reward

A bbie's over at her friend Martha Bisbee's doing home-work so Mommy comes upstairs where I'm laying in bed reading a book. "You want to go for a ride?" she asks. Gretchie looks up at her and whines. "Wanna go? Wanna go?" Mommy says to tease her. Gretchie jumps up and races downstairs barking.

I run and get my shoes and my jacket on and meet her out in the car. The old man's in the front room watching TV. We don't say good-bye or anything since he'd just get mad at us anyhow.

Mommy drives real fast till we're out of town, then she turns off the main road so we can drive real slow and look for coke bottles. The old man says it's a waste of gas just driving up and down, but Mommy says she buys her own gas and she can do what she wants with it.

We play the radio, and I hang my head out the window and look for the bottles in the weeds beside the road. When I find one I holler, "I spy!" and she stops the car so I can jump out and get it. Usually, once I'm out of the car, I see a bunch of bottles all over the place and I run around grabbing them.

It starts to get dark so we go over to cash them in at Neil's Filling Station. We're so close to Tipton, we figure we'll drive over to the A&W for coneys and root beers. After, when I get out of the car to go to the bathroom, I find this watch laying right on the blacktop. It's got a silver band and instead of numbers it's got roman numerals. On the back there are these initials in fancy handwriting. *G. W. H.*

"It's a real classy piece of jewelry," Mommy says. "It's probably worth a lot of money. I'll bet somebody's offering a reward for it."

What we do is we check the paper and there it is under LOST AND FOUND, this ad about the watch. Sentimental value, it says. We called the number and this guy from over in Kokomo described the watch exactly so we knew it was really his. He said he would come over and get it and Mommy told him how to find our house.

He was this really nice guy named Mr. Higginbotham. He gave me this great big atlas with maps of all the states and another one with maps from all over the world. Being honest is a reward in itself, he said. A girl like me will go far. Mommy said after he left it would've been better if he just gave me the money and let me pick out what I wanted, but I never would've got the atlases that way. I never even knew about atlases or that there are so many places in the world you can go. When I'm grown up, I'm going to travel all over the world and then I'll come back and tell everybody in Windfall what it's like the way Reverend Andrews's sister did. She's a missionary that went to Sierra Leone in Africa and she had a slide-show down in our church basement when she came back once to visit.

Before he left, Mr. Higginbotham put his hand on my shoulder and said he couldn't thank me enough. He put his watch back on and kept looking at it like it was an old friend of his. Like if we weren't there he might kiss it or talk to it. He kept holding his arm up to take a look at it while he was talking to us. He had tears in his eyes and everything. "My wife gave it to me," he said. "It was our fiftieth anniversary. She's gone now. God bless her soul."

After he left, Mommy said she couldn't imagine what it'd be like to be married for fifty years. "Fifty years," she kept saying. "Five-o. I'll tell you one thing, I ain't about to hang around with the old man that long. I've given him the best years of my life and what've I got to show for it?"

backlash

Every night after she rolls her hair, Abbie winds her quilt around her shoulders and turns on her side to read her *Modern Romance* magazine. Even though I'm not supposed to, I sneak and read it sometimes when she's not around. It's all about people falling in love and going all the way. I asked Mommy what that meant, going all the way, and her face turned bright red. "Get out from under my feet," she said and swatted my legs with the fly swatter.

Every day at school, my new teacher Mrs. Thorp marches up and down the aisles whacking the desktops with her ruler and talking about how the center of the earth is a core of fire where hell is at. On the first day of fourth grade she made us all stand up one at a time and tell what church we belonged to. When she found out I'd still never been baptized she got all excited and said I had to be saved. She told me she expected to see me in the front pew of her church where Mr. Thorp's the preacher. It's called the Holy Wesleyan Methodist.

Mommy is what you call an atheist. That means she thinks God is dead. She says church is for the birds and you won't ever catch her in a church again even if Michael Anthony hands her a check for a million dollars. She used to go to Sunday school every Sunday way back when she was the teacher for the teen crusaders. That's what they call the high school kids. But then she took them all out dancing at the Backlash one Saturday afternoon and after Reverend Andrews got wind of it he preached about how dancing is the devil's work. That's why she quit.

Abbie quit church on account of after she got baptized and became a member they gave her this great big box full of tiny envelopes for her to put money in every week. They wanted her to say how much she was going to pledge but Abbie wants to keep her baby-sitting money for herself. If you're not a member you can just put in pennies or whatever you want. Nobody knows who's the one that did it when they count it up.

It was fun to go dancing at the Backlash that time even if it did make God mad. Penny's big sister Sonya let me dance with her. She had on a navy blue skirt that swished when she twirled me around and she wore a fluffy white sweater, soft like rabbit fur. Sonya had a red velvet bow pinned on the side of her long brown pageboy. If I was a boy, she'd be the one I'd want to marry.

Every Sunday, Reverend Thorp stands up in the pulpit and tells about how we're all a bunch of sinners. Every last one of us is born bad and we make it worse by not following God's commandments. We forget the holy Bible and we don't pay any attention to God's word. But God has His eye on everything and He knows how bad we are. God will punish us in hell. Reverend Thorp gets so worked up about it he has to take out his big white hanky and wipe his face.

All these people holler back while he's preaching. It's not like Reverend Andrews's church, where you have to be so quiet you can't even move an inch to scratch yourself. I miss going there with Marvella but I don't know what else to do. She says it's OK for me to shop around and figure out what I like but I can tell she's kind of disappointed. I figure maybe eventually I'll go to all the churches in town and then maybe I'll know what to do. But till I get out of fourth grade, I'm stuck. If you even miss one Sunday, Mrs. Thorp announces it to the whole class.

One time at Mrs. Thorp's church, all these different preachers came and had a kind of preaching contest. In the middle of it all, Reverend Thorp jumped up and fell down in the aisle and started rolling around yelling at the top of his lungs and not making any kind of sense. Then all these other folks did it too. I was sitting right beside Mrs. Thorp and she started hollering, "Save me, Lord Jesus." She was shaking around so much, her hairnet came loose and her long grey hair spilled over her shoulders.

Mrs. Thorp made us learn the Ten Commandments by heart.

She explained about coveting your neighbor's donkey and all that. Adultery is when you come home and somebody else's mother is in your kitchen cooking supper for you and your daddy.

remember the alamo

I like to sit with Leota Tupper in her front room. She's got these thick old stamp albums she's had ever since she can remember and one of them used to be her grandaddy's. She tells me things about minting and why some stamps have jagged edges and some edges are smooth and which are the ones worth the most money. She uses a great big magnifying glass to look at her stamps.

"My eyes ain't what they used to be, you know," she says, and her hand shakes all over the place when she tries to get herself a good look. Leota has these thick glasses that make her eyes look like they're about a mile away under water. Her face is covered with tiny wrinkles and when she smiles her lips disappear. She's exactly as tall as me. She says she always was on the runty side.

She gave me a book for me to collect my own stamps and she even gave me some REMEMBER THE ALAMO stamps to get started with. "Mark my word," she said. "When you get as old as me, you can cash 'em in." I sent away for some stamps they advertised in the back of my *Little Lulu* comics. They're from all over the world like Leota's. When they come, I'm going to give her half. She'll be so surprised.

"Do you know what the Alamo is, honey?" she asks me every time we look at her albums. She wants to make sure I don't forget how important the stamps she gave me are. I tell her no even though she's told me about a million times. One time I said yes, but she went right ahead and told me anyhow. The Alamo was this fort in Texas and Davy Crockett tried to save it. "You remember Davy Crockett's motto, don't you?" she asks me to check if I still know it.

"Be sure you're right. Then go on and do it," I say. She nods, all happy.

Davy Crockett wore a coonskin cap just like the one Leota Tupper's got in her house. She let me try it on one time and have a look in her mirror and when I did it felt just like having a cat sit on my head.

Every time Leota shows me her stamp albums she starts crying a bit. She sniffles and dabs at her eyes with a white lace hanky and I get up to have a look at the dried blue hydrangeas she has in a bowl on her table or else I look at the baby doll she's got in a cradle by the door and give the cradle a push with my toe.

I don't think you should ever say anything when somebody cries. Unless they want to talk to you about it, you should just do something else till they're all done. It drives me crazy the way everybody's always going "What's the matter? What's the matter?" or else telling you to quit your bawling.

the fire pole

D uane Flowers fell asleep on his davenport while he was having a cigarette and practically burnt his house down and now the old man can't stop talking about it. He said the worst thing in the world would be to wake up and find yourself trapped in a burning house with no way out. We have to have some way to escape. So what he did was he made us a fire pole. What it is is this pipe stuck in a hole in the ground. It's supposed to be just like the poles firemen slide down when the alarm goes off. He dug the hole under me and Abbie's window and filled the hole up with cement so the fire pole won't fall down. I got to press my palms in the wet cement to make handprints.

The fire pole comes right up to the window outside of our room. If there's ever a fire, what we're supposed to do is we're supposed to crawl out the window and shimmy down the pole to safety. The most important thing, the old man says, is to stay calm. Keep your wits about you. Don't lose your head. Just grab on to that pole and slide down. I'll be right there to catch you.

He won't let us have a fire drill like we have at school where there's a loud bell ringing and all us kids have to line up single file and march out onto the playground with our lips buttoned. We can't even slide down the fire pole once to see if it works. I lie in my bed at night and picture the blue flames rushing up the stairs and me and Abbie trying to squeeze out the window. It's so teensy and close to the ceiling, I'm scared we'll end up stuck halfway out with our legs dangling down the side of the house.

hunting for snipes

W hat's taking him so long?" Abbie says. She has her peppermint pink lipstick on and a blue headband holds her hair away from her face. She takes her compact out and smears her thick flesh-colored blemish stick over the bumps on her cheeks. "Toot the horn or something."

It's the last Saturday in August and so hot the sun is just an orange smear in the sky and waves of heat are coming up off the tar. Mommy and the old man are having what Mommy calls another go-round, meaning if things don't work out they'll get a divorce even if we end up in the poorhouse.

"I don't wanna be the one accused of hounding him," Mommy says, acting all mad about it. "But I'll say one thing. If he's not out here in five minutes, I'm not going." She glances at her watch, then yanks the rearview mirror over and fusses with her spit curls, pinching the ends of her hair into circles on either side of her forehead. A yellow jacket is hovering just outside my window.

We're sitting in the car because we're going to go visit the old man's friend, this guy Ray. We've never been to Ray's before. We've never even laid eyes on Ray or his wife Marilyn. We've never met any of the old man's friends since I don't think he's ever had one before. Ray's this new guy that moved here from Kokomo. According to the old man, the two of them eat lunch together at work when the noon whistle blows. He told us all about how Ray and his wife fixed up this old farmhouse they bought. "They're just starting out," he said. "Remember when we were spring chickens?" he asked Mommy.

When he came home and announced we'd been invited over for a visit, Mommy wasn't too thrilled about it.

"Ray this, Ray that," she said. "I feel like he's at the supper table with us every night as it is."

"Maybe we can pick up an idea or two about fixing up this old place." The old man's always talking about how any day now he's going to finish remodeling our house. So far all he did was make a disaster area out of me and Abbie's room and then rip off the rotten boards around the edge of our front porch so everybody can see this black paper underneath.

"It's nothing fancy," the old man said. "Just a cookout."

"He expects the four of us to show up?"

"Well, Ruthie. C'mon now. You're always going on about how we never go out and have a good time. It won't hurt us. So what if we kill a couple or three hours?"

"Twenty-nine, twenty-eight, twenty-seven." Mommy counts the seconds.

The old man already came out of the house one time and started backing the car up out of the driveway. But then he turned the engine off to go back inside to make sure all the burners were off on the stove. Whenever we all go anywhere together, which is hardly ever, the old man always does that. Then he'll say he forgot his cigarettes. Or he starts patting his pockets looking for his lighter. Or he's convinced Mommy left the iron plugged in. Then he disappears inside the house, leaving us all waiting out in the car for about a million years.

"Three, two, one," Mommy says at exactly the same time as the back door slams. The old man slides behind the steering wheel. When he went back into the house, he had on his grey work clothes. He always wears them no matter what day of the week it is. But now he has on a white shirt tucked into a pair of brown pants I've never seen before. His red hair is slicked back with Vitalis but a cowlick is already poking up in back.

We drive through town heading down the highway and turn down this road I never noticed. Before long, we're way out in the country, further than I've even been before.

Next to a red farmhouse, there's a kid swinging in an old tire that's hanging from a tree. We turn onto a bumpy road and a white dog starts chasing after us, trying to bite the tires. The old man has to speed up to get rid of him. We pass a farmer riding a red tractor across a rutted field. He waves his straw hat at us like we're old friends of his. After a while there's nothing but corn growing everywhere. The long thin leaves flutter in the hot summer breeze. The tassels point up like crosses in a graveyard.

"Check the directions again, Ruthie, will you?"

"I just did. You turned where he said at the Esso station. Then you took the left after the second stop sign. We're on Oak Grove Road now. But there ain't one single oak tree in sight. They must be a couple of hillbillies living way out in the middle of nowhere like this."

"Well, I'll tell you one thing. Ray ain't no suave Humphrey Bogart kind of guy. But he don't come to work with manure on his heels neither. Let's not start, all right?" He reaches over and pats Mommy's leg. She pushes him away and stares straight ahead while a breeze fluffs her dress up and down over her knees.

The whole week before the cookout, Mommy tried on all her clothes so she could figure out what to wear.

"I'd like to whip me up a new dress," she said one night after supper. The old man reached into his back pocket and took out his billfold and handed her a five-dollar bill. "Don't say I never gave you nothing," he told her.

For two nights in a row, the whirring of the old treadle machine shook the back porch as Mommy rocked the pedal. Finally, the day before the cookout, she tried the dress on and stood in front of the mirror.

"What if it's too dressy?" She smoothed the white fluffy material down over her hips and jabbed pins in the sides until it fit her waist just right. She stood on the coffee table and got Abbie to crawl around the bottom of the dress, pinning up the hem while I held the pincushion. Up close, I could see that what at first glance looked like polka dots all over the cloth was really tiny navy blue hearts.

"You look pretty as a picture." The old man looked up from his newspaper. Then he got up slowly and came over and kissed Mommy where the dress left her shoulder uncovered.

"Not now, Floyd," she said.

* * *

104

The old man pulls over and grabs the piece of paper from Mommy's lap. He lights a cigarette. When Abbie starts to cough like crazy, he crushes it out in the ashtray without a word. If Abbie gets worried, just about everything makes her cough. Mommy says it's because she had asthma when she was little, but the old man says it's just her way of trying to get attention.

"It looks like we just haven't gone far enough yet," he says. The corn on both sides of the road is taller than our car and the whole field is full of locusts singing louder and louder, the way they do, with their whining sound getting faster and faster then dying down before it starts up again.

"Them bugs're probably as big as this car." Abbie jabs me in the arm the way she does.

"It's just locusts."

"Not way out here. Don't you know out in the country they've got bugs that're bigger'n you?" She opens her eyes wide, staring at me.

"They do not."

"Do so." She puts her fingers up to her forehead and wiggles them at me like antennas. "And they're coming to get you."

She punches me in my arm again with her knuckles all positioned this special way. She always aims for the exact same spot where she left the last black and blue.

"Knock it off, you two." The old man reaches behind him to swat at us. "Abbie. You're old enough to know better."

He leaves his arm on the back of the seat and slides his hand over to rub Mommy's neck. She lifts it off of her like it's some spider she'd like to squash. The old man's ears turn bright red and start to twitch the way they do when he clenches his teeth.

Up ahead there's a mailbox made out of wood, decorated to look like a red covered bridge.

"That's it!" the old man says.

"I don't know why you're putting your blinker on. It ain't like there's any heavy traffic out here." Mommy leans over the backseat. "Tuck your blouse in," she says to me. "When's the last time you combed your hair?" She takes her big white comb out of her pocketbook and yanks the elastic out of my ponytail and starts combing out the knots.

At the end of the driveway, there's a white house with a big grassy yard and red flowers growing along the edges of the side-walk. The front porch has got a grey painted floor with a ceiling the color of my sky blue crayon. Marilyn told us later, when we stood there under the porch light saying good-bye, how she'd wanted it to be blue like that so on the cloudiest days she could still remember what the sky looked like.

Ray pushes open the screen door like he's been standing there all along waiting for us. He has on overalls, just like the farmer we saw on that tractor.

"What'd I tell you?" Mommy whispers. "Hillbillies."

"This here's the wife and kids," the old man says.

"Well. How do you do?" Ray opens the door on my side. "Hope you didn't have any trouble finding it."

"No siree. Not at all." The old man grins.

Mommy and Abbie get out on their side. Mommy's taller than Ray. When he tilts his head up at her, a dark curl falls into his eyes.

"I feel like I know you already." Mommy's smiling and when her high heels start sinking into the sandy driveway, Ray reaches out and holds her elbow. "I can't have you falling flat on your face," he tells her.

"Floyd, old buddy, I can't believe you're here. We're sure tick-led pink you all could come out. Well," he says, letting go of Mommy when they get to the sidewalk, "let's head on in. The wife's in the kitchen."

Marilyn's chopping scallions and sprinkling them onto this bowl of potato salad. There's a glass of carrot and celery sticks on the counter beside her.

"Here she is," Ray says, like he's the host on a game show pulling the curtain open to show you the prize you just won. Marilyn wipes her hands on her apron. She's pretty with short blonde curls and a red scarf tied around her neck.

"I'm going to give them the old guided tour."

"Honey, did you even ask if they wanted to?" She turns to Mommy. "He's tickled to death over this house. You'd think he invented the hammer and paintbrush the way he goes on about it." She leans back against Ray and wraps his arm around her waist. She presses her cheek up against his. "Did you ever think they might want to sit down and have themselves an ice cold drink first?"

Mommy's lips are all tight. When she smiles, there's a smudge of red lipstick on her teeth. She always says the one thing she can't stand is watching folks act all lovey-dovey like they just got off their honeymoon. I can tell she's wishing she was back home in the bathtub flipping through one of her magazines the way she does most Saturday nights.

"Well, I don't know about any of you, but I'm dying to see this man's castle. It's all he can talk about." The old man is grinning so much his teeth look too big for his mouth. I've never seen him like this, all happy in front of some people we hardly even know.

Marilyn puts her hand on Abbie's shoulders. "You must be Abbie." Abbie nods and gives her the smile she's been practicing, the one where she moves the corners of her lips up just a tiny bit so she'll be what she calls sophisticated. She's looking at Marilyn the way she looks at the movie stars' pictures she pinned up around her mirror.

"And you're Lana." Her eyes are green like a cat's with swirls of black running through them.

"You shoulda seen it before." Ray waves his arms around in the middle of his front room. "Me and the little lady took off— what was it honey?—seven layers of wallpaper. Woo-eee."

"Eight. And each one as ugly as the last. Two of 'em had been painted over. Boy, I'll tell you. That's a job I wouldn't wish on my worst enemy." Marilyn goes over to this shelf they have and takes down a blue scrapbook.

"Here's what I call the 'before' picture." There's a picture of their old front room. It's got exactly the same kind of wallpaper we have in our front room back home—great big white leaves on a background of red and white stripes. The old man shakes his head like he can't believe how bad it looks. Mommy says, "Hunh," and clicks her tongue.

Their new wallpaper is white with thin yellow stripes and tiny yellow flowers all up and down. They have a brown davenport and two matching chairs.

The bathroom's all done up in blue and white. The walls are painted pale blue with white woodwork and white tiles. There's a blue shower curtain and a blue throw rug and a matching blue fluffy cover on the toilet seat. They've even got blue toilet paper. Ray says how he had to replace all the pipes since every single one of them sprung a leak. He even had to tear out part of the floor.

"The damn toilet stool was about to fall clear through to the cellar!" he says.

By the staircase, he shows us the callouses he got on his hands from sanding the stairs and the railings. The wood is shiny and smells the way school does on the first day.

Upstairs, I can tell Abbie's in love with their bedroom from the way she runs her hand up and down on the pink and white chenille bedspread when she thinks nobody's looking. There's one big bed in the center, between two windows. All the furniture is painted white with gold trim. The vanity table has a pink skirt all around it to hide the legs. It looks a lot like the furniture Abbie used to cut out of the catalog.

They even have a guest room. "One of these days, we'll have us a couple of kids ourselves," Ray says. "We'll put 'em in here."

"Then you'll be sorry." Mommy walks over and looks out the window. "That's when the party's over for sure."

The clock on the bedside table ticks real loud. "Well," Marilyn says.

"I've got the coals on," Ray finally says. "Plenty of beer. What d'ya say, ol' buddy?" He slaps the old man on the back like that's a signal for them to go outside. Me and Abbie follow Mommy and Marilyn to the kitchen. At first it seems like they aren't going to have a word to say to each other. I know Marilyn isn't a hill-billy since hillbillies always have chickens in their kitchen. But maybe Mommy doesn't like her anyhow. Marilyn gives me and Abbie each a bottle of Coke.

"What can I get you, Ruth?"

"Oh, whatever you're having."

"Well. To tell you the truth, I'm dying to have me a highball."

"I'd like that. Yes, I'll have one too." Mommy leans back in her chair and takes her cigarettes out of her pocketbook. "Mind if I have a smoke?"

"Go right ahead." Marilyn hands her an ashtray that's bright red and shaped like a heart with I LEFT MY HEART IN SAN FRANCISCO on it in black letters. Mommy turns her chair and swats at the smoke so it won't go in Abbie's direction.

Marilyn puts a tall icy glass on the table in front of Mommy. "This ought to open your eyes up," she says. She sits down and lights one of her cigarettes. They both smoke Winstons. I figure that's a good sign.

Out back, Ray is squirting the flames around the hamburgers with water from an old Windex bottle. The old man is walking up and down with his hands in his pockets, talking.

Marilyn isn't like any lady I ever met before. She does all the stuff ladies do, making the food and all that, but after she clears off the picnic table, she pokes me in the ribs and says, "Who wants a game of tag? You're It." I tag Abbie. The three of us run all over the yard tagging each other. When we fall down screaming, Abbie isn't even worried about getting grass stains on her pants. She just picks herself up and runs after Marilyn, laughing in the same high out-of-breath way Marilyn does. Mommy and the old man and Ray sit at the picnic table drinking.

"I give!" Marilyn puts an arm around each of us and leads us back to the table. My throat hurts from laughing and running so much, and Abbie's cheeks are two bright circles of red.

It's that time of day just when the sun has gone down but it's still light out. An owl is hooting out in back behind the barn.

"You know what a hoot owl is, don't you?" The old man tweaks my ponytail. He's smiling so much he looks like a horse with his teeth flashing.

"What?"

"It's the soul of a dead man that can't get to heaven."

"How come?"

"Oh, Floyd, don't get her all worked up." Mommy turns to Ray and winks. She crosses her legs and her skirt starts to blow up but she acts like she doesn't even notice. "This one'll believe anything. I'll never forget the time I told her she could catch a bird if she could salt its tail. Damned if I didn't look out the kitchen window and see her chasing a robin all over the yard with a saltshaker."

* * *

109

Me and Abbie are standing at the edge of the table, waiting, not knowing what to do next.

"Wanna give me a hand?" Marilyn asks Abbie. The two of them go in the house arm in arm. I figure they're going to bring us dessert since I saw a plate of brownies. But they come back out carrying these brown paper sacks.

"You girls ever go on a snipe hunt?" Marilyn hands me a sack.

"What's a snipe hunt?"

"You don't know what a snipe hunt is? Boy, oh boy, you girls haven't lived."

"Tell us." Abbie's eyes are all shiny the way they get on Christmas morning.

"Yeah, tell us."

"These girls've never hunted snipe? Is that the God's honest truth?"

"Never." The old man swats a mosquito that landed on his neck.

"You like bunny rabbits, right?"

I tell her I do.

"Well, a snipe is kind of like a bunny rabbit, only much smaller. It's all soft and furry and has a little pink nose." She touches the end of my nose. "The reason you hardly ever get to see one is they're real bashful. They only come out at this time of day. And only if you can put a sack over their hole so they think you can't see 'em. C'mon. I'll show you how to catch a snipe."

She walks slowly across the yard, bent over a little, looking carefully at the ground. "There's one," she whispers.

"A snipe?" I almost shriek but Abbie puts her hand over my mouth just in time.

"Quiet!"

"No, sugar. A snipe hole. See here?"

She points to this little hole in the ground that I always thought was where snakes lived even though I never once saw a snake and the old man says no snakes live in our part of the state.

"You put your sack over the hole like this." Marilyn opens her sack and sticks it over the hole. "And as soon as you feel the little snipe sneak up into your sack, well, you grab the bottom and hold it closed real tight." She demonstrates what she means, holding the sack up in the air with her hand clasped around it.

"I think I feel one coming now." We crouch down beside her, our sacks in our hands. I can't hardly hold still. She snatches it up. "Too late. But I almost had 'im. Now you try it."

Me and Abbie creep across the yard, holding our sacks over the holes we find, waiting for snipes. Once, I'm sure something's moving in mine, but when I scoop it up and peek inside, it's empty. I want to catch me a snipe so bad I don't want to give up even though Abbie already quit and lightning bugs've started blinking along the edge of the field. I keep trying till it's getting so dark I can't hardly see the snipe holes anymore.

Everybody's sitting around these candles flickering in the middle of the table. The old man is saying how he'd like to finish fixing our house up one of these days. He says when he bought it, he knew it was a handyman's special, but he had no idea it meant he'd be working on it for the rest of his life.

"I got the thing for you," Ray says. He goes in the house and comes back with a stack of magazines he says is where they came up with all their ideas.

"These are yours for the asking," Ray says. "But first I have to be sure to get the little lady's OK." He holds the stack of magazines in front of Mommy the way the guy holds the Bible on *Perry Mason*. "Now Ruth, you *can* say no." He winks at Mommy. "There's no telling what this fellow will do to your happy home once remodeling fever gets ahold of him."

Mommy smiles and crosses her legs. She swings her foot back and forth, reaching down to smooth her stocking up her leg. "I can't see what harm it'll do," she says, looking up at Ray and smiling. The old man pops the top off another beer and swallows it down fast.

"You catch any snipes?" Marilyn asks. I take a brownie from the plate she's offering me.

"I almost had me one. But just as soon as I squinched up the sack, it ran back in the hole."

Everybody laughs. Abbie cups her hand over Marilyn's ear and whispers something. Marilyn tucks Abbie's hair behind her ear and whispers back.

"What?" I say. "What?" But nobody says a word.

* * *

When we drive off, me and Abbie watch out the back window till we can't see the light from their porch. Then I lean into the front seat and ask, "Can we have a blue ceiling in our room?"

"I don't see why not," Mommy says. "What d'ya say, Floyd?"

The old man doesn't say anything. Mommy takes off her high heels and tucks her feet up under her skirt. Then she scoots across the seat and leans her head on the old man's shoulder.

I curl up in the corner and think about the snipe I almost caught. How if I got one, I'd have it with me right now. I can see it like a miniature rabbit resting in the palm of my hand.

Mommy's giggling and reaching her arm around the old man. "What're you brooding about?" she says. "You had a good time, didn't you?"

Gravel flips up and hits the sides of the car. The old man slams on the brakes and grabs Mommy by the shoulders. Then he wraps his hands around her bare throat. "I could kill you," he says. "I just want to be sure you know that."

He shoves her away from him and she slumps against her window like a rag doll. The old man starts driving again. For a long time, he doesn't say a word. He smokes a cigarette, then lights another one. Abbie's got her window open and her face pressed up close to the fresh air. I can tell she's trying hard not to cough.

"Don't you think for one second I missed one move you made back there," the old man says. It sounds like the words are apple seeds he's spitting out from between his teeth. "I know when you're on the prowl. Don't you think I don't."

"Oh, for Christ's sake. Just drop it, Floyd. You had one too many. You're starting on a wild goose chase over nothing."

"Nothing, my ass." He tosses his cigarette out the window. Red sparks streak out behind us as he drives faster and faster. The car bumps along the dirt road so bad I bite my tongue.

happy homes

A bbie is laying on her stomach on the floor reading *Teen Scene* while her fingernail polish dries. In a little while, she gets up and starts walking around the bedroom with her Home Ec book balanced on her head. She says that's what you have to do to have good posture. When I try it, my book wobbles around and slips off.

The old man is up on the roof tap tapping his hammer. We can hear him thumping above our heads. When he moves, it sounds like sandpaper is scraping across the shingles. Every once in a while he hollers, "Shit!" or "Jesus H. Christ Almighty!" That means he hit his thumb. There's a loud sound like somebody dragging a sled across the roof, then a thunk on the ground under our window.

"Lana!" he hollers. "Lana Marie. Come give me a hand."

"His Royal Highness is calling. You better go," Abbie says.

Mommy's downstairs in the bathtub reading one of the *Happy Homes* magazines Ray gave us. She holds up a picture of a re-modeled bathroom. It has pink and black tiles on the walls. "The tub's built in," she says. "So nobody can see the ugly feet on it. There's even a shelf for you to put your shampoo and what-all." She drops the magazine on the bath mat. "What's wrong with you-know-who now?"

"How should I know?"

"Touchy, touchy. You're getting just like him." She clicks her teeth with her tongue and slides down in the water, making the bubbles break around her chin.

The old man is on the very top of the roof, straddling the peak like he's riding a horse. He waves at me. "You see it? Over there." He points towards the driveway where the hammer is laying in the grass. "Don't just stand there. Bring it up."

I start up the ladder, one rung at a time since I can only hang on with one hand. He edges down the roof and crawls over to the top of the ladder, waiting for me.

"You scared?" He hooks the hammer on this special loop he got at the hardware store to put on his belt.

"Kind of. Are you?"

"Naw. I got me a bird's-eye view of the whole town. Wanna see?"

I let him take my hand and help me up on the roof. The rough shingles scrape me right through my pedal pushers. I kind of crawl ahead of him. My hands feel the way my feet do when I'm walking barefoot on the hot sidewalk.

"Don't worry. I got you. Even if you slip." The old man has ahold of my waistband. "Just don't look down. Don't look till I say 'when.' Then you'll be OK."

When we get up to the top together, I lean back against him and he holds me tight around my waist. There's the town below us. There's the blue water tower with the word WINDFALL painted in big black letters. There's Neila Grimes on Hawthorn Street watering her geraniums. The maple leaves are starting to turn colors already. People are driving up West Jackson Street, walking into the post office and Jack's. Gretchie is laying on the picnic table out back, resting her nose on her front paws. When I call her name, she looks up but can't figure out where I'm at.

When Abbie was my age, she says she got to go to Chicago for two days and stay in a hotel room on account of she won a trip for selling the most newspapers on her paper route. They let her have her own room with two great big double beds in it since she was the only paper girl. All the other kids were boys and they had to share their rooms. Abbie told me she slept in both beds. First she slept in one for a while. Then when the covers were all tangled up, she got in the second bed. In Chicago, they have a skyscraper that's so high you can stick your head out the window and grab a handful of clouds. They feel like cotton candy only they aren't sticky at all.

When I look up, the white fluffy clouds over my head are still too far away to reach. Even the top of the oak tree is higher up than we are. The old man shows me where he's been hammering new shingles on to keep the rain out. Last night, during the thunderstorm, we had to put a bucket right between me and Abbie's beds, the water was coming in so bad.

When I go back inside, Abbie's playing "The Twist." She's in our room twisting and twisting, trying to get it just right. What you do when you twist is you act like you're drying your back with your towel and then you twist your toes back and forth like you're putting out a cigarette. Abbie showed me how.

mighty mouse

I hear them in the dark. Mommy's voice all high and full of tears. "I'm not a fool," the old man says.

"Can't you drop it?" she says. "Can't we just go on like we were before? We were doing so good."

"You call this doing good?" the old man says. "This is what you want? If this is what you want, count me out. I don't want any." He slams the back door and starts his car up, but I never hear him drive away. I don't know if Abbie's sleeping or not. She doesn't say anything to me. I can hear guitars twanging and voices coming out from under her pillow, but I can't make out what they're singing.

In the morning I wake up to the sound of the electric saw ripping through plywood. The first thing I think of is Mighty Mouse coming to rescue some lady that's tied up and moving headfirst towards the jagged saw blades.

When I go downstairs, the old man is standing in a cloud of sawdust in the middle of the kitchen. I don't know what he's making and I'm too scared to ask. He measures a board and draws a thick black pencil line down the middle of it, then tucks the pencil behind his ear and saws some more. Mommy is standing in front of the bathroom mirror holding a wet washrag over her eyes.

empty sack

The old man never mentions Ray at the supper table anymore. And Abbie says she doesn't want to talk about
what it's going to be like when we go visit Marilyn again.
She says she's sick of that one. At bedtime she only wants to talk
about ways to get rid of the old man. She's really ticked off since
our bedroom is still such a big mess. We don't even have real
walls, just silver paper over the pink insulation tacked up. It's got
the words OWENS CORNING THIS SIDE UP printed all over it in big
red letters. I lie on my bed reading it over and over again or else
seeing how many words I can make out of the letters, like *corn*
and *die* and *weeds*.

Abbie says she's the only person she knows that's got to live in
a room the size of a closet and share it with her stupid little sister.
She says we're never going to have a blue ceiling or a door or nice
furniture or anything.

Winter's coming soon and the ground's practically frozen, but
every night as soon as the sun starts to go down, I go out back
with my paper sack to try and catch me a snipe. I don't know if
snipes come out when it's cold. Gretchie follows along behind me,
nudging my hand with her wet nose till I let her have a look in
the empty sack.

accident

F loyd turns on the heater and stands over the floor register,
warming his hands. The dog clicks across the linoleum
and flops near the heat with a groan. He shakes food into
the dog's bowl and starts the percolator going on the gas stove.
Out the window, across the Reebs' yard, past the school playground where the swings hang empty, beyond the dry stalks of
corn, the sun is about to come up.

He lights a cigarette, coughs into his hand, and sips his first
cup of coffee, sitting at the black-and-white Formica table, which
is still sticky from last night's supper. Standing at the stove, he
gulps down three more cups, strong and black the way he likes it.
He spreads mustard over slices of soft white bread and cuts last
night's meatloaf for sandwiches. Packs it all with a thermos of
coffee in his black metal lunch bucket. Zips his jacket up to his
chin, already shrugging in anticipation of the cold air that will
take his breath and swirl it into white clouds in front of him as
he goes out the back door.

He is a man dressed in grey: grey work pants, grey long-
sleeved work shirt, grey canvas jacket, head down, walking to his
grey car. He shivers and clamps his bare hands under his armpits.

The car grinds and gasps, refusing to turn over. He pumps the
gas pedal, careful not to flood the engine, listening for the right
moment to give it more gas. When the engine catches, it roars at
first, then slows to a dull chug. He waits until the defroster is
working, then backs out of the driveway, a cigarette jammed in
the corner of his mouth. There is a light on in the Reebs' kitchen
next door. Bob Reeb, the mailman, will be on the road too in a
few minutes, Floyd thinks. He drives through the sleeping town,

heading toward work where all day he will sit in his booth, his feet sweating in his black steel-toed shoes until the cold and damp of them make his legs ache. He will perch there on his stool reaching again and again for one of the generators that pass in front of him along the conveyor belt. He takes one, puts it on a jig, checks the amps, and bends over his work listening for any off-sounds, while outside his booth, the machines whir and thump too loud for talk even if he did know what to say to the men who work out there.

He drives down West Jackson Street. The yellow light from Jack's shines on the otherwise dark street. There are a few cars parked in front. Men stopping on their way to work for coffee. At the railroad tracks, he stops for the flashing red lights and waits, listening as the train whistle approaches, the clanging bell like an alarm. It is a long time before the train comes rushing down the tracks and passes, but he waits even though he knows he could scoot across in time. When he pulls up in front of a mint green cinder-block house over behind the bowling alley, Audie Wakefield steps out his back door, wrapping the fronts of his red plaid jacket around his big chest. He slides into the front seat.

"Colder'n a witch's tit out, ain't it?"

"Sure is," Floyd says. Then there is the silence that always follows, until Lester Meacham is in back. Audie and Meacham can always keep the ball rolling the whole way, Floyd thinks. They will joke and laugh and he will nod and grin along with them, grateful to have his big hands gripping the steering wheel. Grateful for something to do, for a distraction from the weight, the dull ache he carries in his chest. He pulls up in front of Meacham's house and toots the horn. Floyd thinks he could drive to work with his eyes shut, like an old horse that has been hitched up to a milk wagon so long the driver no longer has to signal which houses to stop in front of.

"Did ya hear the one about the travelin' salesman and the widow woman?" Meacham starts, before he's barely slammed the door. And Floyd sits back, lights another cigarette, waits. He tries to remember their jokes for later. Thinks about how he will tell them too, to others, but whenever there's a chance, all he can remember is the punch line, not what comes before. It seems to him that he will never be able to enter a conversation the way every-

119

body else can, with the ease young girls have when they know the right moment to skip into the swinging rope.

When it happens, he is completely unprepared. He pulls away from the four-way stop like he always does, has looked in every direction beforehand, he's sure he saw no one coming, so how does he miss it? The other car appears from nowhere. "Just like a bat out of hell," Audie will say later, over and over again, coughing and spitting into the gutter when the police are there, when the siren has died down but the red light is still flashing around and around. Floyd sits dazed behind the steering wheel. He can hear Audie shout, "Look out!" and see him press his thick hands against the dashboard, bracing himself.

Floyd waits behind the steering wheel until they open his door and make him walk up and down to steady his legs. The other driver is not hurt. He is a scrawny man in a black overcoat who stands hunched at the curb, twisting his hat around and around in his hands. A preacher, it turns out, on his way to visit a woman who has just lost her husband. "I seen you were about to pull out. There wasn't much I could do but try to steer outa the way and say a prayer. I thank the good Lord none of us're hurt."

Floyd's hands shake as he lights a cigarette. He thinks the accident, his running into a preacher—of all the folks to get into a wreck with, he mutters to himself—must be a sign. But he's not sure what it means. He closes his eyes, tries to concentrate, and sees the black car coming toward him, moving as if in slow motion. His heart is pounding. I am about to have a wreck, he thinks, as he heads right toward the oncoming car. The whole thing happens while he watches, knowing there is nothing he can do to stop it.

"You're lucky you're just shook up," the policeman says. Writing it all down. Taking all their numbers. Checking their papers. "Luckier'n hell. Somebody up there must like you."

Through it all, through the talking and later that day, Floyd feels like the accident is still happening. He is in the car, in the driver's seat, his hands on the steering wheel. Meacham is laughing his high, wheezing cackle behind him. Floyd looks in the rearview mirror at Meacham's red, cracked face, his yellow rabbit teeth. He stops and looks in both directions. He did stop. He did look in both directions. He's sure of it. He can feel his foot push-

120

ing the brake to the floor. Then he gives it gas, and they are flying across the intersection. This is it, he thinks, letting go of the wheel the way he's learned to do in a skid. This is it. There is the thunk of steel crushing steel. The squeal of brakes. The horns. "Look out!" Audie shouts.

That evening, Floyd feels so grateful that when he pulls into his driveway he weeps. There is the dog, running across the yard to greet him. He opens the back door and there is Ruth, at the stove, frying pork chops. There are the voices of his girls, giggling upstairs. He is so overcome he wants to fall to his knees. That night he will say grace before supper, thanking God for watching over him. Ruth will not bow her head with him. She won't say amen. Before bed, he will kneel in the dark at his bedside, praying. But now he just stands in the kitchen, amazed, seeing his home with new eyes. The yellow curtains seem so bright he thinks he might cry at how pretty they are. He is trembling all over when he calls the girls downstairs and tells his family what happened. He takes them out to the driveway to show them the damage: the bumper peeled pack like a sardine can, tied to the hood with a piece of clothesline. He points to where the paint has been scratched down to bare steel. He wants them to know how lucky he feels. How his life seems to have taken a turn. How he's sure he's been given a second chance.

Ruth's hair is streaked with strands of silver he's never noticed. The girls look different to him. Prettier than he remembers. Abbie, with hips beginning to bloom below her waist. Lana, scuffing the toe of her saddle shoe in the driveway, suddenly tall.

At the supper table, he quizzes the girls to see if they remember what he has taught them about safety. He wants to know if they look both ways when they cross the street.

"Do you hold your sister's hand?" he asks Abbie.

"Don't'cha think she's kinda big now?" she mutters, swirling the gravy into her mashed potatoes.

"What? What did you say, young lady?"

"Yes," she says, still looking down at her plate.

"Always?" he asks.

And even though she says yes, he wants her to tell him exactly what she does. Again and again. He asks Abbie, then Lana, over and over until their eyes glaze and they squirm and fidget in their chairs.

His back is turned, he is stacking the dirty plates from the supper table, and the girls are with Ruth beside the sink. He is telling them how the accident felt like being caught in a skid. How he had no choice but to go with it. When he turns toward them, he catches Ruth twirling her finger in the air beside her ear then pointing at him. "So this is what she thinks of me." The thought stabs at him, but he is unable to confront her. Unable to say it isn't true even. "Maybe she's right," he thinks.

The accident clings to Floyd's mind the way the leeches used to hook to his body when he swam out in Lambert's Pond as a boy. His father would light a match to their tails until they dropped off, writhing in the dirt. He wishes there were someone who could light a match to his thoughts. Help him quit going over what happened, quit reliving every detail of the accident. "I hate to think of what might have happened," he says to himself, sure that it's a sign, sure that God's trying to tell him something.

In the shed one night after work, he sands down the edges of a square of plywood and draws the road he was on, and the intersection where the accident happened. He paints in his pencil marks with a line of black paint. Takes two scraps of wood, paints one grey, one black, and when the paint has dried, he sits in his chair in the front room, moving the black and grey blocks towards the intersection, trying to figure out how it could have been prevented.

Every night after supper, he gets Lana to sit across the table from him. She moves the black car toward the intersection and he has her hold the car there at the stop sign, waiting, while his grey car moves forward and crosses the intersection safely, without a scratch.

He tells her he is pretty sure he looked in every direction before he pulled out. "But by God, I should've double-checked," he says. Running his freckled hands through his thick red hair, he looks at her across from him, head bent over the wooden cars, muttering motor sounds. He can smell the milk on her breath.

"It's always better safe than sorry," he tells her. "Count to ten before you step off the curb. Then look again. If only I'd've waited a few more seconds, it never would've happened. Do you hear me?"

something grey floating

M e and Abbie are laying in bed after lights out planning what we'll do when she's old enough to get her license. I want her to drive me over to visit Marilyn and Ray again. Mommy says the old man will never take us because he thinks he's got to invite them over here first and she's not about to have them over to see the pigsty we live in.

"We'll have a picnic out in back of their house," I say. "And Marilyn'll fix your hair in all these different ways and she'll let you try on her clothes," I tell Abbie. "She'll have so many clothes you can take whatever ones you want. We'll even go looking for the snipes that live in her backyard," I say.

"Oh, God. Are you still thinking about that?"

"Well. It would be fun to have one."

Abbie rolls her head from side to side and clicks her tongue. Then she says, "Drown." That means she's ready to play The Old Man's Gone for Good.

"He's out at the reservoir fishing off the bridge and somebody comes and gives him a shove. He falls off the bridge headfirst."

"C'mon," Abbie says and sighs. "Make it more real."

"Well. It could happen."

"He swims too good. You know that. And who's gonna shove him off a bridge?"

"OK, OK. He's out in his boat in the middle of the reservoir. Just him. He's fishing and he gets a really big bite. But he's not really paying attention since he's having a bunch of beers, so he doesn't have ahold of the fishing pole good and the fish grabs it out of his hand. He jumps into the water to get it."

"So? That doesn't make somebody drown."

124

"Well, the thing is he just got done having two of his T-bone steaks and a big bowl of mashed potatoes. He didn't wait an hour the way you're supposed to. So he gets cramps and he can't get back to the boat. It's almost dark out, so nobody even sees him splashing around out there. Nobody even notices when he goes under the last time."

"Good. Good," Abbie says. "Then Gus Riley's driving around in the morning and he sees the empty boat with nobody in it. He sees something grey floating in the water. Yeah," she says. "I like it."

Abbie clicks on her transistor to go to sleep. She has to keep it under her pillow or else the old man will have a fit. I can hear tiny voices coming from her side of the room as I lie in the dark. I pretend I'm all by myself going to one of the places on my maps. I can go to France or India or California. I can go to Canada and even the North Pole. I can see penguins and polar bears and take a boat across the ocean.

I think about that guy Mr. Higginbotham and the way he held his watch when I handed it to him. His hand was big and moist and pink. There were deep lines that crisscrossed his palm like roads on the map.

Mommy's downstairs coughing and coughing. I can hear her cigarette lighter click shut and I smell the smoke. The old man is watching TV and he turns it up so loud I have to bury my head in my pillow but I can still hear Speedy Alka-Seltzer talking so I sit up and look out the window. I can see the candlelight flickering in Mrs. MacAbee's room like it does now every night since Lonnie ended up in a coma. What happened was Lonnie MacAbee and a bunch of other boys went swimming up at the reservoir. They were all jumping off the railroad bridge into the water even though there's a NO TRESPASSING sign. Nobody knows exactly how it happened but Lonnie fell and instead of landing in the water, he landed on the rocks.

The boys in school are still talking about it. They say how his brains were smeared all over the place by the time Gus Riley got there and the ambulance took him away. All he does now is lie in a hospital bed all covered up with a white sheet. He doesn't even wake up when they make his bed. He doesn't talk or cry or anything. If you jab him with a pin he doesn't even jump and he can't even eat. They have to feed him with some kind of sugar water in his veins and I don't know what they do about him going to the bathroom.

His desk at school still has all his books and papers in it like any minute he'll be back shooting spitballs. We all made him get-well cards and sent them in a big envelope to the hospital. I drew a picture of an egg frying on the sidewalk so he'd remember his favorite thing to do in the summer, but I don't know if he can see things or not in his coma.

Abbie says he might as well be dead. It makes me think how my whole life could be over any minute. Everybody says Mrs. McAbee sits by Lonnie's bedside holding his hand and praying for him to come to, but his hand is cold as ice. She talks to him night and day, but she might as well be talking to a corpse.

reading the dictionary

The old man is sitting in his chair reading his red cloth-covered dictionary. He does this practically every night after supper. He likes to know what everything means so he's planning to read the whole thing one of these days.

He wants me to sit on his lap, but I say I'm too big. He moves his lips this funny way like he's all disappointed. "OK, Miss Smarty Pants. If you're so grown up, tell me what's the biggest word in the dictionary?"

"I don't know."

"You don't know or you don't remember?"

"I don't know." I have my little comb out and I'm running it down Gretchie's back. She rolls over and lets me comb her belly. Mommy's in the hospital again. Yesterday I got to stand on my stilts and look at her through the window.

"Antidisestablishmentarianism," he says. "Ain't that a mouthful?"

"Anti what?"

He says it again. Then he tries to teach me how to spell it.

"When you want to learn how to spell a word, you have to be able to see it in your mind. Close your eyes while I tell you the letters."

I get up to the *h,* but then I can't see after that.

"Maybe my mind's not big enough yet to hold all of them letters."

"Maybe not," he laughs. Then he starts quizzing me on my spelling words. He got this special book that's supposed to help you practice. It's full of a bunch of words I never heard of. The old man says the meaning's not as important right now as the spelling. I can always look it up later. But every night he teaches me the meaning of a new word.

"I'd be mighty proud if you won the spelling bee," he says. "But I wouldn't be arrogant. You know what that is?"

He looks it up and reads it to me. "Pride's one thing, but arrogance is another," he says.

I almost won the spelling bee at school, but I missed on the word *amateur*. I closed my eyes and everything like he said. But even though I could see that it was "t-e-u-r" in my mind, I still said "t-u-r-e." Now he wants me to get ready for next year.

"You win the County Champion, they'll send you off to the state capital," he says.

"I got to be the best speller in my school first." I'm already the best one in fifth grade.

"We're working on it. We're working on it. Spell *deliberate*," he says. And I do even though I don't remember what it means. The old man looked it up for me the other day, but I forget. It's got something to do with accident. Mommy said it was him going on and on about that damn accident every other second that put her back in the hospital this time. She said let him try to take care of us kids on his own if he's looking so hard for something to feel bad about.

"Spell *gubernatorial*," he says. And I do even though I don't remember what it means. I can spell a whole bunch of words even though I have no idea what they mean. That's because I'm getting what the old man calls a photographic memory. That's what President Kennedy has and everybody knows he's smart.

sing along with mitch

T he old man went out and got himself a tape recorder. Ever since Mommy got back from the hospital he plays it all the time. He says it's fascinating how modern science has made such a thing available to your average man. Mommy says she knows the old man is under a strain, acting the way he did after his wreck like he'd seen his own ghost, but the tape recorder is the last straw.

At first, we all get to use the tape recorder too and it's a whole lot of fun. We've never had anything like it before and none of us have ever heard what our voices sound like. It's really something how you can hear yourself talk every day and then when you tape-record it, it's like hearing a stranger's voice. The only way you can be sure it's you is if you remember the exact words you said.

We play the *Sing Along with Mitch* record we got for Christmas and sit together on the davenport taking turns singing into the microphone, acting like we're famous. Mommy and the old man don't even have to read the words to half the songs. They know them all by heart since they sang most of them when they were kids. Mommy feels so good she keeps getting up and doing a tap dance to "East Side, West Side All Around the Town" and I tape-record her shoes clicking on the floor. We pass the microphone around and take turns singing solos and then we lean in close together, singing all at once. When we're all done, we rewind the tape and play it back to see how we sound.

Mommy says the old man has always got to go too far. He's never satisfied doing a little bit. He can't just practice his singing and cut up a little, he has to turn into some kind of FBI agent.

What she means is the old man's been taping us sitting to-gether at the supper table then playing it back later on. He finds some part and rewinds it to listen to over again. Then he starts picking a fight with Mommy about some stupid thing she said. I mean, it seems like she just said some really dumb thing like "Who wants some more potatoes?" He asks her just exactly what she meant by that. He acts like he's Perry Mason talking about the tone of her voice when she said it, making her listen to it again.

He even tape-records their fights. In the middle of the night, he plays them back full blast. When I sneak downstairs to go pee there he is sitting in his chair in the dark with the tape reels wind-ing around. "You lousy son of a bitch!" Mommy's voice shrieks from the tape recorder. He doesn't see me walk by. He doesn't even notice me standing at the foot of the stairs. But I know he's awake because I can see the red tip of his cigarette move up to his mouth.

whispering

I keep having this dream over and over again. What happens is I dream I'm laying perfectly still on my bed with the covers pulled up over me, even over my face. I try to move and loosen the covers but I can't budge. Then it dawns on me I'm dead. Mommy and Abbie come in my room and I can hear them whispering, standing at the foot of my bed. They don't know I'm dead. I try real hard to say something but no words come out of my mouth. I try to move, but I can't even wiggle my toes. So then I start trying to get them to read my mind. Once I read in this book if you stare real hard at somebody that's not looking at you, after a while they'll turn their head and look at you. Even though I can't see Mommy and Abbie through the covers, I stare in their direction. I want them to look over and notice I'm dead. I want them to start to cry and feel bad about all the times they were mean to me. But they just stand there whispering and whispering and I can't make out a word they're saying.

orchid corsage

Maudie Purtlebaugh got killed when her and Iggie were driving home and their car ran out of gas on the railroad tracks. The old man can't quit talking about it. "Now there's an act of God if I ever heard of one," he keeps saying. "He just comes and plucks you right up when your time is ripe."

Out in the barn, Marvella opens the door to her black potbelly stove and shovels more coal in. The chimney pipe rumbles kind of like a train going down the tracks. They say Maudie just froze right there in her seat when the train was coming. Iggie tried to yank her out, but she wouldn't budge. In my mind, I can see Maudie Purtlebaugh standing by the cash register at the grocery store, talking to me in her high, scratchy voice, asking if Gretchie would like a Milk-Bone from the box she keeps under the counter. Iggie's in back by the meat case, wiping his hands on his stained white apron, his white hair combed carefully over his pink scalp.

It's so warm I have to sit on a stack of newspapers till I quit feeling dizzy. The damp mossy air is like the garden after it rains. There's a big white box on the table. I lift off the lid and unwrap the green waxy paper. Inside, there are red roses with their petals curled up tight. Seeing them all lined up under the paper makes me think of dead people laying in their caskets all still.

Marvella takes out these pink and white carnations from the icebox and I start wrapping the stems with green tape so we can hook them to the pins to make corsages. She's standing at this big table across from me separating yellow and white pompons into two stacks.

"We got to get over to the funeral parlor before four. They're having the viewing tonight," she says. "Maudie Purtlebaugh was a good soul. Everybody'll want to come by and pay their last respects."

"Can I go?" I clip the ends of the yellow and white pompons and start handing them to her one by one. She weaves them in and out of this wire frame. The countertop and the floor are covered with leaves and flower petals. Marvella raises her eyebrows at me and puts her hands on her hips. She shakes her head.

"You're only ten. That's too young for such a thing."

I've never seen inside the funeral parlor. When we deliver the flowers, we just leave them in this back room by the door. But Abbie told me what it was like. She knows since she gets invited over to Martha Bisbee's house all the time for slumber parties. Since her daddy's the undertaker and they live upstairs over the funeral parlor, at night after her parents go to sleep, Martha takes Abbie and the other girls on a tour.

Abbie says they've got one whole room filled with caskets all lined up with their lids open wide so you can see inside and choose whether you want the blue or red velvet or the white or pale blue or pink satin. They even have a tiny casket painted white with white satin lining that's supposed to be for a kid.

There are three rooms and sometimes there's a dead person in each one waiting to have their funeral. Martha acts like the dead people are just regular people sleeping. She tiptoes around, patting them on the cheek and touching their hands and saying "nighty-night." Abbie says a dead person looks a lot like somebody that's all dressed up ready to go to a party in their best clothes, only when you touch them, their skin is cold as ice. If you look at a dead person long enough, you'd swear to God you saw them scratching themselves or twitching a little bit.

"Where'd you go? Never-never land?" Marvella nudges me with her elbow. "Cut me a nice long strip of white ribbon. That thick one." She lays the ribbon down on the table and writes on it with glue, holding the glue bottle like it's a pen. She lets me sprinkle silver glitter all over it and when I shake it off, it says *Heavenly Rest*. She ties the ribbon across the wreath and starts putting the roses and some ferns into these two cardboard vases.

"Lemme show you something." Marvella wipes her hands on

her skirt and takes something out of the icebox. "This here is an orchid. It came clear across the country, all the way from California. I sent for it special for Maudie to wear."

There, in a see-through plastic box, is a lavender-and-white flower that looks like some kind of fancy spider. She lifts it out real careful and lets me fill this tiny glass tube with water. Afterwards, she pokes the stem into the tube so the orchid will stay fresh.

sleeping beauty

Mommy and Abbie are going out to deliver Nova since a bunch of new stuff just came and all the customers are waiting. Before they go, her and Abbie sit in the kitchen packing it up in the little white bags that you put all the orders in. I don't get to help on account of I'm sick and I have to lie still, but I'm downstairs in Mommy's bed so I can hear them adding up how much money they're going to make if everybody's at home. Every time they start whispering, I can tell it's about me. Mommy acts like I got sick just to make her mad. After they go, the old man comes in to check up on me.

"Hey, Sleeping Beauty," he says. "How's my daddy's girl? You sick of being sick yet?" He puts his hand on my forehead. "You don't feel hot anymore," he says. "Say 'ah.'" I stick out my tongue. "Nothing in there either, partner," he says. He pats my knee. Then he rubs my foot. He thinks I'm still just a little kid. Abbie says I'll always be his Little Lana. She's glad it's me, not her. The old man's fingers creep up my leg. I pinch my knees together tight and hold my breath.

"I'd sure like you to get better." He pulls the blankets down to my knees and starts rubbing my belly. I feel like Doc Havey is hitting me all over with that rubber hammer he's got. I shut my eyes and act like I've got a big ball of gauze. I wind and wind it all around me till I'm covered from head to toe but when that don't work I start trying to name the fifty states. *Kansas. Florida. Kentucky. Montana. Nevada.* There's a big map in my head kind of like a jigsaw puzzle with a bunch of pieces missing. *California, Indiana, Texas.* Then my head gets all achy and I can't think of any more. *Texas,* I say, over and over again. *Texas.*

This feeling rushes down my belly like somebody's waving a sparkler around me too close. I open my eyes a tiny crack and there is the old man looking at himself in the mirror above Mommy's vanity. Then I remember *Maryland* and that song starts going in my head. What did Della wear, boys, what did Della wear?

intercoms

This here house's a regular firetrap. But once I get this set up right, I can protect us from anything." The old man's downstairs in his room fiddling around with the intercom he just got. Even though he's talking to himself, all of us can hear what he's saying because the old man stuck the brown plastic intercom boxes all over the house and all the wires lead down to the control box he stuck on his bedside table. There's a switch on the front of his box so he can turn it off or on whenever he wants to. When it's on, he can hear everything all over the house. And when he wants to tell us stuff, all he has to do is switch on the "Talk" button and presto. Having the intercom is kind of like having walkie-talkies only there's a whole bunch of receivers and only one control box. We can't make him listen to us unless he's already got the "Listen" button turned on. But anytime he wants to, he can tell us stuff and we can't turn him off.

"Let's test her out again." His voice crackles over the intercom. "Ruth? We ain't through yet."

To test it out, what the old man wants Mommy to do is keep crumpling up a paper sack so he can see how good he can hear. He says the crumpling paper sounds just like fire crackling. She's crumpled up about a million sacks already. She sighs and rolls her eyes up at the ceiling like she's asking for God's help.

"Be sure now and crumple up them sacks in every corner. You never know where a fire's going to break out."

Mommy gets up off the end of my bed and takes a new sack and crumples it up right in front of the intercom that's between me and Abbie's beds.

"He oughta be able to hear that!"

Abbie sticks her pillow over her face to keep from laughing out loud. The old man hates it when we laugh. No matter what we're laughing about he thinks we're laughing at him.

"Go back in the closet again."

Mommy thumbs her nose at the intercom and crumples up a sack in the closet.

"I can hear it real good. Now try the stairs again."

Mommy grabs another sack and crumples it over by the stairs. Her eyes are all shiny and red from trying not to laugh. She's always saying how there ain't nothing to do but humor him once he gets started. But I can tell she's about to flip her lid.

"OK. That oughta do it for now. Over and out." There's a click. The old man must've turned off the "Talk" button. The thing is, there's no way to figure out if he's still got the "Listen" button on or not. Mommy starts scooping up all the crumpled sacks. "I'm gonna take these out back and burn 'em. Maybe he'll hear the fire crackling clear out there."

the reckless driver

When me and Abbie play The Old Man's Gone for Good every night before we go to sleep, we put a blanket over the intercom box so the old man can't hear us. Sometimes when we start to giggling, the old man stands at the bottom of the stairs and threatens to come up with his belt off and smack us good if we don't quit it. But as soon as he walks away, we play it. It's the only way we can fall asleep.

The way we like the old man to die the best is when he gets killed in a wreck on his way home from work. He's driving home in the rain so he can't see too good. All of a sudden, up ahead of him on the road, there are these blinding headlights.

Whenever it's Abbie's turn to tell the story and she gets to this part, she gets all excited and acts like she's on a TV show. She sits up in bed real straight and pushes her thick hair away from her face and whispers, "It's the reckless driver!" She says it in a way that makes each word sound important, like she's saying, "The mark of Zorro."

What always happens is the old man can't get out of the reckless driver's way in time. Sometimes, he ends up going headfirst over a cliff. Sometimes, he crashes right into a telephone pole. In the end, there's a big funeral and everything and we all cry and act like we're sad. Then the three of us live happily ever after.

going back home

Remember that time Mommy forged one of the old man's checks and took us back home with her?"

"Yeah. That was something, huh?" Abbie looks up from her magazine.

"I wish we'd a stayed."

"Me too. But she didn't have any choice. He said he was going to go to a lawyer and have her arrested if she didn't hightail it home."

"You think she'll ever really leave him? I mean for good?"

"I hope so," Abbie says. Then she starts reading again. When I try to talk to her she hums. That's her signal that she doesn't want to say anything else.

It was back the summer I turned eight and Abbie was thirteen. That was just two years ago but it seems like about a million years. What we did was when the old man was at work—it was his turn to be a rider instead of a driver so his car was home in the driveway—we packed up and left for Auntie Thelma's. We took a whole bunch of our clothes and toys and stuff and the food that was in the icebox, even the old man's T-bone steaks. "Won't he be surprised when he comes home and we're all gone," Mommy said. "He'll get the coals all ready to grill himself a nice fat steak. He'll be thinking of sinking his teeth into it and it won't be in the icebox."

Mommy had to forge one of the old man's checks at the bank so we'd have enough money for gas. She practiced writing his name the way he does till she could do it good, then she made out the check. She said she felt like a siren was going to go off when she handed it to the teller. Gretchie was in back with me all fat

140

because she was going to have puppies any day. Her belly dragged on the seat. "Shut your eyes!" Abbie hollered as we got out on the highway. "Shut 'em for a second and you'll miss Millersburg." We sang along with the radio. "Lipstick on Your Collar" and "I'm a Wanderer." The windows were all down and Gretchie's ears were flapping. We stopped and cooked the steaks in a rest stop in Illinois. It was late at night when we were going up this hill in Pennsylvania and the car started sounding like it was crying and it puffed smoke so Mommy had to pull into a gas station. "Just in time," she said. But it was closed and we had to sleep there till it opened up. It's the fan belt, the guy said. Abbie counted up the money. "I could kick myself for not taking more," Mommy said, "but I was scared it'd bounce." I took Gretchie over to the back so she could get some water. I remember how she peed real careful, looking up at me with her sad eyes. Gretchie knows every single thing there is to know about me. She always knows what I'm thinking. When I'm scared, she wags her tail a little bit like she's saying it's OK. I don't know what I'd do without her.

I went to get the key for the bathroom and fill her can with cold water. *No belts no pins no pads.* One of these days I'm going to stick a nickel in there to find out what that means. I figure it's got something to do with being a teenager since they have an ad about it in Abbie's magazine, too. When I'm a teenager, if there's one thing I'm not going to do it's lie around reading magazines all the time like Abbie does and getting all moony-faced about movie stars. That just seems like the stupidest thing.

The big surprise was how when I came out Gretchie was lay-ing on her side licking puppies. There were four of them, all blind and squirming in the dirt. She licked and licked and licked. I ran and told Mommy but she didn't even listen. Abbie came and helped me carry them to the car. Gretchie was barking and trying to climb up my leg. "Careful. Your smell might bother her," Mommy said. "She'll eat them."

When the car was all fixed we drove to a grocery store and Mommy got us a quart of milk and them little packs of cereal. The milk bottle was icy cold with big drops of water on the sides. That was the best milk I ever tasted. We ate the cereal right out of the box, just like it says you can, cutting on the dotted line with Mommy's nail file. Gretchie was panting like crazy on the floor and the puppies crawled all over each other trying to get at her. I smiled at her and said I love you inside my head the way I do when anybody's around. When it's just us, I talk to her. But once Abbie heard me and she said I was crazy as the old man so usually I just do it in my head. I said a little prayer to God and asked Him to please not let Gretchie eat her puppies and she didn't.

"It must be a hundred degrees out," Mommy said. She opened her new pack of cigarettes and lit one up. "Come on, Bessie, you can make it," she said. She patted the dashboard and started it up. I waved out the window at everybody that passed us but nobody waved back. "Count the white lines on the road," Mommy said. When I woke up, we were in a parking lot and Mommy was looking at a map. She said after we got more gas we could have ice cream. "I smell the ocean," I said. Abbie said, "That's just all in your stupid head. We ain't anywhere near the stupid ocean." I only saw the ocean one time that time we all went back East for a vacation when I was three. I remember how Mommy said I'd have to wait till the next day to go in the water but the second she wasn't looking I jumped right in with my dress on and everything. Mommy said how first we'd spend the night at Auntie Thelma's and then we'd drive over and see Grammy at the dog-collar factory where she works but what happened was while we were sleeping at Auntie Thelma's somebody came and stole our car. Mommy left the keys in it the way we do here all the time and they just jumped in and took off.

Auntie Thelma said she was fixing herself a cup of tea when she heard the car door slam. She saw the car drive off but she figured it was Mommy mad about something the way she gets so she didn't think anything of it till Mommy came down for breakfast. Then they called the police. We finally got the car back but we didn't get any of our clothes. Mommy said whoever did it must've been pretty desperate to keep our stuff. We had to tell the old man about it and everything and as soon as we got the car back, we had to drive home. "I'll put out a warrant for your arrest," he told Mommy, but he never did.

communion

F loyd looks back at the accident he had and thinks of it as the beginning of the end. He uses those words, says them to himself over and over, whispering under his breath, *the beginning of the end*, the words running around inside of him like the reels from his tape recorder. He's sure there's a message he's not getting, sure he's being given a sign, but he is unable to figure out what to do. *The beginning of the end*, he says, bending to whisper into the microphone, flipping through his Bible saying *Alpha* and *Omega*, like passwords to a door that never opens.

This is what sends him creeping down the cement steps to the church basement, this and the colored lights that flash and swirl in front of his eyes. "Just like rainbows," he told Doc Havey when he went in for a checkup. With the doctor thumping his chest and back, listening to his heartbeat, looking in his ears, Floyd tells him, "It's started to get so's I can't sleep a wink at night. I've always had trouble sleeping. But not like this."

"You look healthy as a horse to me," Doc Havey says, shutting off the light he just peered into Floyd's eyes with.

"It's like somebody's pulling rainbows from out of my eyes. Like these long scarves of real pretty colors all lit up are being pulled out of me. I'll pass a car on the highway and start crying over how pretty it looks."

Doc Havey is on his way out, has his hand on the doorknob. Is, in fact, turning the latch, when Floyd says this.

"You sound to me like a fellow that's under a strain." He glances at his watch. "You ought to take it easy," he says, closing the door behind him.

Floyd doesn't mention that he also has the distinct sensation he is being watched no matter where he goes, like someone is always behind him, shadowing every move. That even now sitting on the paper-covered table with his pants folded on the chair beside him, someone is behind him, waiting for him. Every once in a while Floyd gets a glimpse of a hand out of the corner of his eye. A man's hand with the nails scrubbed clean, cut close to the fingertips. A dark head bent over a pad of paper, writing and writing like he is keeping track of everything Floyd does.

He feels himself being watched as he creeps down the basement stairs of the church, on his way to the meeting, the crunch of his tires on the driveway as he drove away from home still echoing in his ears. Ruth, her mouth an angry snarl, had flung her wedding band at him. "This doesn't mean shit to me," she'd said. And he'd driven right over it.

He creeps down the stairs, the whole time wanting to turn around, rush into the evening air filled with the calls of mourning doves. He wants to go home, sit in his chair. Get a case of cold beer and take it easy, like Doc Havey'd told him to. He wants Ruth to be there, playing solitaire in the kitchen, her cards slapping onto the table, the radio playing. She'll smile up at him when he walks in the back door. Look at him the way a wife is supposed to. His girls will be upstairs. Abbie trying on makeup, walking up and down the stairs with a book balanced on her head. Lana sitting on her bed pretending to drive to China or wherever it is she's planning to go that week. Ever since she'd gotten those maps, there was no shutting her up about places she could go. He wants to walk in the back door, scratch the dog behind her ears, open up a cold bottle of Black Label and tip back his chair with his feet up, watch TV, and forget about how his marriage is almost over. Forget about how he's sure he's losing his mind.

Just as he is about to turn and leave, there is Reverend Andrews. "I thought I heard somebody." His voice is loud, bellowing up at Floyd. "C'mon down and join us. Don't be bashful. We're just about to get started."

He grips Floyd's hand, clamping on to it like he's afraid Floyd will slip away from him. "It's real good to see you," he says, pumping his hand up and down the same way he did that day after church.

"Just a little get-together. For prayer and God's merciful guid-ance. We'd sure love to have you, Floyd," he'd said last week, pumping Floyd's hand up and down while all around them the congregation pressed close. Floyd had gone to church that Sun-day because he felt sorry for Lana.

"Marvella says for us kids to bring somebody from home next Sunday," she'd said when they were all sitting around the supper table. "It's Family Day."

"What'll they think up next?"Ruth had scraped back her chair and gotten up from the table to start clearing away the dishes be-fore the food was even gone. "Putting kids up to that crap. Ain't it enough they've got half the town in pews? Why can't they take care of them that wants to go and leave the rest of us to go to hell in peace?"

Floyd wasn't exactly sure how he felt about going to church, though he'd been thinking it over a lot lately. He'd watch Lana march off on Sunday morning with the handful of pennies he'd given her and try to picture what it'd be like to walk along with her.

The organ is playing when they walk in the door. Seeing the sanctuary filled, ladies in pink and white and black hats, men in their Sunday-best starched white shirts, along with the organ's whining notes, the smell of perfume and aftershave, the lemon oil he rubbed into the pews the day before and a breeze through the half-open windows make Floyd dizzy. Lana leads him into the first empty pew. The colors around him are so bright he feels as if he's never seen colors before, the light through the stained-glass windows sparkling like diamonds. He is filled with an immense joy. "Alpha and Omega," the voice whispers. And he knows he's finally been led to the place he's meant to be.

His stomach flutters with excitement. Here I am, his whole body seems to be saying. I'm ready. There is even a tap on his shoulder but when he turns around, it's only Bob Applegate, the owner of the drugstore, already snoring softly. Beside him, his wife, Viola, thumbing through her hymnal, doesn't even look up.

Floyd can barely sit still. It happens right in the middle of the sermon. With Reverend Andrews working himself up over the scriptures: "There appeared to them tongues as of fire, distributed and resting on each one of them." His voice crackles down the aisle, Floyd jumps as the flames rush along the backs of the pews. He looks all around him, but no one else seems to notice. There is no smell of smoke, no heat, just the crackle of flames along his thighs and across his chest and back up along the pews. He knows he is the only one who can see it. He rubs and rubs at his eyes, telling himself to calm down and then the fire is gone, as quickly as it came. There is Lana beside him, so still she seems to be barely breathing. He looks down at the line of scalp beneath the part in her hair. His chest aches. Tears keep rushing to his eyes and he has to blink hard to keep them from spilling down his face.

"You are a child of God," he wants to say. He wants to pick her up in his arms. Grab her close the way he did when she was small, before she'd begun to shrink from his touch. How she used to squeal with pleasure, pressing her face into his neck and he would inhale her sweet, clean smell.

The congregation is moving down the aisle, singing, "Let us break bread together on our knees." They crowd around the alter, row by row. Floyd follows, kneeling on the soft red cushions. He kneels, barely letting his weight rest on the cushions, nervous that he is doing something wrong, afraid he doesn't belong, and everybody will know. It has been so long, he can't quite remember what to do. He glances at the lady beside him, her eyes closed in prayer, her hands cupped in front of her, and he does the same.

"This is my body, broken for you," Reverend Andrews is saying. "Do this in remembrance of me." The tears are coming so fast now Floyd gives in to them, swallowing his sobs, the saltiness running into his lips. He waits, his hands open in front of him, for the bread of forgiveness of all sins. Surely this is what he was called here for. Surely he is being given another chance. Surely this is the moment God has been leading him to. Even with his eyes closed, the beautiful lights dance in front of him. This time he isn't frightened. He knows he isn't drunk or crazy, like they accused the disciples of being. He knows the truth. He knows God is sending him visions and dreams. Soon all the true believers will see it too.

At first he thinks the preacher has run out of bread. That he will return with more and place the soft white cube in Floyd's palms, but then the tray of thimble-sized glasses rattles in front of him. He lifts one out, keeping his head down to hide his tears. "This is my blood, poured out for you." Floyd swallows the sweet grape juice.

A finger taps and taps on his shoulder but this time he doesn't turn around. He knows there is no one there. "Forsaken, forsaken," a voice whispers in his ear. He can see Ruth with her hair loose around her shoulders, laughing as if she will never stop. He is desperate for the taste of bread. His belly is empty, hollow, as if he hasn't eaten in weeks and he's been deprived of the one food he needs most.

When the service is over, Floyd and Lana step out into the bright sunlight. The church bells are ringing. Reverend Andrews grabs Floyd's hand, looks him right in the eye, his voice low, urgent, telling him about the prayer group. "We'd love you to come, Floyd. It's just a little get-together. To pray for God's merciful guidance."

All that week Floyd replays the scene at the altar. He sees his cupped hands waiting and empty. When Ruth picks a fight with him—he doesn't remember what it's over this time; it doesn't seem to matter anymore—he climbs into his car, knowing he is headed for church, for that meeting. He backs out of the driveway, backs over Ruth's wedding band. The next day, he will see it there, a circle of gold ground into the dirt. He won't even try to pry it loose.

There they are at the bottom of the stairs, sitting on wooden folding chairs, borrowed Bibles open on their laps. How Ruth would laugh at the sight of them. "Neila Grimes praying her heart out one minute, and telling the whole town what everybody else prayed about the next," she'd say. Reverend Andrews is reading from his big Bible in his singsong voice, standing at the head of the circle, his voice echoing in the basement. "Ask, and it shall be given you; seek, and ye shall find; knock, and it shall be opened unto you."

Floyd turns the thin onionskin paper, searching for the place.

"Let us pray for those who are troubled. For those who need God's guidance." Reverend Andrews bows his head. Around the

147

circle people begin to murmur the names of those they have come to pray for.

"Be with my sister Merle," Dorcas Carey whispers. "She needs you to ease her pain."

"I'm here to give thanks for all the blessings in my life. My family. This church. Our wonderful community," Mary Cordle says loudly, as if doubt never crossed her mind.

Floyd wants to say, "Pray for me. Floyd Franklin. Now there's a fellow that could use a little help." But he is silent when it comes his turn. Silent except for his heart thumping and thumping in his chest.

independence day

The old man got laid off from his job so he's out back in his lawn chair all day long in the hot sun where the whole world can see him out there in nothing but his teeny black swimming trunks. The weatherman on the radio claims it's the hottest summer in decades. All day long the locusts whirl and click up in the trees and the old man lies out there baking in the sun with his eyes shut. Him and Mommy aren't talking to each other. The old man says it's like the cold war and Mommy's Russia. He says if she could she'd build the Berlin Wall down the middle of the house.

"You try bringing home the bacon for a change," he told her. So Mommy went out and got a job working on the graveyard shift over at the canning factory in Elwood. The old man said they're only hiring girls because they can pay them half as much and still get away with it. Mommy gets home right about the time the rest of us are waking up. We have to tiptoe around the house all day so she can get what she calls her beauty rest. We can't flush the toilet or slam the screen door or anything as long as she's in her room with the blinds pulled shut.

I'm sitting at the kitchen table trying to figure out how many words I can make out of the two words *Independence Day*. I like to do this every time a holiday is coming up. The most words I've ever got are fifty-seven from *Merry Christmas*. That's a good one since there's an *s*. That's like getting a double word score in Scrabble. So far, I've only come up with six: *depend, end, pen, den, deep,* and *need.*

The old man is whistling like a cardinal. That's his signal that he wants me to get him something. I keep trying to find more words. There's *pain, pin, din,* and *in.* If I had an *r* I could make *rain* and *dinner.* He whistles again.

When I get out back, he waves at me like he thinks I can't tell where he's at. "C'mere, little lady," he says. "It's high noon." He acts like I'm supposed to know what that means. A jet streaking across the pale blue sky makes a loud boom and the old man jumps in his chair and slaps his chest like he's been shot. "They got me that time." He hangs his head like he's dead. I'm supposed to laugh.

"A fellow can sure develop a powerful thirst out here on a day like today. What d'ya say you bring your old man one of them ice cold beers?"

The bottom shelf of the icebox is stacked with brown bottles of beer. The old man bought two cases. Usually when he gets a case of beer he sits in the front room and drinks one bottle after the other till he drinks them all up. Then he either turns into a mean drunk or a happy drunk. You can never tell which one it's going to be. This time he claims he's spreading them out. He's only having six beers a day. That way, he won't have to buy any more till Friday hits. On my way out with the beer, I slam the back door by mistake. Mommy groans.

"What am I supposed to do, partner? Open it with my teeth?" He pretends to bite the cap off.

Mommy's in the kitchen boiling water for coffee. Her pink rubber curlers are half falling out of her hair. She's got on her underpants and a blue blouse hangs open over her bra.

"He starting already?" she asks, stirring her coffee and tapping the spoon on the edge of the white cup. "Tell him I said it's just a matter of time before he steps off the deep end."

The old man pops open his beer and flings the cap under his chair where all the other caps are half buried in the tall grass. "Did you hear the one about the nut in the nuthouse?" he asks. He tells that stupid joke at least five times a day. It's all about some doctor that asks this guy if he puts manure on his strawberries since they're so nice and juicy red. Whenever the old man gets to the part where the guy says, "Hell, no. I put cream and sugar on 'em and they think I'm nuts," the old man starts slapping his bare thighs like it's the funniest thing he ever heard but I don't say it's funny or anything. Every time the old man hears somebody say the word *funny,* he starts going on and on about do you mean funny ha ha or funny *funny?* Just exactly which funny do you mean? he wants to know.

When he reaches over and wraps his fingers around my wrist, I feel like I'm locked in handcuffs. I can see the words *Independence Day* in my head. *Nice, dice, ice,* I think. *Pay, pie, die.*

He flips up his sunglasses and says, "They say the worst thing about going nuts is how you're the last one to know it."

On Independence Day, we always used to sit out on the front porch to watch the fireworks go off in Tipton, but now I'm the only one that wants to watch. The whole sky above the cornfield across the road lights up all red and blue and white and green. Once, when I was a little kid, we all drove in to see them up close, but I got so scared I wouldn't get out of the car. I couldn't believe something that pretty could make so much noise. I hid my head in the corner of the backseat and covered my ears. I was practically crying my eyes out. We ended up having to leave before it was over since I was convinced the world was coming to an end and nobody could talk me out of it.

the white leather bible

I'm sitting up in the maple tree when this blue station wagon pulls up out front. This guy takes a big black suitcase out of the back and climbs up the front porch. The old man comes to the door eating a baloney sandwich. All he has on is his black swimming trunks. He shakes the guy's hand and acts all interested when he opens up his suitcase.

"This here is genuine cowhide leather," the guy says. He hands the old man a white Bible.

"See here. It's a King James Version. In back here, there's a study guide so's you can find whatever you're looking for. Here's Daniel in the den of lions. And here's Lot's wife aturning into a pillar of salt." The Bible salesman is acting all tickled pink because he knows he's got himself a customer. He's got a high whiny voice like a mosquito humming in your ear. "If you want to find mention of water, it's right in this index in back."

"I'm mighty glad you stopped by." The old man is running his hands all over the Bible like he's never held one before. "This sure is a pretty one."

From where I'm at, I can see that salesman grinning from ear to ear. Abbie would say he's got dollar signs in his eyes. "Everything Jesus says is in red. Thataway you can find it quick. And there's fourteen color illustrations." He leans in close to show him.

The old man finds the story of Lazarus coming back to life and starts reading it out loud. He reads slowly, putting feeling into it.

"I was pretty near saved from the dead myself. Had me a wreck. A close call, you could say. Just the other day I was reading in the paper how more folks've died from all the car wrecks we've had than've died in every U.S. war combined. Can you imagine? I had a near miss myself, but I escaped that one. I sure did."

He finds the part where Jesus is picking his disciples and starts reading that. Pretty soon, all that salesman does is scratch at the back of his neck and rub his thick red hand over his bald head like he's polishing it. He starts drawing a circle with his toe on the porch, staring at it like it's the most interesting thing he's ever laid eyes on. I can tell he's wishing he could figure out some way to get away. But once the old man starts talking nowadays, that's the end of that. You can't ever get a word in edgewise.

Mommy says when she first met the old man, he was so bashful he hardly even spoke one word. I can remember back when he hardly ever said much of anything. Now he talks all the time but he doesn't make a whole lot of sense. He'll talk to anybody that'll stand still long enough to hear what he's got to say.

"I just know there's the answer to life between these pages," the old man says. "This here book'll sure as shooting show me the way. I'm mighty glad you stopped over with it. They say you never know when one of God's messengers'll show up. And looky here. I've got one right on my doorstep."

The pages of the old man's new Bible have gold trim and there's a gold zipper around three sides.

"This here's a sign from heaven," the old man says. "Sure as shooting, a sign from above." He walks around zipping and unzipping his Bible and he reads it out loud. "I'm getting the answer in here," he says. "The meaning of life is right here between these pages. Listen to this." And then he starts reading about some valley of dry bones dancing and Mommy tells him to knock it off. She's sick to death of Bible study.

what if?

I'm out back trying to teach Gretchie how to roll over and play dead. Everybody says you can't teach an old dog new tricks, but I'm still trying. Whenever I tell her to roll over, she sits and tries to give me her paw. Penny says maybe it's because she's a dash hound. Maybe she speaks German on account of that's where she comes from, but I don't know the German words for it. I lift her up so she's standing, then I push her over on her side again and say, "Roll over." Gretchie wags her tail and smiles at me. I'm not kidding. She really does smile. She lifts her long nose up in the air and pulls back her lips a little bit and shows me her teeth. Gretchie's the best dog there ever was.

Penny is out back helping her daddy drown the moles. What they do is Mr. Reeb sticks the end of the hose into one of the mole tunnels that crisscross their yard. Then Penny turns the water on full blast. Afterwards, they walk on top of the tunnels till their backyard is flat as a pancake.

"C'mere, kiddoke." The old man's smearing Coppertone on his legs. Abbie says if he stays out back long enough he's going to look like one giant freckle.

"Tell me something. What if you were old Adolf Eichmann about to get hung for being in cahoots with Hitler?" He grabs me around the neck and makes a choking sound. "What would you have for your last meal? They give you whatever you want to eat, you know, just before they do you in. I'd have me a big plate of chicken and dumplings myself."

I'm trying to figure out what I'd like to have when he starts asking me something else. "What if the house was to catch on fire and you could only take one thing, what would it be? What would you take first?" he wants to know.

"I'd grab Gretchie quick and stick her in my pillowcase," I tell him. "Then I'd carry her down the stairs over my shoulder. I'd hold the top tight so she couldn't squirm out."

"What if the stairs caught on fire?" the old man wants to know. He frowns and his forehead gets all crinkled up. "You'd shimmy down that fire pole I made you, now wouldn't you?"

spin the bottle

Winona's come over to give Mommy a home permanent to celebrate the old man getting called back to the factory. The whole house stinks of it, but Mommy says that's a small price to pay to be a knockout. Winona says she'll do me one too but I like my hair just the way it is now that I got a pixie cut even though Penny says I look like a boy and ought to let it grow.

Winona and Mommy are drinking about a million highballs. They keep clinking their glasses and laughing their heads off over everything. Mommy doesn't even care if I make fudge, so I am. I'm stirring it about a hundred hours waiting for it to boil.

"You keep tasting that the way you're doing and there won't be a damn thing left," Winona tells me. She's cracking open a tray of ice, biting her cigarette between her teeth the way she does. Her teeth are small and yellow like a rat's. She smears more glop on Mommy's hair and rolls it up on these little plastic curlers. Winona gave herself a perm last week and it's all curly like a poodle. That's the name of the hairdo. She says it's the latest style.

"I had this frigging dream last night I can't get out of my head for shit. I'm in bed with Duane and Syd Sizelove," Winona tells Mommy.

"You sure that wasn't a nightmare?"

"Listen. I'm serious. I never thought of Syd thataway but the dream really says it for me. I mean there we are. Duane in the middle whining about how he can't keep a hard zonger anymore and Syd there leering at me like there's no tomorrow. I wake up thinking about how I'll go into Syd's and say I bet you're just my size, lover boy."

"His teeth'll fall right out of his head if you do."

"Ruthie. I think that about does it." Winona snaps her rubber gloves off and tosses them in the sink then ties a blue hairnet around Mommy's curlers before she pours them each another drink.

"Mommy?" I ask. She doesn't even hear me so I say it again but she's too busy clinking glasses with Winona. Winona's kids all went to see their grandma in Idaho so she's been over to our house just about every second since Mommy quit working. The graveyard shift was too much for her; she said she never had time for any fun.

"How'd you ever end up with a man like Duane?" Mommy asks.

"Shit. I knew him one goddamned night. And I mean knew in the biblical sense. Then wham. I get stuck with a bun in the oven."

"Mommy? Can I have another Coke?"

"Mommy. Mommy. Mommy. Miss Whiny Butt. Have whatever you damn please just stop calling me Mommy like you're two years old. And keep your trap shut for once. I'm trying to have a talk with my friend. How'd you like it if every time you and Penny were talking I kept butting in on you? Where is Penny anyhow? Why aren't you out playing on a day like this?" she asks me, taking a big gulp of her drink. "Did ya do the white dress bit and all?" she asks Winona.

"Christ, yes. Bridesmaids, the works. I think that was the last time I had a frigging dress on. Jesus. I sure had my head up my ass back then. What's the story on you and Floyd?"

I get the hammer out to tap a nail into the cap of my Coke. I like to drink it that way best, sucking it out from the little hole. I tell Mommy I don't know where Penny's gone to but I do. She's at Debbie Mendenhall's birthday party. I saw her leave a little while ago all dressed up with her shiny shoes on. She was all excited about it because it's both boys and girls and they're going to play Spin the Bottle. I didn't get invited but I wouldn't have gone anyhow. I'd rather drop dead than have to kiss some boy.

"We got hitched right before Floyd was shipped overseas.

'Send our boys overseas with a grin on their faces,' everybody said. I knew that man a total of six weekends. Not enough days to add up to a month and there I was promising to spend the rest of my life with him." Mommy stirs the ice in her drink with the tip of her finger then licks it. I've only heard a little bit about how her and the old man met. She usually says about how good looking he was and all that, but when I ask her to tell me more, she gets mad and says it's not worth wasting her breath on. If I ask the old man, what he does is he takes his billfold out of his back pocket and shows me this picture of him and Mommy. "Here we were before you came along," he'll say. Or, "Here we are, two young pups, before we tied the knot." He's kind of sitting on the hood of this old-fashioned black car and Mommy's on his lap with her legs crossed and her skirt riding up. He's got ahold of her leg to keep her from sliding off. He has his uniform on with his hat tilted funny and what he calls a shit-eating grin on his face. But if I ask him to tell me about the olden days, that's all he does is show me that picture.

"The ceremony we had. If you can even call it that. Was over before the bless-you after a sneeze. But we waited so long for our turn I swear I could feel my fingernails growing." Mommy looks at her hands like she can still see it happening.

"You mean your wedding?" I ask. "Is this when you had your wedding?"

"Yes, Big Ears. But it wasn't exactly what you'd call a wedding. More like a funeral." Winona hums the funeral song and takes Mommy's cigarette to light one for herself. "That room was packed," Mommy says. "All them soldiers in uniform and girls with their best clothes on trying to act like they weren't scared half to death. I can still see myself sitting there on one of them wooden folding chairs like I was at Sunday school.

"Floyd stood across the room smoking a cigarette the way he still does, fiddling with it like he can't figure out what else to do with them hands of his. This girl behind me had a big fat baby on her lap crying its eyes out. I was so stupid I counted my lucky stars Floyd was willing to marry me before it went that far. I'll tell you a secret. I was never even sure it was his. Back then, one minute a girl was having a ball dancing with some fellow, and the next thing you knew she was knitting baby booties. Shit, Winona.

What'd you put in these drinks? Truth serum? What're you, the FBI?"

Winona laughs and puts her bare feet up on the table. The bottoms are black as coal and there are smears of dirt between each toe. I can see her blue underpants up the leg of her short shorts. "It does you good to get things off your chest once in a while. It'll keep your damn frown lines from going too deep."

"How long has it been?" Mommy reaches up to touch her head.

"Nuh-uh-uh. It has to stay put just the right time or else you get waves, not curls. You got a while yet."

My fudge is bubbling now pretty good so I keep testing it by dripping some in a glass of water, but it's not time to add the butter yet.

"I haven't thought of all this in years. The fellow that married us? The justice of the peace? He had this real thin head of hair swirled every which way around the top of his head and a beard pointing out of the end of his chin just like some goat. His hair was black as shoe polish and the roots on his scalp and chin were pure white. Now just what kind of man dyes his hair?"

"Skunk man," Winona says.

"Pee-you," I say, laughing.

"What're you laughing at, little sister?" Winona asks me.

"I'm planning on telling it from beginning to end if you're going to listen." Mommy crunches her ice and looks at Winona like she's mad.

"I'm all ears," Winona says. "But lemme make us some fresh ones."

"Floyd got me a corsage of pink carnations. He acted all pleased and bashful, pinning it on my jacket like he'd never laid a hand on me before. Wouldn't you know carnations are the only flowers I can't stand?

"It figures."

"I had all I could do to breathe with them damn carnations pinned up under my nose. There I was with one hand pushed against my belly. I'm already starting to show. And I'm about to puke from the smell of them. I barely spit out 'I do' before Floyd slips the ring on my finger and that's that. My mother and my sister Thelma throw a handful of rice at us and I toss my corsage at

Thelma. She catches it with one hand, grinning her stupid grin, with those big horsey teeth of hers. Do you know she was the only virgin left in that town after the war was over?"

"Mommy?" I want her to check and see if she thinks the fudge is ready. I take a swig from my Coke. "Mommy?" I say again.

"What the hell are you doing sucking on that Coke like it's some baby bottle?" She smacks at me and tells me to go outside. "And call me Mom like I said to or don't call me nothing."

"My fudge's still cooking."

"I don't care. Get out of here this minute."

"Frigging kids. Last week I caught Tammy sucking on Little Duane's baby bottle. She sticks it in her lunch bucket for Christ's sake. I said don't you give a shit what the other kids say about you?"

"The other day I read in the paper how an octopus dies after it lays its eggs. Maybe they know something we don't."

"Christ, Ruth. You're getting grim on me. Better have another."

I'm out on the back step eating my fudge out of the pan. I'm still listening to them but I can't figure out all of what they're saying. Sometimes when Winona and Mommy—I mean *Mom*—get going it's like they're talking some foreign language half the time. I don't see what the big deal is about *Mom* or *Mommy*. Abbie calls her the old bag behind her back when she makes Abbie do something she doesn't want to. I wonder how she'd like it if I called her that.

"Floyd never was a talker. You know that. We used to just hold hands and every once in a while I'd catch him staring at me this way he had of doing. It only meant one thing to me then. Romance. I sure fell for the secret, silent type. How was I to know he'd end up nuttier than a pecan pie? Maybe I could make me some money writing about it for one of them stories in *True Confessions*."

"Then I'll write mine. I married the man that wasn't there. He sits at the table. He sleeps in the bed. But he ain't really there."

"You can call it 'I Married Casper.' Mine's there when he can get a foot in the door. But he's not all there in the head."

"You two have a honeymoon?"

"Not exactly. Floyd borrowed my brother Slim's car and we

drove over to this roadhouse on the edge of town. Friendly Fred's."

Slim is Mom's baby brother. She told me once how she loved him like there was no tomorrow. He had thick blonde curly hair and baby blue eyes and a heart of gold. I never did meet him because what happened was Slim got married to some lady named Orkida when he was stationed in California and they lived out there with palm trees in their front yard and a lemon bush by the door. Then one day he got up and went to work like he always did only he never came home again and nobody ever heard from him since. I wrote a letter to Bob Barker to see if he'd put Mom and Uncle Slim on that TV show of his where he reunites everybody. It was going to be a surprise for Mom's birthday. But I never even got an answer back.

"Yeah. Fred was friendly all right," Mom says. "They used to say he was so friendly there wasn't a girl in town he hadn't had. There we are, drinking beers at Fred's. Floyd pats my hand, running his thumb back and forth across my ring. Let me tell you, it started feeling tighter and tighter, pinching into my skin, like it was cutting off the circulation. It sure slipped on easy enough."

"I bet it did," Winona says. "It slipped *in* easy enough too."

"Go on now!" Mom starts giggling so bad she has to run to the bathroom so she doesn't pee her pants. When she comes out Winona starts fussing with the curlers. I watch through the screen as she unrolls them till Mom looks like she has a bunch of tight little spools all over her head.

"I'll say one thing," Mom tells Winona, holding the mirror up to see what she looks like. "The minute I waved him off, I spit on my finger real good and yanked that ring off. I didn't put it on again till VE Day.

"When Floyd came back from the war, it was like he'd seen his own ghost. Never slept much to speak of. Half the time, he still sits straight up in bed in the pitch dark, slapping at his arms and legs like he's on fire. He never talks about it. Just tells the one story about some French broad that begged him for table scraps. How she'd squatted in the dirt licking their supper plates like a dog."

"I think it looks good on you," Winona says. "Go in the crapper so you can see the back."

161

"I like it," she says. It hardly even looks like Mom anymore with all those curls every which way.

"Why'd you go with him, anyhow? I mean, what was it about him?"

"What was it about Duane?"

"Duane. Christ. Would you believe it? He had a frigging car? That was it. A car. He was the only damn boy in the senior class that did. It didn't matter that he was all skin and bones and looked like he'd just crawled out from under some rock. He had wheels and every girl in town wanted a ride. But I'm the one that got him. Ain't I a lucky bitch?"

"I met Floyd at a dance. This was before your time. What were you, ten, eleven back then?"

"I guess about that."

"Well. If you'd've had a few years more, you'd've loved it. There were more fellows than I'd ever laid eyes on. Hundreds of 'em, roaming the streets and all of us living like there was no tomorrow. I could've had me a date every night of the week for the rest of my life. Thelma said I'd go after anything with brass buttons on. She was right about that. I'd find my dream boat, then I'd turn around and see something I liked better. You could say I left behind a regular trail of broken hearts. Then I met Floyd. When he walked into that room, he was so tall he had to duck his head when he came in the door. And you know how hard it is for me to find a man that's taller'n me. One look from them green eyes of his and I was gone. Even with all that red hair of his, he made me think of Clark Gable, he was that good looking."

"So what about the honeymoon? You gonna get to the good part or what?"

"Don't hold your breath. We had us a rented room waiting. My mother got it for us. She said a married couple ought to know more than the backseat of a car. It was August. Hot and dusty. We were driving over to the room when we came up to this country fair out in the middle of nowhere. Floyd turned to me and asked, 'What d'ya say, Ruthie?' I used to swoon over that accent of his. You have to understand, Winona. Before the war, I'd never met a boy from outside the state of Massachusetts. When Floyd opened his mouth, folks'd ask him what language he was speaking. How was I to know the whole damn state of Indiana talked just like him? We pulled off the road and parked in some weeds."

Winona laughs the way she does, smacking at her thighs. "Uh-oh. I see it coming. Jesus, Ruthie. You're still pulling into the weeds for the same thing."

"Quit it! I'm trying to be serious." Mom starts laughing up a storm.

"You want to be serious, have one of these." Winona is pouring them each another drink.

"Shit. I haven't thought of any of this in so long. It's like my life is flashing before me. You think an old tornado's about to come and carry us off?"

"Drink up," Winona says. "Here's to letting your hair down."

"Let me tell you. There we were at this god-awful country fair and it's so hot and me all dressed up. And there's Floyd grinning from ear to ear saying how it reminds him of the state fair back home. It was just a bunch of farm ladies selling molasses cakes. A bunch of washtubs full of ice cold beers. So, there we were. A married couple. Walking up and down, me in my high heels feeling silly. There were all these oxes with wooden yokes clamped around their necks standing there chewing their cud. Dumb animals. Funny how you can have a day like that, and every last detail comes back in living color, even after all this time. I guess you could say it was just like having my last day before I was sent to the gas chamber. The oxes were supposed to pull this wooden board piled with cement blocks. Each block must've weighed nearly a ton. The object, the whole point of the ox pull, was to see which pair pulled the most weight the furthest. I don't know why this has stayed in my mind all these years. I can still picture this black ox and tan ox yoked together. The black one was much bigger and didn't want to do a thing. It had only one horn and the farmer grabbed it and tried to lead it but it pulled away from the yoke and dug its hoofs into the dirt and yanked with all its might in the other direction, twisting its nose up in the air like it wanted to pull its whole body right through that yoke. That fellow was all red in the face yelling, "Pay attention!" Then he wheeled around and punched the ox. Even way up at the top of the bleachers, I could hear his fist smacking that animal's skull. It looked around for a second, stunned. But it still wouldn't budge."

"Some honeymoon," Winona says. "About as much fun as me having morning sickness at Niagara Falls."

"Wait. That ain't all. So we get to our room and Floyd cracks open the whiskey and we're cutting up, having a good old time. He pulls me back on the bed and I think he's laughing, then I see tears running all over his face. I should've known right then and there he had a screw loose. What kind of man bawls his eyes out on his wedding night?

" 'I got something to tell you,' he goes. I pour another drink and sit by the window. If there's one thing I can't stand it's the sight of a grown man crying. 'Ruthie,' he says. 'You're not the first.' I have all I can do not to laugh. He's getting all worked up over that? Then he starts in on this whole long song and dance. About some girl he knew in high school. Grace something or other. How the two of them took a trip down South somewhere. She had cousins or something. Jesus. It's hotter'n hell in that room and I'm starting to feel like I can't keep my eyes open and he's droning on and on about how the two of them're out in the middle of some lake, diving off the side of a boat, horsing around. He's teasing her, trying to yank her bathing suit right off of her, so she swims away. He's half crocked so he can't keep up with her. He keeps telling me how she was such a good swimmer. 'I can still see her long white arms flashing up over that water,' he says, going on about it like I'm not even in the room with him. The next thing he knows she's screaming and flailing around. He figures she's pulling his leg and he laughs and climbs back in the boat like he's leaving without her. Come to find out by the time he circles back around, it's too late. 'I'm caught in barbed wire,' she hollers. 'Help me. I'm all tangled up.' She's thrashing around and Floyd's trying to pull her in the boat without tipping the thing over. He kept saying how them white arms of hers were streaked with blood. It turned out she was caught up in a nest of water moccasins."

"Jesus," Winona says. "Now don't that give you the chills? If there's one frigging thing I hate it's snakes."

" 'Boo hoo hoo,' he goes. 'I swore to God there'd never be no-body else but her.' He's looking all pitiful as can be. I feel the way you do when it suddenly dawns on you the party's over and you're the only one left. I married me a soldier. A hero. What a crock of shit.

"So anyway, they ship him overseas. For months I don't hear one word. I keep telling myself, 'Ruth, you're a married woman now.' But I don't feel that different. Then the baby's born and the doctor says he nearly lost us both. I remember I just laid there with her all wrapped up in a bundle beside me and wished he had. All I could picture was this thick calendar in front of me with all the days of my life numbered one after the other. I wanted to yank the pages off by the handful and watch them blow away." Mom lights a cigarette and turns to look at me out the screen. "You getting all this down?" she asks me. I don't know what she means so I don't say anything. I'm thinking about the old man and that lady tangled up in the snakes. I only once had to save anybody's life that time Mom cut her hand on a broken glass reaching in to wash dishes and she started bleeding something awful. I was only in second grade but Mrs. Zugel taught us all about tourniquets that year so I tied a dish towel around Mom's arm even though she said it was too tight and I called Marvella and she raced over and drove Mom to Doc Havey's. He said I'd saved her life because she sliced an artery. He said how I ought to be a nurse when I grow up and maybe I will. But I think I'd like to be a vet better. I like animals more than people.

"I bet you didn't even know I had the one before Abbie, did ya?" Mom says to Winona. "Shit, I wished I'd had the sense to get out when I could've."

I know what Mom's going to say all about Shirley Jean since she tells me it sometimes. How she named her and about how she slept in a bureau drawer and all.

"She was always sick. I could hardly keep a drop of milk in her. She'd cry and spit up. Meanwhile, Floyd's letters come. With checks, thank God. He writes how it's so damp he finds mold on his boots in the morning. He says he's got a hankering something awful for a mess of fried catfish. At the end of each letter he draws a heart with our names inside of it. It could've been anybody sending me them letters. He finally told his mother he was married. She was all surprised to find out he had a wife and baby girl. 'Why don't you come down to Indiana and meet your in-laws?' she wrote. I'd never been more than ten miles away from home, so I figured I'd better go see what I was in for. I left Shirley Jean with Thelma. That was the end of that. Thelma could never even look me in the eye again after we buried that baby. She said no matter what she had on her mind, no matter what she was doing. Even now all these years later, she'll be driving that school bus up and down all over the hill towns and out the corner of her eye, there's Shirley Jean's little face with her skin all blue and her lips pursed in a tiny o."

"What'd you do then?"

"I went to work at one of the defense plants. I don't know what the hell we were making. All I know is I was raking in forty bucks a week. That was good money back then. I figured when Floyd came home we'd go our separate ways. I don't know why I ever gave in to him. Seems like that's the story of my life. One minute, Floyd had his arm around me telling me how he would've come home in a box if I hadn't been waiting for him. The next minute, Abbie was on the way."

"I know what you mean. With me, I had 'em one after the other. Bam. Bam. Bam. I swear the minute Duane'd pull out of me I'd be hunting down the maternity clothes. I had two sets of twins that died. Didn't carry the first ones more than five months and the second ones for six. Imagine if they'd all lived? Me with seven snot-nosed brats. I had my plumbing yanked after Little Duane. I said you got your boy now let me live. Now I can do whatever I want and I don't have to worry about getting caught."

"Me too," Mom says. "I got rid of mine after you-know-who. She was two years old and I thought I was knocked up again and I was ready to swallow a can of lye before I had another and Doc Havey just took it all out for me. I'll tell you something. If they didn't make such a big deal out of love in all them picture shows, the human race would've died off a long time ago. Just like the dodo bird."

"You said it. Just give me the hot and heavy," Winona says. "The longer, the better, and I do mean size as well as time."

Mom's laughing and smacking Winona's arm. She doesn't even notice when I come back in to get another Coke. She's making little moaning sounds with her hands on her hips and her eyes closed. "Johnny Roudebush turned out to be short and sweet."

166

"Too short to be rowdy in the bush?"

"Winona!"

"Well. I've had me some I've had to say 'Is that all?' when they pulled it out."

"Well. He *was* a little short now that you mention it." She's laughing like some kind of hyena. I don't get what's so funny, but looking at her with her mouth wide open like that she reminds me of Cruella DeVil.

Out the back door, I see Penny coming down the alley home from her party. I think about going out to ask her what it was like but she'd just go on and on about how wonderful it all was and then she'd want me to come in her room and stick on makeup. I take another Coke and go upstairs to my room where I can drink it however I want. When I grow up, I'm not going to get married. I'm not going to have any children either. I'll have a house all my own like Leota Tupper does and I won't let nobody inside that I don't want to come in I don't care who it is. I'll read all the books I want whenever I want, even while I'm eating supper.

"Oh. I need me somebody now," Mom says. "I'm what you call a ripe peach."

"Well, I'm free as a bird tomorrow. Duane's got his bowling league. The only night off he has a week and that's his idea of fun. We'll go out stalking. There oughta be somebody out there worth dropping our drawers for."

the world is an apple

In the middle of the night I wake up to the sound of the old man's cha-cha music. He's down in the front room dancing around counting one-two, cha-cha-cha. Three-four, cha-cha-cha. He keeps turning it up louder and louder till the whole house rattles with it. Mom says just stay out of his way. She's working on getting rid of him.

Eventually Gus Riley comes knocking on our front door.

"Pipe down, Floyd," he says. "You're keeping the whole neighborhood up."

When he leaves the old man starts talking into the tape recorder about all the ideas he's got, things that don't make any kind of sense like, "The world is an apple." Every night after supper he makes me sit down and listen to him play it back like he's one of them preachers on TV with an important message from God above.

"You see. Folks are like ants crawling over the surface of an apple," his voice says. He grins over at me, clicking the top of his ballpoint pen in and out. "God's got that apple in his palm."

Mom laughs right in his face half the time, asking him does he have a screw loose, but I have to sit there and listen to him without making a peep.

shakin' all over

The old man drove up out front in a bright red convertible with the top down. He sat out there tooting and tooting till we all came out. Mom forgot she was giving him the silent treatment. "What's this?" she said.

"It's a car, Ruthie. A dream of a car."

"I can see that," she hollered. "What I mean is where'd it come from?"

"I bought it. With cold, hard-earned cash. This beauty was sitting uptown right across from Jack's with a For Sale sign on the dashboard. Looked to me like it had my name on it." He patted the white leather seats.

"The summons you're gonna get'll have your name on it too." She slammed the door.

The next day, Mom came back from the bank and told us the old man was in hock up to his eyeballs for his stupid car. He'll be paying through the nose till he's old and grey she said.

He never lets any of us ride in it or anything. Mostly he sits behind the steering wheel putting the white leather top down then making it come back up again. All he has to do is unlock these hinges and press a button and the whole thing lifts up and folds down.

On Saturday afternoon, after he's all done baking himself in the sun, what he does is he stands out in the driveway wearing his swimming trunks and washing his car. He blasts the record player he keeps in his shed, piling up all his favorite records. While the music plays, he dries his car with one of our good towels and polishes it with car wax. It's so shiny you can see yourself in it like you're looking in a mirror. When that song, "Shakin' All Over" comes on, he dances around with the hose, wiggling like he's Elvis.

That's what he was doing when Gus Riley showed up with the papers and told him he had to pack up and get out. He didn't even act surprised. He just whistled and put his shirts and socks and underwear in his old suitcase. He took his T-bone steaks from the freezer and drove off tooting his horn.

Every night he drives back and forth in front of the house blasting his radio. Once he went by with this lady squeezed up close to him. She had blonde fluffy hair like Marilyn Monroe.

I ran in the house to tell Mom.

"I can't imagine who'd want to ride around with the old man," she said. "Who'd be that hard up?"

"There he goes again," I said. I was watching from behind the venetian blinds. "He's still got that lady with him."

Mom and Abbie ran over to have a look.

"It's Gravel Gertie," Mom said, shaking her head.

"Who's that?"

"She's this tramp that'll go to the gravel pits with any Tom, Dick, or Harry that asks."

"Oh God," Abbie says. "Who d'ya think's seen him?"

"Who *hasn't* seen him?" Mom says. "That's what I'd like to know."

queen for a day

I got something the matter with me but nobody knows what it is. Mom took me over to see Doc Havey and he said he never saw a thing like it before and maybe she ought to take me on over to Indianapolis to see a special doctor. He said it might be something to do with female trouble and I might need a pelvic. Mom said wasn't I too young for that to start up? But Doc Havey said with female trouble you never can tell. They talked about me the whole time like I wasn't even there. I sat on the crinkly paper with my white gown wrapped around me and my bare feet dangling down off the side of the table.

When we got out in the car I asked Mom what female trouble was but she just started up the car and said not to worry about it. I looked *pelvic* up in the dictionary but they had so many words I never heard of before, I got a great big headache thinking about having to look them all up.

The whole thing started when I got itchy all over and started to feel real hot. My arms got red spots on them like when I had the measles. Mom let me bring my pillow downstairs and lie on the davenport watching TV. Every day I watched the lady get crowned Queen for a Day. I always used to want Mom to go on that show. I even wrote a letter telling them all about her. Mom said forget it, they don't take real people. The whole thing is rigged to look real. Anyhow, being queen for a day wouldn't be enough for her. She'd need to be queen for a year for it to make a dent in her life.

I laid around watching TV for a week and then the itchy bumps went away. Later on, me and Penny are playing potsies in

171

the school yard when all of a sudden I can't hardly talk, my throat hurts so bad. I've got these two lumps under my ears.

Mom's home, sitting at the table having a cup of coffee. Winona Flowers is there too with Little Duane sitting in the middle of the kitchen floor messing up my dot-to-dot pictures. I tell them I have the mumps.

"We were all cooped up a couple of winters ago with you and the mumps." Mom touches my throat and says it sure feels like the mumps to her. Winona touches it too. "Doc Havey says it's her glands," Mom tells Winona. "You know what that means," she says, rolling her eyes.

"I'm still all itchy, too," I say. I lift my blouse up in back so Mom'll scratch me good.

"Least you don't have Cupid's itch," Winona says. She snorts her cigarette smoke out her nose like she's some dragon.

"Oh, come on. She's just a kid."

"Well, they say the clap's going through this town faster than the flu. Half the fellows up at Syd's've had a dose."

When Abbie comes home she says I probably have leprosy. Or maybe elephantiasis. That's when you turn into an elephant. "You'll have to sleep out in the shed," she says. Mom tells her to let me alone. Then she says I might as well take her and the old man's bed downstairs since I'm so tired all the time and it's the only room with a door I can shut. She'll sleep up in my bed next to Abbie and the old man'll sleep in his chair in the front room, only half the time he comes in and sleeps with me. I want my bed upstairs back but Mom says it's not fair to Abbie to have me sleeping all the time. She's got to live her life too, she says.

I lie in bed staring up at the ceiling trying to make things out of the cracks. I find a castle and a shoe and a witch's face. The old man comes in to see how I'm doing. When he sits on the edge of the bed it gets all lopsided and I feel like I'm going to slide off.

ether

What happens is I end up having to go to the hospital. Doc Havey says they're giving me some tests. Mom comes to visit and she's all happy saying thanks to me she's got grounds to get rid of the old man for sure this time just wait and see. I lie in this bed that's so high up off the floor I need a footstool to get in and out of it. I have to wear this little white nightgown with bows you tie down the back and everybody can see my underpants. The thing about a hospital is it's so clean and every day this guy comes and washes the floor again. I like that. The nurses change my bed for me even though I just slept in it once. They can even change it with me in it.

Candy, the nurse with the red pageboy, comes after suppertime to give me a sponge bath and a back rub. She says I can talk to her. I can tell her whatever I want. "I can keep a secret," she says, and winks. Candy can roll her tongue into a tube and make her ears wiggle. When she does this the starched white cap on her head moves too. I can't do either one but she says it's not something you can learn. It's genetic. That means it's passed down from your parents in your blood. "That's what makes everybody a little different," she says.

I tell her all about Gretchie and how she lets me put clothes on her and take her out riding in the basket on my bike. I tell her how Gretchie will only give *me* a kiss, not anybody else in my family except for maybe Abbie only Abbie would never let Gretchie kiss her on account of dog germs. Marvella came to visit and said she had no idea and if she could she'd fix it so I could live with her but it's out of her hands. She brought me a planter that's a donkey pulling a cart and in the cart there's a little plant called a dogtooth ivy since the leaves are shaped like a dog's tooth. I tell Candy how one time Abbie was running around the house trying to make Gretchie bark since when we first got her she wouldn't bark no matter what and Gretchie was chasing after her slipping on the linoleum and she got all excited and just after she finally started barking, she grabbed ahold of Abbie's bobby sock and one of her teeth got yanked right out.

I don't really feel all that sick anymore. Doc Havey says they just want to do some more tests and pretty soon I'll be good as new. Mrs. Adams comes in with all these glass tubes rattling and she ties a big band around my arm and jabs me so she can take my blood. Candy says sometimes when something really bothers you it does you good to get it off your chest. "You just remember I can keep a secret," she says. I know she's wanting me to talk about the old man. They made me come here because of him, I guess. But I don't feel like talking about it. I'm thinking about how when I was real little, back before I even hit kindergarten, I had to come to the hospital to have my tonsils out. I always got these real bad sore throats and Doc Havey was always poking a stick down my throat making me almost throw up till one time he said they have to come out. Mom told me I could have ice cream after it was all over. I can still remember how this lady tied my hands down and my feet too then Doc Havey put this black rubber thing over my face. "This is ether," he said. "It'll put you out like a light. Just count to ten. You know how to count, don't you?" I felt like I couldn't breathe and it tasted like poison and I was sure they were going to kill me then the next thing I knew I was awake and had the worst sore throat of my life. Mom was there sitting by the bed with her lipstick on and her flowered dress. "What flavor do you want?" she wanted to know. "Strawberry? Chocolate?" But I didn't feel like eating a thing and my throat hurt so bad I couldn't even talk.

remember when?

Remember when the old man had his boat?" I ask Abbie. She's sitting at her vanity table trying to roll her hair up this special way they've got a picture of how to do in her magazine. She smacks her comb down and rolls her eyes at me in the mirror.

"Yes, I remember. How could I forget?"

"Remember how we had to watch him waterski till our heads about fell off from craning our necks?"

"Remember when! Remember when! Is that all you can say, remember when? Of course I remember. I just don't want to! I don't want to remember when about anything. Get that through your thick head. Just because you think it's fun to lie around and talk about the good old days doesn't mean I have to, too."

I'm home from the hospital now and I'm still supposed to take it easy so I lie back on my bed and close my eyes. When I think of the old days, I can watch it all over again like I'm looking at a movie. I do that a lot with stuff I remember. Sometimes I can pick what it is I want to look at, but other times as soon as I close my eyes, the movie just starts playing and I don't have any choice.

The old man is waterskiing using just one ski while Mom drives the boat and me and Abbie turn in our seats to watch him. It's our job to tell Mom when he falls or when he points at the shore meaning he's ready to quit so she'll slow down and he can let go. He keeps going for a minute even though the boat's not pulling him anymore and then he sort of sinks down and takes his ski off. I can hear the motor and smell the gasoline and everything even though I'm in my bedroom and it all happened a long

175

time ago when I was only seven. I can see the old man's head bobbing in the water, waiting for us to pick him up. Mom used to say one day she was going to just drive off and leave him floating around out there. Everybody but the old man ended up hating that boat and he was the only one that was sad when he had to sell it to get the bill collectors off his back.

Mom and Abbie both got to ski once in a while but the old man said I wasn't old enough since I couldn't swim or anything, just float around in my life jacket. I still can't swim even though I'm getting ready for sixth grade. I'm probably the only one in my whole class that can't but I don't care because I'm never wearing a bathing suit again anyhow. Mom says I have to have Abbie's old one and it's got this foam in the top to make it look like you've got a bust and I'd never be caught dead in something like that. She says I can't always be having new and I'm too old to go swimming in just my shorts with no top but I don't care. I just won't ever go again if I have to wear that one.

When we went out in the boat, we all had to wear these big puffy orange life jackets except for the old man. He had this special one that was like a belt strapped around his waist. I kept wanting to ski too and finally the old man built me a surfboard. It was this board with a rubber bath mat nailed onto it and ropes to hold on to and what I'd do was I'd sit on it and he'd pull me around. Abbie said I looked like a raving lunatic out there but it was kind of fun. I'd be out in water over my head and sometimes I'd hold on with one hand and wave at people in the other boats. "You don't have a thing to be scared of," the old man said. "Just hold on and watch the world go by. Whatever you do, just don't let go and you'll be fine."

After a while I figure out how to stand up on my surfboard and the old man starts going faster and faster and I'm zooming along like crazy behind the boat and one time these waves start coming from a big cabin cruiser that passes us and I try to sit down because I'm scared I'll fall off. I hold on real tight and nod my head like crazy, which is my signal I'm ready to come in, but nobody's watching. "No matter what don't let go," the old man always says every time I start out, so I hold on and the water rushes up my nose since I can't hold my breath anymore and I can't get my head out of the water. Abbie's supposed to be watching me but she's looking in another direction.

When I remember that, it makes me think how come if God is watching everything you do then why didn't He come and help me as soon as I started going under? I was choking and crying and the old man was hollering like crazy and he smacked Abbie so hard he left a red handprint on her cheek.

"How come you didn't let go?" he says and he yanks me into the boat by my arm so hard it feels like it'll come right out of the socket. Mom says, "She's a stupid shit, that's why." I have goose bumps all over me even though the sun's real hot. I can still picture it right down to the little blonde hairs sticking out of each goose bump. I wrapped myself up in a wet towel and Mom said, "You watch now because the old man is having his turn." But I just kept looking down at my feet, shivering. I didn't even turn around to see.

the house of blue lights

Everybody in the whole town of Windfall except for me's already seen the house of blue lights. The whole school's talking about it. What it is is this house way out on the Crooked Creek Road where this guy Chet Osgood keeps his wife Arletta in a white coffin in his front room. Arletta was his one true love. When she died he just couldn't stand the idea of her getting buried and leaving him behind alone, so he keeps her in her coffin. He stuck blue Christmas lights all around it since blue was her favorite color. Everybody says when you drive by you can see them blue lights flicker. The whole thing gives you the creeps real bad.

I never saw anybody dead before except the Indian mummy they keep in a glass case over at the courthouse in Tipton. But that doesn't really count since you can't see much of anything. Just some guy wrapped up in a bunch of rags like some kind of giant cocoon. They wrapped him up like that to keep him from turning to dust. The sign they stuck next to the mummy says he was found buried in some cornfields in the olden days. Indians used to be all over Indiana back when the farmers first got here.

I keep trying to figure out how it feels to be dead. Abbie says if you want to know, just lie real still and quit breathing. But no matter how long I hold my breath I never feel any different. The old man says being dead is one of the things you only get to do once. That's why nobody can say what it's like. Once you're dead you're not around to talk about it.

Mom and Abbie are spritzing on hair spray and dabbing on lipstick from the tiny white plastic samples Mom gets to show to her Nova customers.

"Are you guys going out?"

"What'd you think? We'd get dolled up to sit around this dump?" Mom says. She blots her lips with a tissue.

"Can I go? You said we'd go see the house of blue lights."

Abbie groans and twirls her finger around her ear. She looks at Mom in the mirror. "Should we tell her?"

"Tell me what?"

"You ever hear of watching TV in the dark, pea brain?"

"What's that got to do with anything?"

I lean up close to the mirror and shut my eyes then open them just enough to peek through to try and see what I'd look like if I was dead.

"See?" Abbie says. "She's hopeless."

Mom laughs.

"What's the big joke?" I ask.

"You are." Abbie flicks me in the side of the head.

"I am not."

"You are too."

"Oh, don't go getting your bowels in an uproar." Mom smacks me on the bottom like I'm a little baby. Everybody around here is always acting like I'm about two years old even though I'm eleven.

"You guys'll be crying your eyes out when me and John Glenn go up in outer space." John Glenn sent me back a picture of him with his space suit on. Abbie says he probably sends that same picture to anybody that's stupid enough to write to him. But I wrote back anyhow and told him I wanted to be the first kid in outer space.

"Dream on," Abbie says. She slides around on the linoleum in her bobby socks singing along to the radio. It's that song about the party lights. Mom twirls Abbie around like they're on *American Bandstand*.

"Don't be such a Pitiful Pearl." Mom's slip rustles when she comes over and pinches my cheeks to make it look like I'm smiling. She has her white button earrings clipped on. "We'll bring us home a treat. So quit moping."

After they drive off, I go out back and stand on the edge of our yard. You can tell right where our yard ends and the Reebs' yard starts. The Reebs're always out there raking or mowing or

179

clipping around their house. Or else yanking crabgrass out of the sidewalk cracks.

Tonight Sonya and Christie and Penny Reeb are all hunched up digging dandelions out of the grass with trowels. Mr. Reeb puffs on a cigar and comes along after them scooping the dandelions into a bushel basket. Mrs. Reeb hardly ever comes outdoors but she watches everything they do from her kitchen window.

Penny waves at me but she can't come over and play. When she's working out in the yard, that's all she can do.

The very second they dig up the last dandelion, Mrs. Reeb sticks her head out the back door and hollers, "Bath time!" The Reebs have a special time for everything.

A light comes on in Penny's room. "Psst, Lana," she says in a loud whisper. She's all shadowy in the window. I run across the grass. "Penny!" her mother hollers. "Get in that tub right now or else." Penny holds her hands up and I press mine against them through the screen. "Tomorrow," she says.

A car is coming down Carrigan Road. When it gets out front, I see it's the old man, so I hide behind the oak tree. He's got the top down on his red convertible. He has sunglasses clipped over his glasses. Mom says he acts like he's some kind of playboy driving around in that flashy car.

He goes real slow and toots his horn then turns around in the Reebs' driveway. I edge around the tree so he won't see me. If he sees me, he'll want to stop and try to take me for a ride. But Mom said he's not allowed to take me anywhere anymore and he'd better never try. If he even sets one foot on our property, he'll be arrested so fast he won't know what hit him.

Across the street as far as I can see, the green corn plants wave like long fingers. I wonder how many mummies are buried out there. Every time the farmer plows, me and Penny run over there hoping to find a dried-up hand or a foot or a bit of mummy rags but there's only old brown corn silk that looks just like hair tangled up in the dirt.

When I go inside, I turn on the back porch light and the kitchen light and I go in the front room and turn on the lamps. We hardly ever go in there anymore since the old man started remodeling. There's plaster dust all over from this big hunk of wallpaper that fell off the ceiling.

180

Mom says what the old man did was he went on a remodeling rampage. "It wouldn't've been half as bad if he could've just finished one room before he tore up the next one," she said. "But you can't ever tell that man how to do a thing."

What he did first was he ripped out the kitchen cupboards with a crowbar. I got to help him and we found a newspaper from way back when there was the Great Flood of 1937. There was a picture of a lady shoveling mud out of her front room and another one of a house turned practically upside down.

The old man drew plans of the new cupboards he was going to make. "You'll feel just like the Queen of Sheba in here," he said to Mom.

On weekends, his electric saw shrieked and whined like some pig having its throat cut. The boards clattered when they hit the floor and the house filled up with sawdust. He whistled and measured, stopping to have himself an ice cold beer. After he was all done cutting the wood he started hammering. But in a little while he was cussing pretty bad and yanking the boards out of the wall. He had everything all measured out but he couldn't get the pieces to fit together.

That's when he got this special machine that turns water into steam and started steaming off the wallpaper in the front room. He held it up to the wallpaper till it got good and wet and kind of shriveled up. We took turns pulling it off in long soggy strips.

Now the walls look the way Mom's back does when I pull her skin off after she gets a sunburn. And we have to keep our dishes and stuff in cardboard boxes. The old man said fixing up an old house like ours could take a fellow his whole lifetime.

A little while after Mom got Gus Riley to serve the old man his papers, he started calling her up to try to talk her into taking him back. But she's still giving him the silent treatment. When the phone rings, I always have to pick it up.

Last night when he called, Mom was in the bathtub with a blue towel wrapped around her hair. She leaned over and shut the bathroom door.

"How's daddy's girl?" The old man's voice sounded all happy and fake.

I picked at the bits of wallpaper stuck to the wall beside the telephone. "How's Mommy?" he asked. "She ready to take me back yet?"

"Any day now," I told him, even though Mom never even asks me what he says.

I go upstairs and get in bed with all my clothes on. I pull my sheet up over my face and shut my eyes and smush my fingers against my eyeballs. Red and yellow and blue and white lights swirl around. It's raining out a little. It sounds like somebody's tapping on the windows.

I picture the old man stopping by the side of the road to put the white top up on his convertible. As soon as he laid eyes on that car, he said he knew it was his. "See that bird there? That's a thunderbird. The Indian symbol of happiness without end," he said, tracing the edges of the bird's wings on the back of his car. "You just get one life. You might as well live it."

When Mom's car comes down the street, way before she even gets here I know it's her car because of the funny clickety sound it makes. When she turns if off, it rattles and knocks like it doesn't want to quit. The whole house shakes when the back door slams. "This house's lit up like a birthday cake," Mom says. Abbie is laughing all high and out of breath the way she used to when we ran around outside together after supper playing Red Light-Green Light.

"You want some i-c-e?" Mom hollers up the stairs. She still calls it that from when I was a little kid, back when her and the old man were trying to talk about ice cream without me knowing it. They always spelled out everything they had a secret about. The old man says that's probably why I ended up such a good speller.

I don't say a word. I stare at the light bulb to see how long I can look straight at it without blinking. The stupid spoons clink in the bowls. I wrap my covers around me and hold my breath and act like I'm the mummy. I can still see the light bulb with my eyes shut. I remember how at school, back in fourth grade, Mrs. Thorp showed us this picture of how on the inside of your eye, everything you look at is really upside down. I wonder if the last thing the mummy looked at is still hanging upside down inside his eyes.

"Guess what, squirt?" Abbie sets a bowl of ice cream on my bedside table. She punches me in the arm the way she always does. "I got me a date."

Abbie sits at her pink vanity table looking in this special mirror she's got that makes your face look gigantic. Her neck has pink splotches on it like she gets when she's excited about something. She smiles at herself with her mouth closed. Then she smiles with her mouth open a tiny bit, turning the mirror so she can see herself sideways. She tries it once more with her teeth showing. She can't ever decide on the best way to smile.

"A-OK," I tell her, holding on to the edges of my bed and making splashing sounds like I'm coming in for a landing.

"Oh, for crying out loud! Quit living in never-never land!"

"A-OK," I say. "I'm reading you loud and clear."

She rolls her eyes.

"He followed us all around. Every time Mom speeded up, he'd speed up. When she slowed down, he slowed down."

"Who?"

"Donnie Merchant. My date, you numbskull. It was so exciting. He flashed his headlights off and on. Then he passed us. Mom said all the guys do that when they want to get to know you. 'Take a good look,' she said. 'If you like him, we'll tail him next.' So anyhow, we followed him right up to the A and W."

"Did you guys get coneys?"

"No. Just root beers. My heart was thumping so loud I figured he must've heard it." Abbie stared off into space like she was looking right into Donnie Merchant's eyes. She blew a big bubble and sucked it back into her mouth with a pop.

"He's built like a football player. And he's graduated already. He works over in Blanketport. Mom asked him why didn't he hop in back. That's when he asked me out. Now both me and Mom've got dates tomorrow."

"She's going dancing with Billy Boy?"

"Billy Boy? What've you been doing? Living in another century?"

Abbie starts telling me what she's going to wear on her date, but I'm not really listening. I'm thinking about the parade they'll have down West Jackson Street for me and John Glenn. The school band'll play. We'll sit in the back of a big black convertible waving at everybody. Then we'll drive over and have a good look at the house of blue lights. Chet Osgood'll be leaning over the coffin holding Arletta's pale white hand.

Abbie hangs her head upside down and starts brushing her long hair. She counts every stroke. Abbie says if you want to be beautiful, you've got to brush your hair at least a hundred times every night. She never misses one stroke. Even when I start counting backwards and shouting out a bunch of numbers, she still goes right on counting. Abbie brushes and brushes till her hair crackles with electricity.

I shut off the lights so I can see the tiny blue sparks fly around her head. When me and John Glenn go to outer space, stars'll fly by our space capsule. We'll swig Tang from special straws hooked up to the inside of our space suits and lie back, side by side, watching the sun rise and set and rise and set. When we pass over Windfall, everybody in the whole town'll turn on their lights for us as we go whirling by.

the dairy hut

P ut some water on for me, will you?" Mom says. She
throws the newspaper and the box of donuts she just
bought on the table and starts untying her head scarf. I
hear her but I act like I don't. I'm almost through with my Social
Studies homework. Only two more questions to go.

"Knock-knock," she says. She taps on the back of my head
with her knuckles. "Anybody home?"

She sits down and puts a spoonful of coffee into her empty
cup and scans the front page. I don't see why she can't put the
water on herself, but I get up and do it anyhow.

Abbie's upstairs getting her beauty rest since she was out late
with Donnie Merchant last night. We don't have any regular
times when we all do things together anymore now that the old
man doesn't live with us. We eat breakfast whenever we feel like
it. Usually we eat supper in the front room with the TV on, but
none of us sits in the old man's chair. Half the time we just eat
sandwiches and potato chips. Mom says she no longer has to be
a slave to her kitchen now that she's a single girl.

After she looks through the whole paper without really reading any of it, she turns to the STAR GAZER so we can figure out
what kind of day we're supposed to have. "Let's see. Mine's
twenty-seven, thirty, thirty-five. 'Red letter.' Did I say thirty-five?
Lemme see. 'Red letter day.' Sounds good so far. Now it's thirty-
eight, forty-one, forty-eight. 'You achieve goals.' Red letter day.
You achieve goals." She takes a sip of coffee and looks over the
top of the paper. Her eyes are so blue they look the way the sky
does on the first sunny day after a week of rain. The old man's

185

always saying how if she'd been born with brown eyes it might have made all the difference in the world.

"What's my fortune?" I ask.

"Yours's got a frowny face."

"Oh no! Lemme see."

She hands me the paper and I look up my numbers. " 'Use caution with electrical devices. Check faulty wiring.' That's so dumb."

Mom laughs. "Just don't go sticking your fingers into any light sockets. Maybe my surprise'll be me getting another job." She turns the pages till she gets to the "Help Wanteds." Ever since she quit her job over at the canning factory she's been hoping to get another one. The money the old man gives us to live on isn't enough. We ended up having to get free lunch tickets at school, only Abbie gets Donnie Merchant to buy her a sandwich instead. She says she doesn't see why the whole school has to know we can't afford to buy our own lunch.

" 'Help wanted, female,' " Mom says, leaning over the paper to read. "Lemme see. They're still looking for an LPN and some girl to type them address labels. I wish I'd a studied business in high school. What else is there? Two full-time beauticians. Hey. Now wait. Here's the one for me. 'Girl over twenty-one for dairy bar work.' That's me. I'm sure over twenty-one!"

"You going to try it?"

"I think I just might." She lights a new cigarette from the tip of her old one.

"What kind of job would you get if you could get any one you wanted?"

"Oh. I don't know."

"What if you could make any wish for any job and it came true? Say you could pick any job to have. What one would you pick?"

"Well. I figure I'd marry me a millionaire. How's that? Me the wife of a millionaire. But none of them're knocking down my door. 'Ruthie,' " she says. " 'It's time to get off your fat ass and go looking.' "

I know what job I'd like to have. I still want to be an astronaut like John Glenn but I don't mention it because Mom acts like it's a big joke. I do know one thing. I'm never ever going to marry some guy, no matter how much money he's got.

I lick one of my fingers and pick up the donut crumbs next to the box. I lift out a cinnamon donut and take small bites all around the edge. Then I flip through the paper for the obituaries. I always read them first. I like seeing how many people died the day before. Usually it tells how they did a bunch of nice stuff in their life and where they went to church. They'd never say if you were selfish or slept in your clothes or drank beer. Half the time, you have to guess what killed them. It just says after a short illness or after a long illness but it hardly ever mentions what was the matter.

Four people died yesterday. Two old ladies in the Sunset Nursing Home. One of them had four kids and twenty grandkids. The other one was ninety-two. She never got married so they don't stick in a whole lot about her. There's this guy from Tipton that was a famous Boy Scout leader forty years ago. It tells how he was having chest pains and went to the hospital for a checkup. Before they could find out what was wrong with him, he kicked the bucket. The last one is about this lady that was thirty-nine years old, the exact age Mom is.

"Listen to this." I read it out loud.

"Christ Almighty! Do you have to be so gruesome? I swear, you're as morbid as an undertaker. Gimme that." She tries to grab the paper away from me but I hold it up in the air so she'd have to get up out of her chair if she really wanted it. "Why can't you read the funnies like any other kid?"

I don't answer her. She'd never get how it makes me feel kind of good to read about the people that died. Like I'm lucky or something to still be here. I have another day more than they got and maybe it'll be the day when my whole life changes. I take a donut with chocolate icing and peel the icing off slow, saving it for last. When I get up to pour myself some more milk, Mom taps her cup with her spoon and I pour more hot water into it.

Usually after breakfast on Saturdays what we do is we go into the front room, me still wearing my sleep clothes, and Mom lies on the davenport with the ashtray on her stomach, smoking. I turn on the TV and we watch shows till Abbie comes down. Then we make toasted cheese sandwiches. But today, when I go into the front room, Mom doesn't follow me. She's in the bathroom running the water. Then she goes into her room and opens and shuts her drawers about a million times. When she comes out, she has on her pink skirt and a white frilly blouse. She comes in singing, "It's Now or Never." She dances around in front of me with her eyes shut, imitating Paul Anka. He always sings with his eyes shut. She knows how I can't stand that. She's got the newspaper clamped under her arm. "Wish me luck," she says.

Her car door slams and the car roars like an airplane about to take off. She backs down the driveway and toots her horn as she goes past the window. At first, when I can't hear her anymore, there's nothing but dead silence. Then some crows call to each other and the Reebs' lawn mower buzzes.

Gretchie's whining and scratching at the back door to go out. I put one of her rhinestone collars on her and hook on the leash and take her for a walk uptown. In dog time Gretchie's way over twenty-one. Sometimes when I'm filling up her bowl, I tell her she's old enough to go out and get a job and pay room and board if she expects to eat since Mom's always saying that's what we'll have to do if me and Abbie don't move out the minute we come of age. Mom says I'm not even funny when I say that, but Gretchie wags her tail and smiles.

When I'm sad, Gretchie gets sad too. She lies on my bed with me and pokes her nose into my armpit and moans a little bit and her skin shivers while I pet her. If I start crying, she sits up and looks at me with her head cocked to the side and her forehead wrinkled.

We stop first over to Leota Tupper's to see if she wants anything uptown, but she has her door shut and the blinds closed. That means she's sleeping even if it is in the middle of the day. Leota Tupper's so old now she sleeps pretty near all the time.

Marvella's out in her backyard clipping back her lilac bushes. Vernon's sitting in a lawn chair brushing the lint off his pants. "What you up to?" Marvella asks me.

"Nothing much."

"If you come by tomorrow," she says. "I can use some help getting ready for the Boyer twins' wedding. We got a bunch of corsages to put up and bouquets like you never seen."

I tell her I'll be over. Vernon's head is hanging down on his chest and he's snoring. Marvella holds her finger up to her lips and I wave good-bye.

Penny and these other girls are uptown looking at magazines in Applegate's Drug Store. I wave but I don't go in or anything. Penny looks at me like she doesn't even know who I am. All she cares about lately is boys. She has her hair all teased up and she's wearing a pair of tight red pants. Everybody says she changes into them and puts makeup on when she's over at her friend Trudy Hubbard's house because her mother'd never let her go out of the house looking like a tramp.

It seems like just the other day me and Penny were sitting by the road shouting at everybody driving by on their way out of town, "Take a picture, it'll last longer." But Penny would never do that now unless there was some boy driving the car. I don't get what the big deal is about boys. If you ask me, the whole thing makes me sick.

When Mom comes home she's so excited, she can't hardly stand still. "I got the job," she says. "Let's celebrate. I'll get us a pizza."

The three of us drive over so she can show us where she's going to be working. It's this place that looks like a giant green gumdrop. On the roof there's a sign made out of a board cut and painted to look like a strawberry ice cream cone with THE DAIRY HUT in big red letters. OUR ICE CREAM IS OUT OF THIS WORLD, it says underneath.

"They've got fourteen different kinds of sundaes." She acts all proud like she's the one that thought them all up. "The man that hired me—Mr. Fowler his name is—he said pretty soon he's going to open up a whole chain of Dairy Huts all over the state. There'll be a Dairy Hut in every county. Plenty of opportunities for advancement." She says it like she's reading one of her "Help Wanteds." "If I play my cards right, I could end up a bigwig. Then we won't need the old man's measly support payments."

gentleman friend

om's leaning against the kitchen counter with the groceries half put away reading *Something for Everybody,*
this magazine they sell up at Purtlebaugh's Grocery.
People put ads in there when they want to sell stuff they don't
need anymore: old tires, used Frigidaires, baby cribs.

Abbie's sitting under the hair drier reading *True Confessions.*
I'm at the kitchen table doing my math. "Listen to this," Mom
says. " 'Lost eighty-five pounds. Selling my whole wardrobe. Size
forty.' What size do you figure she is now? A thirty?"

"You sound like one of these problems I've got to figure out."

"My little bookworm. For pity's sake," she says, shoving the
cans of soup up on the shelf. "It's Friday night. You're probably
the only girl in town doing homework."

"It's real hard. You try it."

I tell her the problem I'm trying to figure out. " 'From a point
on a straight road, John and Fred ride their bicycles in opposite
directions. John rides ten miles per hour. Fred rides at twelve
miles per hour.' "

Mom slams the cans up on the counter. "OK, OK," she says.
"That's enough to give me a headache for the rest of my life."

She sits down at the table with one of her highballs and a box
of crackers. I draw a chart like the one in the book. How many
hours will go by for John and Fred to end up being fifty miles
apart? I can't imagine riding my bike for fifty miles. The furthest
I ever got was five miles and my legs hurt so bad I had to walk
halfway home.

Mom starts laughing and laughing. She's laughing so hard
she's got tears running down her cheeks.

"What's the big joke?" I ask.

She smacks herself on the thigh, gasping. She leans over and lifts up the edge of Abbie's hair-drier bonnet. "I got a good one," she says. " 'Wedding gown. Size fourteen. Worn only once.' " She starts laughing again. It sounds like she's saying hee-hee-hee.

"What's so funny about that?" I ask.

Abbie rolls her eyes and flips to another page of her magazine.

"Well, what'd she expect? To wear it every day? Put it on to take the trash out in? Wear it to work?" She swirls the ice cubes around in her glass and takes a swig. "Picture how desperate you'd have to be to buy yourself a used wedding dress."

Mom flips to the ads in back where people want to find each other and go out on dates. She's always trying to figure out if there's anybody for her to write to.

"Here's a doozy," Mom says. " 'Looking for a Christian family man.' Now what kind of moron'd advertise for that? Just go to any church if that's what you want. There's plenty of 'em lining the back pews."

" 'Retired fellow,' " Mom reads. " 'Don't drink or smoke. Looking for that special someone.' Bet he's a real barrel of laughs. Probably thinks your feet'll fall off if you go dancing."

" 'Ruthie'," she says, talking to herself the way she does. " 'It's Friday night. What would you like to do?' I ought to stick my own ad in here. That's one way to get me a date."

"It'd be some total stranger," I say.

"So?"

"Wouldn't you be scared?"

"Of what?"

"I dunno. Just scared."

"You watch too many of them late-night movies."

"Well. You never know."

"He'd have to write me a letter first. Some ax murderer's not going to go through all that trouble just to lure me out of the house." She takes my pencil and starts filling out the squares on the form that's on the back. I read it upside down. *Fun loving lady seeks gentleman friend,* her ad says.

"Gentleman friend?"

"Well. I can't exactly say boyfriend. Me here with more grey hairs that I can count. What else am I supposed to call it?"

When she shows her ad to Abbie, Abbie asks her what George Purkey'll say.

"Who's that?" I ask.

"Where've you been, outer space?" Mom says.

"Georgie Porgie," Mom says, winking at Abbie. "He kissed this old girl but I'll make *him* cry."

to tell the truth

I 'm home!" Mom hollers. She flings her car keys on the kitchen table and unzips her skirt, wiggling her hips till it slides down her legs and falls to the floor. She yanks her blouse off over her head before she even finishes unbuttoning it. "Did I get any mail today?"

What she means is did anybody answer her ad. Even though there's nothing but junk mail, she looks through it real careful to be sure I didn't miss anything. Then she stands at the sink in her slip, running cold water over her clothes—a black skirt and a white blouse with a floppy red bow she calls her Dairy Hut Getup. She scrubs at the pink and brown stains from where the ice cream and syrups dripped down the front.

"Don't ask me why I bother with this. It's not like the morons who come to get an ice cream'd notice. But old Finicky Fowler's got an eagle eye." The way she always talks about him, I figure all her boss does is follow her around breathing down her neck looking for an excuse to fire her.

I made tonight's supper after school even though I had a ton of homework. It's this special recipe I got from a magazine. It's called Scalloped Tuna Surprise. They don't even ask what the surprise is. All during supper, Mom and Abbie just talk about what kind of guys might answer her ad. Abbie says maybe there'll be one that looks like Paul Newman. Mom acts like she's about to swoon. After Abbie leaves to go driving around with Donnie Merchant the way she does nearly every night now, we turn the TV on and Mom lies on the davenport flipping through a magazine. She stops at a story called "September Eve." There's a picture of a blonde lady leaning back against a dark-haired man in

193

a blue sweater. The lady's eyes are half-closed. Mom throws the magazine on the coffee table. "Look at me sitting here like some kind of nun."

I go get the Chocolate Dream Bars I made for dessert and carry them in to her. "Ta-da!"

She sits up and pats the cushion beside her. We watch TV a while and then she lets me brush her hair. She keeps it up in a french twist now that her permanent's grown out. When I take the bobby pins out, her hair falls down her back like syrup.

"You find any grey hairs, you know what to do."

"I don't see any," I tell her, even though there are a whole bunch of thick white hairs in the back. I can't stand yanking them out.

"I'm not getting any younger, you know. So you tell me. When's this old girl gonna start having some fun?"

I lift her hair and pull the brush through in long strokes. While I'm brushing I can see Mr. and Mrs. Reeb sitting on their davenport watching their TV. They've got on *Cheyenne*. I think about everybody, all up and down the streets of Windfall, sitting in front of their TVs. I don't know why, I can't explain it, but thinking about that makes me cry. I have to blink my eyes like crazy so Mom won't notice.

To Tell the Truth is almost over.

"It's got to be number one," Mom says. "Ain't he got a guilty look all over his face?"

"Nuh-uh. It's number three. You can tell by the way he looks right at you when he answers."

"Will the real Ray Fetty please stand up?"

The three guys all start to stand up at once, the way they always do to trick you. But the guy in the middle is the one that stays up. Nobody on the show guesses right, either.

"I'll be damned." Mom closes her eyes. "Just tell me one thing." She grabs my hand to make me quit brushing. "Just tell me now. Is it my imagination, or is every single guy in the whole goddamned state of Indiana already taken?"

model homes

The Merchant and Abbie're going steady now. He gave Abbie his high school ring and it's so big she has to wrap angora yarn around it so it'll stay on her finger. She has a whole bunch of different-colored yarn to coordinate it with whatever she's got on. Today it's pale pink to go with her new sweater.

We all started calling Donnie "The Merchant" one time when he was over horsing around with Abbie in the front room and it stuck. He says the name suits him to a tee since he's going to be a big businessman rolling in the dough someday. He's studying up to go into business for himself by taking this mail-order course. They're going to give him a certificate with his name on it and everything when he passes the test at the end. Now he works at Mack's Magic Carpets. He's the one that goes out and puts new rugs in folks' houses. The best thing about him and Abbie going steady is they take me out with them sometimes on their dates. Today it's a big surprise. He won't tell me or Abbie where we're headed. He just keeps driving and driving and every once in a while he looks over at Abbie and smiles and pats her hand.

"Here we are," The Merchant says, driving through this gate with a big sign over it that says BREEDLOVE'S MODEL HOMES. Blue and pink and green balloons are tied to the gateposts.

He parks the car and we all get out. Abbie and The Merchant walk up ahead holding hands. I hop along on one foot after them, acting like I'm their kid.

This guy dressed up as a clown with a red rubber nose and gigantic green shoes waves at us and hands Abbie a little yellow basket. "For the lady of the house," he says, and squeezes his nose. It sounds like he's tooting a bicycle horn.

"What'd you get?" I ask Abbie, leaning up close.

"You don't have to breathe on it," she tells me. There's a wooden-handled scrub brush for doing your pots and pans, a blue box of Wonder detergent that's the size of the smallest box of crayons you can get, a set of green plastic measuring spoons all hooked together on a ring, and a pad of paper with a tiny red pencil that slides into this loop on the side of it.

There's a loud crackle and then a voice comes over this loudspeaker just like the principal does at school. "Welcome to Breedlove's Model Home Village," some guy says. "The place where dreams come true."

In front of us, there are all these houses the color of candy mints. The Merchant is explaining about how you can have a look at them and then pick the one you want to live in.

"It all comes on the back of a truck," he says. "Then they put it together for you wherever you want."

All the houses have signs out front with their names on them. The doors are open and you can just walk on in and have a look. We go in the Cozy Cottage first, this yellow house with green shutters that smells like sawdust and varnish. This guy and a lady are standing in front of a picture window that's so big you can see everything outdoors. The carpet is so thick, I can see the footprints they made walking on it. They look up at us then go on with what they were saying. The lady is telling the guy how they have to have three bedrooms. "They say these houses are easy as pie to add on to," he tells her.

In the kitchen, another lady is opening all the cupboard doors and looking inside. She's going on and on about how all you have to do is push a button, and presto, everything's done for you. There's a breakfast nook with pompon curtains on the window. Upstairs, there are two bedrooms that've got bedspreads with matching curtains. Abbie calls them drapes. You can open and close them with this special string.

The Contemporary Ranch has got drapes that look like leopard skin and a sliding glass door in the kitchen so you can get to your patio out back. It has an oven with a blue door built right into the wall. The blue stove is what you call a stove top and it's built right into the counter and has got a copper roof on top with a fan that takes away all the smoke. This guy shows us how it works by holding his cigarette up under it.

There are houses that're all on one floor or else houses that have got an upstairs and a downstairs. I'm upstairs in the Modern Manor throwing a Kleenex down the laundry chute that's under this secret door in the floor of the closet when Abbie says, "It's time for you to get lost."

"What d'ya mean?"

"What d'ya mean?" she says, imitating me. "What I mean is make like a tree and leave."

She's looking at herself in the mirror, fussing with her hairdo. It looks like a cone of cotton candy balanced on top of her head. She takes out her lipstick and smears it on her lips even though she's already wearing some.

The Merchant is in this room that hasn't been finished yet so you can see what the house looks like before they put up the walls. Some guy with a hat on is telling this bunch of guys about how the houses are built. Some of the guys're writing stuff down on their little pads of paper. The Merchant takes his comb out of his back pocket and runs it through his hair. It stands up perfectly straight like a scrub brush on top. I go down the stairs and out the back door to the next house.

Every time I go in one of the houses I hope I'll run into Abbie and The Merchant, but I don't see them for an ice age. I'm in the Split Level Estate when I see them coming up the sidewalk out front so what I do is I sneak into the bathroom and hide behind these shower curtains covered with big blue daisies. When they come in to have a look, I'll jump out and scare the living daylights out of them. I stand there waiting and waiting, trying not to breathe too loud. I'm leaning up against these blue tiles when I hear footsteps clicking up the stairs into the bathroom. I peek out, but it's not them. It's these other folks that've come in to have a look. The lady has a navy blue hat on with a little net hanging half over her face. The father's holding on to their kid's hand.

"I don't know about keeping it clean," the lady says. She flushes the blue toilet and watches the water swirl down. "It'd be kind of hard to drag the vacuum up and down all these stairs."

The kid is looking right straight at me. He doesn't smile or point or anything. He looks at me like I'm part of the decoration. Then he sticks his pink thumb into his mouth. I don't know what I'll do if the lady yanks the curtain back.

After they leave, I walk around acting like I'm OK and I don't mind being the only one there by myself. I keep thinking about how all the houses come in these big flat pieces. This doll house I got for Christmas once was like that. It came all in pieces and the walls had pictures of sinks and stoves and fireplaces and windows with curtains stamped on them, and you just had to hook it all up by sliding these metal flaps into these slits they made in the floor and roof. Then you bent the flaps over and you had your house.

The Split Level Estate has a boy's bedroom and a girl's bedroom. The girl's has dancing ballerinas on the wallpaper and a pink ruffled bedspread on the bed. The boy's room has wallpaper with cowboys throwing lassos around these cows. I try to picture that little boy going to sleep in the middle of a room like this, his mommy coming up the stairs and lifting up the veil on her hat to kiss him good night, his daddy coming in with a glass of water in case the boy gets thirsty.

I'm hoping this is the house Abbie and The Merchant pick out because I'd like to have this room for myself. They don't know it yet, but I'm planning to live with them. I'm thinking about laying down on the bed to see how it feels, when the closet door flies open behind me and Abbie and The Merchant jump out yelling, "Boo!" I about have a heart attack. Abbie and The Merchant sure do know how to have a good time.

On the way home, The Merchant's pretty stirred up because every one of them houses has got wall-to-wall carpeting. "You know what that means for me," he says, looking over at Abbie then back at the road. Him and Abbie are trying to figure out what house to get. Maybe they'll get the Split Level Estate, or else they'll get the Modern Manor, the one that has a sunken living room and a dining room with a lamp you can raise and lower depending on if you want the light to be bright or dim. If you ask me, the best part about getting one of them model homes is it would really be something to live in a house where everything is completely brand new, even the icebox. Imagine a house where nobody has ever fried a hamburg in your kitchen before and no stranger has ever even sat down on your toilet.

mr. right

When Mom's first letter finally comes, it's a long white envelope with her name and address printed on the front in red pencil. Mom doesn't read it out loud. She stands in the kitchen moving her lips as she reads it to herself. Her face is pale and I can see the flecks of powder on the soft hairs of her cheeks. When I was little, I used to put my hands on either side of her face and give her a kiss. I can still remember the taste of her lipstick and how her cheeks felt like ripe peaches.

"He put in his phone number. 'Give me a ring,' he says, and signs his name. Bus Arbuckle," Mom says. "What kind of man calls himself Bus?"

"Maybe it's short for Buster or something," Abbie says. "What else does he say?" Mom hands her the letter.

"What d'ya think, Ab?" she says.

"It's worth a try."

After supper, Mom takes one of her bubble baths and I do the dishes. Abbie whips up some egg whites and smears it over her face after she wraps her head in a towel. She says it's supposed to make your skin soft and new like a baby's. Mom keeps the door open so she can talk to us when I'm not running the water. I fool around with the suds, letting the cups fall like space capsules landing in the ocean.

"I have never once in my life called some guy up on the telephone," she says. She acts like her hand'll shrivel up and fall off if she does.

"What am I supposed to do?" She sloshes the washrag. Steam is so thick on the kitchen window, drops of water streak down the dark glass. I stand on tiptoe and wipe it away. My own face looks back at me, like I'm some stranger peeping in the window.

Mom comes out and starts pacing back and forth, her slippers making sticky sounds on the linoleum. Finally she says she'll talk to this Bus Arbuckle if Abbie dials his number. As soon as it rings, Abbie hands her the receiver. While they talk, Mom twirls the black phone cord around and around her elbow. When she hangs up, she does a little tap dance across the kitchen.

"What'd he say?"

"He wants me to go out for supper with him at Meryl's Highdecker. He says he just loves taking a pretty lady out to eat."

The next day, she comes home with a brand-new dress, this black sheath dress that zips up the back. It's got scalloped edges around the neck. "It was on sale," she says, like she's apologizing. She tries it on and models it for me and Abbie.

On the night of her date, she spreads her clothes out on the bed. Her white slip, clean underwear, stockings, her black dress. I watch her powder herself all over. "Jayne Mansfield I ain't," Mom says, tucking her falsies into her bra. Abbie comes and helps her pull her dress on without mussing her hair. She stares in the mirror, dabbing her cheeks with rouge.

"He *is* some total stranger," Mom says. She looks at the back of her head in the mirror. She groans and snaps her purse open. She puts on more lipstick and blots it with a Kleenex. "I can't do it," she says, crumpling the Kleenex up and flinging it on the floor. "I can't go out with somebody I've never even laid eyes on."

She kicks her shoes off and throws herself on the bed.

"He'll be here in five minutes," Abbie says. "What're you gonna do?"

"You want me to turn out the lights?" I ask.

She lies perfectly still, staring up at the light bulb like it's some crystal ball. "I'll tell you what." She smiles. "Let's lock the door and go upstairs. I can get a good look at him before I go anywhere."

The three of us crouch in the dark, our eyes on the driveway. When the big blue car turns onto our street, we all hold our breath. The door opens and Bus Arbuckle, a skinny old hunched-up guy with thick white hair, gets out. He's got a red-and-black-checked hunting jacket on. When Mom lets her breath out, she sounds like a beach ball going flat.

"He's an old coot," she says, letting go of the curtain and sitting back on her heels. There's a loud knock on the front door.

"I'm not answering it," she says.

Bus Arbuckle is knocking and knocking.

"Go tell him I got sick." Her whisper smells like toothpaste and cigarettes.

"Not me," Abbie says. I don't say anything.

"Well, all right. He'll get the hint eventually. Unzip me, will you?" She turns her back to me. I slide the zipper down and she pulls her dress off and lays it carefully on the end of my bed. Bus Arbuckle knocks again.

"I ain't so hard up I'm ready to go out with somebody old enough to be my own father. Not when Mr. Right's out there waiting for me." She stretches out on my bed, her stockings rustling under her slip. She seems to shimmer and glow in the dark room, her long legs glistening like marble polished smooth.

furnished room

Floyd sets down his cardboard suitcase inside the thickly varnished door and kicks it shut behind him. He puts his tape recorder on the bureau and sighs as if the weight of these two things is something he has carried too long, has been longing to let go of, though it was only a short trip from his car parked out front up the stairs to this room. He trips on the torn edge of the linoleum rug. It is golden brown, stamped with a design meant to resemble wood. Floyd traces the cracked edge with the toe of his heavy black shoe and thinks of it as a road, leading off into the desert of the golden brown linoleum. Underneath, there is a swirling pattern of green and white.

The walls of the room are covered with pale green paint slapped up over so many layers of wallpaper it is crusty like blistered skin and bulges in the corners with crumbly plaster. The slanted ceiling is low enough for him to smack his head if he doesn't watch out. Above the light switch, where the green paint has already worn down to the blue roses underneath, there are two signs written in wavy script. A dried gnat is caught in the thick yellow curl of tape along the bottom of the first one: GOD BLESS THIS HOUSE AND ALL THOSE WHO ENTER IT. The sign beneath: NO LADY FRIENDS ALLOWED.

In three steps, Floyd is across the room, parting the curtains—some flimsy greying cloth thick with dust and stained in the center from who knows how many hands before his, holding the curtains aside to peer down at what? A dank overgrown backyard from which the sour stench of rotting weeds wafts through the black screen, making Floyd feel seized with panic, like when he was a boy, diving into deep water, sinking like a dead weight

203

until he touched bottom and pushed himself up again. Floyd lowers the venetian blinds with a snap.

"You like the room?" the old lady asked when he had descended the stairs the first time. The staircase listed to the side so bad he had to hang on to the railing with every step, climbing down like a child learning to walk. She stood fingering the worn green bills he had handed her, folding and unfolding them like she was pleating a skirt. She squinted up at him. Her pale blue eyes were covered with a film that made them seem watery, almost white, through the thick lenses of her glasses.

"You like the room." She answered herself. "What do you think of that, Sammy?"

Sammy, a yellow hound with stubby legs barely able to hold him up, flopped at her feet, his long ratlike tail sweeping the floor. As she spoke, the dog looked up out of the corner of his eye.

Floyd had stopped at the first house in Sheridan with a sign in the window, had climbed the wooden steps, thinking how good it would be to sleep again with a roof over his head. His footsteps creaking across the soft worn wood of the porch floor had given him the sensation that he was walking in sand, with waves lapping around his ankles, burying his feet. The clapboards of the house were speckled with scabs of yellow paint. He knocked and stood scratching off chips of paint, waiting. He knocked again, and was about to turn away, thinking there was no one home, when there was a movement in the window. He peered in at an old lady coming toward him, her thick black-heeled shoes scuffing the linoleum, her twisted fingers grabbing on to the edge of the dark wooden table—so wide it nearly filled the room. She grasped the chair backs and pulled herself forward like an exhausted swimmer hauling herself up out of a whirling current.

Floyd had been sleeping in his car for weeks, pulling over onto the dirt road beside the White River and passing out in the backseat. In the morning, he shaved with cold river water dipped into a can, scraping his cheeks in the rearview mirror. "Like some kind of hobo," he muttered to himself.

It had never gone on this long before. Had never been more

204

than a week or so before Ruth relented. Said, "Come on home. We'll give it another try."

This time she wouldn't even talk to him. At first he didn't care. It had felt good to walk out of the house thumbing his nose at her. It had felt good to drive off in his shiny red convertible. And there had been Gert Fostich. How easily she had taken him into her bed. He still got a chill when he thought of her long legs wrapped around his waist. And then, just as quickly, she had let him go like they had never even spoken, let alone shared all those nights in bed, her trailer rocking on its flimsy foundation.

One night after work, Floyd walked into Syd's and saw Gert at a booth with Lyle Mosbaugh—she didn't even look up at him when he came in the door. Floyd had been so shocked to see her leaning across the black table top with her face up close to Lyle's that he had walked right through the bar and out the back door without stopping.

Now he called home every night to try to talk some sense into Ruth. But Lana was the only one who answered. He couldn't tell if she was lying or not when she told him her mother wasn't home. This time it looked like she was going through with it. He'd received papers from her lawyer. He'd been to court twice already and was making support payments. The guys at work said he'd better get a lawyer of his own, but he still hadn't done that.

He felt desperate to talk to Ruth. If he could just look at her or hear her voice, he could make everything all right. But the way it stood now, he couldn't even go to his own home without being arrested.

Once Floyd had called Ruth in the dead of night, standing in the phone booth in the cramped space between the doors to the toilets at Syd's. All around him, men calling to one another, the TV too loud, and him listening, his hand cupped over one ear, while the phone rang and rang. He could picture the house empty. All the rooms stripped bare of furniture, the curtains taken down from the windows, the closet doors hanging open. Ruth and the girls gone somewhere he'd never be able to trace. Gone. He drove past the house only to find it the same as it had always been. A light on over the kitchen sink. Ruth's car *crouched like a green toad in the driveway. He could almost hear them breathing through the walls. He could imagine the warmth rising up out of the blankets as he slipped into bed. But of course the doors were locked and he couldn't get inside.*

He tried calling again, last night, after midnight. In the smoky haze of the bar he imagined the black phone on the wall in the alcove off the kitchen, the chalkboard underneath where Lana drew her pictures, thinking, "My phone. My kitchen. My kid, for Chrissakes. Ruth. My goddamned wife." He could see her smoking in bed, cussing the phone like it was his face.

"I know who this is!" A lady's voice, a stranger, shrill and accusing. Floyd was so startled he held the receiver away from his ear and stared at it in disbelief. The ringing had gone on so long, so endlessly, with him perched on the tiny stool in the phone booth, staring through the glass at the men lined up at the bar on the red vinyl stools, nudging one another, mugs of beer in front of them, the click of pool balls behind them. He had been in the phone booth so long he'd forgotten what he was there for. Who was that answering his phone? He cleared his throat, lifted the receiver back up to his ear. "Decent folks are trying to get some sleep," the voice was saying. "This has got to stop." Neila Grimes. Of course. That old busybody on their party line. She would stick her nose in this, too.

Floyd kicks off his shoes and, after lighting a cigarette, sinks into the center of the sagging bed. Six o'clock. On the dot. He watches the second hand jerk slowly around the numbers. Six-o-one. Six-o-two. "How the hell am I ever going to get through this night? Sunday night, and all the bars closed," he thinks. "The liquor stores locked up. I'm heading from bad to worse. Here I am, a family man. A husband. The father of two girls shut up in this furnished room like some kind of bachelor."

When he pulls the thin lumpy pillow out from under the brown bedspread, turns to ball it up under his head, there is a greasy stain on the wall where some other man's head has rubbed. And higher up, a dark smudge where the same man must have sat leaning against the wall.

The room is clammy, like someone just took a shower in it. It smells of mildew. Black dots of mold are sprinkled around the *edge of the window frame. Floyd worries that he will suffocate there in the night with the wallpaper caving in around him.*

Downstairs, corned beef and cabbage is simmering on the stove. He can almost taste the slivers of pink meat. The green translucent cabbage. Canned laughter drifts up through the floor grate. He leans over, peers through the metal slats. There is the old lady, a grey blanket wrapped around her knees, sitting perfectly straight like she's in church waiting for the next hymn to be sung. The blue lights flicker across her face.

Floyd shuts his eyes. He is in his red convertible, the top down, the sun on his face, the wind in his hair. He is driving toward mountains that rise up from the horizon casting dark shadows across the road ahead of him. He will drive west until he is free, until whatever connection he has with his life here is severed, snaps like a frayed rope pulled too tight.

Waitresses in diners alongside the dusty roads—he will only go on back roads—will smile when they set steaming cups of coffee in front of him. Girls in tight dresses, their large hips grazing him as they pass by where he sits with his knees tucked up under the counter. He will reach out and slap their flesh the way other men do and the girls will turn toward him, their dark eyes glowing.

He will be someone going somewhere. Someone strangers will wonder about. The kind of fellow girls dream will return to them. One day, walking down the street of some town he has never been in before, a girl who served him coffee at the counter of a diner in the middle of nowhere will come up to him, her cheeks flushed, her chest heaving the way girls' chests do in the movies. She will say, "I saw you once. Back in Sparksville, South Dakota. And I never forgot it."

"I'm Mrs. Hopkins," the old woman had announced in her cracked, too-loud voice. "Mrs. Henry Arnold Hopkins." Her head nodded and shook, bobbing like a doll's head on a spring. Floyd had stood in the dark front hall like a schoolboy, cornered, waiting it out. The room reeked of mothballs—their thick smell like the taste of some soft, too-sweet candy melting on the back of his tongue and trickling down his throat. He tried to be polite. Called her ma'am. Grinned foolishly.

"This here's my dear Henry." She thrust a gold-framed photograph at him. Floyd couldn't see Mrs. Hopkins in the voluptuous girl behind the lacy veil. A dark-haired man, his fingers barely grazing her elbow, stared straight into the camera's eye like he had been on the verge of divulging some long-held secret when the shutter clicked. At their feet, the train of her dress spilled across the glossy floor like a puddle of milk.

"He looks like a nice fellow," Floyd said.

"It's a terrible thing to be the one left behind," she said. "I've been left alone here going on nine years now, waiting to go. And here I am, still alive and kicking."

Floyd tried not to stare too hard at the thick flesh-colored hearing aids jammed into her ears. His eyes, despite his effort, traced the thin wires that disappeared down the front of her navy blue dress. "Why, she's so old," he thinks, "she's got to plug herself in." There is a sudden hysterical rush of a laugh in his chest, like a bird trapped in a dark room, its wings grazing the walls, searching for light. He cleared his throat, turned abruptly to the cabinet in the corner.

"Those were Henry's. Yes. They belonged to him. Ain't been used since the day we lowered him in the ground. God rest his soul."

Three polished rifles were lined up on a rack behind the glass doors. "He always kept 'em loaded and ready to go. But I'm the one that held on to the key." She threw her gnarled hands up in the air and cackled, her thin lips spread wide over her shiny, too-white-to-be-real teeth. "You like the room," she said again, as if thinking of it for the first time.

She was clasping a change purse in her hands and she opened it now and dug out a key. An old-fashioned black key with a bit of red Christmas ribbon tied to it. She dangled it up at Floyd.

Floyd thought at first she was offering him the key to the cabinet. He could feel the weight of a gun, the cool iron barrel in his mouth. One click of the trigger was all it would take. One click, and it would be over. Fast.

"I leave the front door open till ten-thirty," she said. "This is a Christian home."

Floyd realized that the key she was giving him was the key to his room. He took it from her and put it in his shirt pocket.

Now Floyd is upstairs in Mrs. Henry Arnold Hopkins's house

listening to silverware scrape across a plate and dog tags clink against a ceramic bowl. Floyd is hungry too, but he doesn't have the heart to do anything about it. The hot plate on the table is the last straw. He lies there, his head throbbing, the darkness filling the room.

shit-assing schertzie

Every night, Earl Schertz—the last guy that answered Mom's ad in *Something for Everybody*—comes over and parks himself in our front room. "Hi, honey," he says, coming in without even knocking. He acts like he owns our house, kissing Mom on the cheek like he's been doing it his whole life.

He was the third guy that answered her ad, but the only one she went out with. The second guy never even got out of his car. When Schertzie came up the sidewalk, I thought Mom was going to hide in the dark the way she did with the other two, but she said he didn't look bad. She hiked up her dress and undid her garters to readjust her stockings while he knocked on the door. Then she put her hand on my shoulder and slipped one shoe on, then the other. Before she ran downstairs to let him in, Abbie fussed with the back of her hair.

Me and Abbie stayed upstairs with Gretchie. I had to hold on to her collar so she wouldn't follow Mom. She moaned a little but then she settled down and let me scratch her chin. I hate meeting strangers and anyway, Abbie said he might not be interested if he knew Mom had two kids. "We don't want to mess up her chances," she said.

I laid down on my bed and thought about how Mrs. Zugel used to try to teach us how to meet people, about who's supposed to say how do you do first and which hand to stick out. There was the spritzing sound of Mom opening up a Coke for him. Then she got a glass out and poured it. Or maybe he poured it. I couldn't tell which. He said she looked real nice and I could hear her giggling.

When they left, she didn't even holler good-bye. Me and Abbie stood in our dark room watching him hold her by the elbow and steer her down to his car where she stood with her arms dangling like she'd never used them before in her life. He opened the door and helped her in.

"He's a real gentleman," Abbie said.

But I could tell something was funny about Schertzie right away. I just didn't figure it out till it was too late.

"Shit-assing Schertzie's what you call a good catch," Mom keeps saying. She calls him that behind his back but to his face she calls him Earl Baby. "Looks ain't everything, you know," she says. "Who would've thought a guy like him'd be uptown all this time and I never even noticed?"

Half the time her and Abbie are in Mom's room whispering and giggling about him like he's some kind of movie star. But if you ask me, she has to make excuses because Earl Schertz is the ugliest guy alive. He isn't just ugly, though. The thing is, old Schertzie is only about five feet tall. The old man is six two and Mom's pretty near five feet nine. Schertzie wears these special shoes that have lifts in them so he can pretend he's taller than he is but he still has to stand on his toes to kiss her. Only a moron would act like it's normal to have gigantic soles that raise you up off the ground like that. As if that's not bad enough, he goops up his black hair so it stands way up high off his head. His pink scalp shows through about two inches below his hairdo.

Schertzie's the one that decorates the cakes at Molly's Bakery uptown. Half his cakes look like they're covered with corduroy because of his special technique. What he does is he covers the cakes with a thin layer of white icing. Then over that he squeezes colored lines of icing real close together. On top of that he writes his message in swirly letters.

I've seen him up there with a white apron tied around his belly standing behind the counter. Before I knew him and knew he made the cakes, I used to stop and look in the window. Once there was a Father's Day cake that looked like a straw hat and another time there was this cake for a boy that was shaped like a train. There's always one with some girl doll shoved into the center of a cake decorated to look like her frilly skirt.

Schertzie gets whatever's left over at the end of the day. Mom always opens the white box he brings over and says something only a nitwit would say, acting like he made it special for us. "Would you look at this, Lana?" she says, showing me a box of broken sugar cookies or a layer cake covered with green coconut that says *Happy Birthday, Coreen* in swirly letters on top.

When him and Mom first started going on dates, Schertzie took her to the movies and out dancing at the Backlash. Once she brought home a paper umbrella she got in her drink when they ate in a fancy restaurant. Now they never go anywhere. When I have to go downstairs, the two of them are always sitting on the davenport with the TV on but they don't really watch it. They just start looking at it when I come down. When the old man calls to talk, Mom turns the sound up real loud so I can't hardly hear what he's telling me.

gravel gertie

T hey found it in the trash. In the ladies' room. Wrapped up in paper towels and whatnot." Winona Flowers is grinning like she's all excited.

"What?" I say.

"Go on, now." Mom gives me a shove. "This is grown-ups' talk. You go on and play."

I act like I'm going up to my room but I sneak halfway down the stairs again so I can still listen.

"Syd Sizelove said he thought it was some cat that got in from the alley. You could hear it crying clear out in front. So he sent Charlene in there and she came back out just as white as a sheet."

"Oh. Don't it just give you the chills?" Mom says.

"Syd had to grab her so she wouldn't fall flat right there on the floor. It was Syd himself had to go in there. He came out carrying that baby all covered in bloody brown paper towels crying its eyes out. A little boy. Had no arms and no legs to speak of, just little flippers. Said he'd never seen a thing like it. They called Gus Riley and the ambulance both. Turns out it was Gertie Fostich's. Nobody even knowed she got herself knocked up again since she never shows. How many kids you suppose she's got the state raising?"

"Gert Fostich?" Mom says. "Gravel Gertie?" She gasps a little like she's just seen a mouse.

"You know who I mean, right?"

"I know *of* her," Mom says.

"Seems she was in to Syd's having herself a good old time and then she started having the worse cramps of her life. I bet she was scared shitless seeing that thing come out from between her legs.

Must've thought she was giving birth to something from Mars. She didn't know what to do with it. They say it's a criminal act what she done, leaving it in the trash thataway."

"Whose do you suppose it is?" Mom says.

"Could be anybody's, from what I hear. They don't call her Gravel Gertie for nothing."

moon pies

Abbie's spraying her hairdo when The Merchant pulls up outside and toots. She can see me watching her. "All right," she says, looking at me in the mirror like that's my real face. She acts like I asked her something but I didn't make a peep. "Get your shoes on and let's go."

While Abbie goes out to warn The Merchant that I'm coming, I stand in the doorway so I can see what Mom and Schertzie are watching on the TV. Schertzie's got one of his gorilla arms around Mom's shoulders, his idiotic onyx ring squished onto his pudgy pinky finger. There are two tall glasses half-filled with Coke on the coffee table. Schertzie's got his shoes off and his feet are propped up on the table next to a green bottle of rum. He's wearing black nylon socks just like the old man wears. He starts tapping his fingers on Mom's arm and whistling. Then he jiggles one of his legs up and down up and down, practically shaking the whole house.

Some guy on the TV's all excited about these spiders that live underwater. There's a close-up of a spider swimming along holding this bubble of air between its back legs. The spiders take the air underwater with them somehow so they can breathe later when they're down in their nests or whatever it is you call a spider's home. The guy doesn't say.

"I'm going out with Abbie."

"I know," Mom says. "You be good." She crosses her legs and smiles. "Don't do anything I wouldn't do."

Schertzie acts like that's the funniest thing he's ever heard. He crosses his arms over his chest and snorts. The two of them look at each other like they have some secret and clink their glasses.

Last week, Schertzie and Mom went out and bought new wall-paper for the front room. They tried putting it up on one wall, but it came out crooked. It's not at all like the kind of wallpaper the old man would've picked out. It's blue and white with these scenes of an old-fashioned man and lady. In one, they're dancing with their arms up in the air. In another, the lady is swinging while the man plays a flute. In the last scene, the lady has a blind-fold on and the man's leading her down a road. When I was little, the old man used to tie a scarf around my eyes and take me for walks so I could see what it was like to be blind. I can still re-member the way it felt when he lifted my hand up to touch the brick walls and the tree bark. Seeing is just one of your senses, he'd say. But you've got four more. He'd hold a stone he'd pried out of the ground under my nose or the husk of a hickory nut and ask, What's this? He used to always want to know what sense would you do without if you had to give one up but I could never decide. Mom said she could do without feeling. The old man looked at her like she was crazy. You'd die, he told her. You'd burn yourself or cut yourself or freeze to death and not even know it. But Mom just laughed and said you asked me and I'm telling you that's what I'd pick.

The Merchant toots for me and I run out. He's sitting in his car out in the driveway with the motor running. Abbie's in front up close to him like she always is. I get in the back. "Hi, squirt," The Merchant says to me. He's wearing the blue sweater Abbie got him for his birthday and he's got his hair combed real careful so the little hairs in his crew cut stand straight up. The whole car smells like Old Spice.

"Where to?" he says.

Abbie says she doesn't care. "All Alone Am I" is playing on the radio and Abbie turns it up and starts singing along. Abbie knows all the words to just about every song that comes on the radio and she knows who sings them and even what number they are. The Merchant starts driving around town a little bit. He never cares if I put my feet on the backseat, so I do and lean up against the window. The leaves are all red and yellow and it seems like just about everybody in the whole town is outside raking them up into big piles by the side of the road. We go down West Jackson Street and then turn around and go back the way we came. Shreida Huckaby's walking back and forth over the railroad tracks talking to herself a mile a minute. She's got her hair up in curlers and she's wearing a pale green chenille housecoat and a pair of black rubber boots.

"Maybe she's hoping to get hit," Abbie says.

The Merchant toots at her but she doesn't look up. I stare at the back of his head. His hair swirls around and around in circles starting at the tiny pink spot where his cowlick would be if he had enough hair for one to grow. I don't talk to them or anything since Abbie's always saying I can go along with them so long as I keep my lips zipped.

"Hey, hey, what d'ya say?" Rocking Robert comes on the radio and starts talking about this big shindig going on up in Indianapolis to celebrate the opening of the new shopping center they've got. "Shake, rattle, and roll on down here," he says. The Merchant turns the radio down. "What d'ya say we go on over and have us a look?" Abbie sits up and looks at herself in the mirror, fussing with her hairdo the way she does when she's all excited.

I've never seen so many cars before and there's a whole bunch of people walking around this really big store called the Giant Store. It's so gigantic they claim a whole airplane can fit right inside of it and there'd still be room for all the stuff they've got on sale. I feel kind of dizzy, it's so bright and the racks and racks of clothes go on for miles.

The Merchant takes Abbie over to a rack full of blouses and starts holding different ones up under her chin to see what she looks like. He tells her the ones he'll get her when his business is going good. They've got clothes in all sizes from little tiny babies on up to grown-ups and they've got both men's and ladies' stuff right in the same store. I've never seen so many clothes in my whole life. We start walking up and down the aisles just to look at everything.

"The thing I can't get over is how they've even got music playing in here," Abbie says. "I never did go to a store that had music playing before." She says that's what she likes the best. There are

217

these big signs hanging down from the ceiling to tell you where everything's at. One section has nothing but shoes and then off to the side they've got Housewares where there's a bunch of kitchen stuff and iceboxes and rugs. There's even swing sets and lawn mowers in the back.

"I'll betcha they've got as much stuff as the whole Sears Roebuck catalog," I say.

The Merchant laughs. "And you probably want one of everything."

After we look over all there is to see, we go outside. They've got a whole bunch of other stores all lined up but most of them are still empty except for one store that just sells ice cream. Red, white, and blue balloons are hung up on the front of it.

"C'mon. I'll treat you." The Merchant has his arm around Abbie's waist and he kind of steers her ahead of him into the store.

"Looky here. Fifteen different flavors." He starts reading them out loud. I can't pick between Cherry Vanilla or Chocolate Chip so he lets me get a scoop of each.

"You going to spoil our kids thataway?"

The Merchant's whole face turns bright red, even his ears. He stands there looking at his shoes and grinning. We sit on one of the little benches they've got out in front and watch everybody walking around.

"Someday I'm going to try me every single one of them flavors."

"I bet you will, squirt."

Abbie's so happy she doesn't even give me any dirty looks for saying stuff. "Yeah," she says. "And you'll end up as big around as Mrs. MacAbee!" Abbie's stirring her ice cream around and around in the paper cup. She can never eat ice cream unless she mushes it up like soup first.

"Evidently there's going to be shopping centers all over the world one of these days," The Merchant says.

We hang around waiting till they announce the winners of the door prizes. Abbie's got her heart set on winning the sewing machine so when the guy reaches into the big fishbowl to pick the winner I start praying "Dear God, let it be Abbie's number" over and over again. But it's some little girl. Her daddy lifts her up in the air and kisses her when she says she's going to give the sewing machine to her grandma. After the prizes are all handed out, this guy in a black suit starts doing some magic tricks that're all fake. He reaches into what looks like an empty hat and unhooks this secret compartment to take out handfuls of penny candy he tosses at us. On the way back to the car, Abbie doesn't say anything but I can tell she's feeling gypped.

When we get home, they drop me off the way they always do. "I've got a secret to tell Donnie," Abbie says and laughs.

All up and down the street little piles of leaves are burning, glowing red at the curbs. Now that Mom's kicked the old man out forever, I don't know who's going to rake up all our leaves. I tried it but I got so many blisters I had to quit before I even had one pile. I can't picture Schertzie out there with a rake. The yard's covered like a thick red and brown and yellow quilt of leaves.

The only light on in our house is in the kitchen. A huge brown moth is flinging itself against the screen door. Mom is laughing with her head back, blowing smoke up at the ceiling. She has on the pink quilted housecoat the old man let me pick out for her the last time we went Christmas shopping together.

In the middle of the table, there's a plate of moon pies, marshmallow seeping out the edges of the big round chocolate cookies. Schertzie is straddling a kitchen chair, a moon pie in his hand. His pants are undone at the waist and he has a white ribbed undershirt on. There's a greenish blue tattoo of a snake circling his bare arm.

The door smacks shut behind me. They both look up, their eyes wide, their mouths open, like I just snuck up and took their picture.

visitation rights

Mom finally got this paper that says the old man is addicted to a violent temper and he'll be arrested if he comes near us. She's really going through with the divorce this time, but the judge ended up telling Mom he's still our father and he has the right to see us kids. From now on every Saturday from two to eight we have to be with him and there's nothing Mom can do about it.

We have to go over to Reverend Andrews's house and wait for the old man to pick us up since he's not allowed to even drive up our driveway. Mom says the two of them can't be anywhere near each other without sparks flying. Anyhow, she's got absolutely no desire to lay eyes on him again as long as she lives. She says us kids are going to court with her next time so we can tell the judge we feel the same way, but I can't picture me saying what Mom wants me to if the old man's there listening.

"How's my girls?" the old man says in a loud, too-happy voice. Abbie rolls her eyes and grabs me by the shoulders to steer me out to his car. The old man shakes hands with Reverend Andrews all polite.

"I figure we'll swing over to Sheridan to take in a picture show." He looks at me and Abbie like we're a stack of pancakes on Sunday morning and he's ready to sit down at the table and help himself.

"You mean the movies," Abbie says.

"Yeah. Well. Whatever." He jabs in the lighter and pops a cigarette in his mouth. He grabs my hand and squeezes it.

Abbie sighs. "Can I turn the radio on?"

"Sure, sweetheart. Whatever your heart desires."

She leans over the front seat and fiddles with the dial till she tunes in her favorite station.

She's in a bad mood because The Merchant couldn't get time off today. Usually he follows us around and then when the old man leaves us out in the car for an ice age to go up to his furnished room the way he always does, The Merchant parks nearby so Abbie can run over and sit with him. It's my job to be on the lookout and toot the horn when the old man is coming so Abbie can jump back in. The old man can't stand The Merchant. He thinks Abbie's too young to be having a boyfriend. He'd have a conniption if he knew what was going on.

The old man pulls up in front of the movie house. *How the West Was Won* is playing.

"We saw that already with Donnie," Abbie says all mean about it like she hates his guts. The old man gets this look on his face that reminds me of the time he drove us over to have a look at the house where he was born and when we got there, it'd been torn down and this factory made out of grey cinder blocks was standing there instead.

"Well," he says. "Well. Let me see what I can do. You two wait here. I'll be back in a jiffy."

He walks right up to the lady sitting in her glass booth and takes his billfold out like he's going to buy us tickets anyway and then he walks away down the street and disappears.

"What's going on?" I look back at Abbie. She's got her arms wrapped around her chest.

"You know," Abbie says.

"What d'ya mean?"

"Don't even ask, if you can't figure it out."

I scoot over and sit behind the steering wheel.

"Let's go to California." I act like I'm happy and we're sitting out in the driveway like in the old days when one of our favorite games was acting like we were going on a trip. Sometimes we'd do it in the car parked out in the driveway and sometimes we'd sit on the ends of our beds and pile our dolls around us and go anywhere we wanted.

"Oh, grow up why don't you?"

That's all she ever says. That or "act your age not your IQ."

221

"I'm not in any big hurry to turn into you." When I'm a teen-ager I'm not going to go around in a bad mood half the time.

She taps the back of my head. I figure I won't even act like I notice. Sometimes all she wants is to get into a fight. I'm at the beach with my shoes off wading in the water. It's warm as a bath. In the rearview mirror, I can see Abbie hunched down in her seat with her collar up around her ears. She draws a witch's face in the steam on the window.

"If he's not back in five minutes, I'm walking home."

"It's too far."

"I don't care. I'm not sitting here freezing to death waiting on him."

We wait for about a hundred hours. This big crowd comes out of the movie, all these kids holding their parents' hands and act-ing all excited. Then a whole bunch of other people start lining up to go in.

"It figures," Abbie says. "What'd I tell you?"

The old man is walking down the street like he's liable to fall down. When he gets in, the car fills up with the smell of whiskey and cigarettes and peppermint gum.

I stare out the window and act like I'm not there. The old man drives real slow hunched over the steering wheel like he's about a million years old. He acts like he doesn't even know we're there anymore even though Abbie's in the backseat singing along to the radio at the top of her lungs. He doesn't say anything after he parks the car. He just gets out and goes up to his furnished room. My fingers are so cold they feel like long thin icicles. I put them in my mouth and suck on them till they tingle and itch.

"I got X-ray eyes," Abbie says. "I can see right through your head. It's empty inside."

I don't even say anything back to her. She just acts mean when she's trying not to act scared. That's something you have to do when you're acting grown up.

"I'm going to go get him."

"Suit yourself."

I stand on the front porch, ringing the bell, feeling like I do when I go trick-or-treating. I wish I had me a mask to put on. This real old lady with her back all hunched up opens the door. "What is it, dear?" She's so short she has to look up at me.

"I'm looking for Floyd Franklin."

"Who's that?" She cups her hand behind her ear and leans closer.

"Floyd Franklin," I say louder.

"Why, yes, Mr. Franklin. Such a nice quiet man. He's right up at the top of these here stairs. I think he came in a little while ago, dear."

An old dog is laying on the floor in front of a kerosene heater. It thumps its tail like it wants to get up so I can pet it, but it's too tired. The stairs are covered with sticky red linoleum and lean to the side like in a haunted house. I hold on tight to the rail and kind of pull myself up. I take my time.

The old man doesn't answer when I knock, but the door's not locked or anything so I go on in. He's sitting on a kitchen chair just like the pink vinyl-covered ones we have at home. He has this pad of yellow paper in his lap. He still has his coat on even though the room is warm. He looks up from what he's writing.

"I know you came to get me. But I'm not ready to go yet. You'll have to court-martial me." He sort of salutes me.

On the bed, there's a paper plate with a pile of dried-up beans and a shriveled-up hot dog with a plastic fork stabbed into it. There are soup cans on the windowsill filled with cigarette butts. Crumpled balls of yellow paper are all over the floor. Practically every inch of space on the table has yellow lined paper with stuff written all over it. *We know that all things work together for good to them that love God,* it says in big black letters on the page on top. There's stuff about the world being an apple. How the core has to have seeds in it, but it can be rotten. *Get at them seeds before it's too late to do some good,* it says. There are all these arrows pointing in different directions and a drawing of an apple with a leaf stuck to the stem.

On the wall he tacked up this picture from a magazine of a man on fire standing in the middle of the street with his arms up in the air and the orange fire all over him. All these people are in a circle watching, not doing anything, just watching. The *Ed Sullivan* theme song is on downstairs. I can smell chicken cooking on the stove.

"Daddy, it's me. Lana. 'Member? Me and Abbie want to go home."

"I know who you are. Don't you think you can trick me! Oh no. I'm not falling for that this time. There's always one ready to turn against you. I know." He jumps up and runs over to the table like any minute I'm going to steal his papers. His face is white as a ghost. He looks like Abbie did that time before she fainted.

He backs out the door and goes down the hall. A toilet flushes and then water runs into a sink. I try to figure out what to do but mostly I can't even think straight. For some reason, what I do is I take that picture down from the wall and fold it up and put it in my pocket. Then I go downstairs.

Mom's all excited when I call. "This is it," she says. "This proves he's unfit. You sit tight. I'll be right over. This'll be the end of it."

bread and water

I feel like playing me a game of Monopoly," Mom says. She says it real loud to lure me downstairs so me and Schertzie'll have to try to be friends. "It won't hurt you to talk to him," she's always saying.

I figure I'll go downstairs since there's nothing else to do. It started snowing today. Big white flakes have been falling and falling since I woke up this morning. We all sit around the kitchen table where there's a box of old cupcakes with gobs of pink and white icing that're as big as the cupcakes. Old Schertzie eats a cupcake in two bites. He gulps down half his drink in one swallow. They've got the game already set up and since Schertzie has to be the banker, the money's all lined up in front of him on the table. He keeps straightening out the piles and every time he does I swear to God he sneaks a hundred-dollar bill onto his own pile. Every time he passes Go he gives himself three hundred dollars instead of two. I say something about it but he says I'm seeing things.

"Why would I go and do that?" he asks in his high whiny voice. I keep my eye on him but I can't be sure. No matter how many times I collect rent from him, no matter how many properties he buys, he's still got more money than me and Mom put together even though she owns all the railroads and he lands on them every single time. Then I catch him sneaking extra motels onto Marvin Gardens. What he does is he passes one of his white doughy hands across the board real quick then starts scratching the back of his head. There are two new motels on his property and he didn't buy a thing. He whistles the way he does, sucking

225

his breath in like some kid that hasn't figured out how to do it yet.

"You cheater!" I scrape my chair back and stand up, throwing my money every which way into the middle of the Monopoly board. I feel like smashing one of them cupcakes in his face.

"Lana," Mom says, all shocked. "Watch your mouth."

"I saw him with my own two eyes. Slipping them motels onto his property. He's stealing money too."

"Oh. She's just a sore loser," Schertzie says. He leans back in his chair, flipping a stack of five-hundred-dollar bills.

"Clean that up," Mom says. She starts straightening her money, lining up the edges of her property cards. "I'm not going to play if you act like that."

"I saw him. Didn't you? What's the fun in cheating?"

Schertzie just stares straight ahead the way he does with his pale pig eyes all squinty, like it hurts him to keep them open. I take the edges of the game board and slap it together so all the hotels and motels fly out all over the floor.

"I hope you drop dead," I tell him.

"Lana. I'm warning you."

"I hope you trip and fall into one of your ovens and can't get out."

Schertzie acts like he's going to bite his cigarette in two. He tips back in his chair, rocking it back and forth.

"Get out of my sight, young lady," Mom says. She goes over to the sink and starts running water full blast over the dirty dishes. She's slamming the pots and pans around.

"Honey?" Schertzie asks. He never ever says Mom's name. I don't think he even knows what it is. She's always Honey or Darling or Sweetheart but never just plain Ruth. "Why don't you get her to do that for you?"

" 'Cause I can't stand the sight of her. Now go, I said." She comes over and gives me a shove. I can't stand to go upstairs and listen to them gripe about what I did so I go get Gretchie's little red sweater and put it on her. She runs ahead of me towards the door, her tail wagging in circles like a propeller.

"The next thing you know that dog'll be wearing boots," Schertzie says.

The snow is already up past my ankles and it squeaks and

226

crunches with every step I take. Gretchie whines a little since her legs are so short her belly drags. She has to kind of leap like she's a seal jumping through hoops. It's so quiet I can hear the snow falling on my shoulders. The strange thing is it's not even that cold on account of it's so still. There's no wind and the snow's all piled up on the bare tree branches and telephone wires making peaks like meringue on a pie. It's what the old man calls ice cream snow. On a night like this, he'd go out in the snow and make ice cream from this special recipe his papaw taught him. Every winter after the first snow—it has to be the first snow or the recipe won't work right—he'd whip up the ice cream in the white mixing bowl we have. It'd be all sweet and watery and taste like vanilla. But nowadays you're not supposed to eat the snow on account of all the fallout. It's poison or something.

Gretchie bites the snow and sneezes. "You want some ice cream, girl?" Her tail brushes the snow and she watches me like she's waiting to see what I'll do next. I hold my arms out and fall backwards. Snow falls on my face and my cheeks and my eyes and my lips. It's cold on the back of my head and some of it trickles down my neck. I start waving my arms and legs to make an angel. Gretchie's rolling on her back beside me like she's making a dog angel.

I don't know if there's such a thing as an angel or not, with wings and halos and all that. There are in the Bible, but I mean in real life. Marvella told me once that somewhere in the world, if you look hard enough, you'll find somebody just like you that's your heavenly twin. Kind of like an angel, I reckon. I'm laying there thinking about all this when I hear the back door slam. Mom comes out and stands over me. I don't say anything. Schertzie's with her and he's got his fat fingers wrapped around his key chain.

"Well," Mom says drawing the word out like she's singing opera on *The Ed Sullivan Show*. Her head's already sprinkled with snow. Big drops of water are dripping from Schertzie's hair.

"Earl's going to get pizza. What d'ya want on it?"

"I'm not hungry."

Schertzie stares at this spot on my forehead. He always does that, never looking anybody in the eye. Then he just takes off.

227

"He wants to be your friend," Mom says. "Give him half a chance."

I don't say a thing. I listen to her feet crunch away and the back door slams but I just lie in the snow with Gretchie biting at my sleeve and moaning. I figure I may never say another word as long as I live. When I was a little kid, once for about a month, I refused to talk to anybody but Abbie. When Mom or the old man tried to get me to say something, I just acted like I was a great big rock. The old man would get so teed off he'd threaten to take his belt off and give it to me good, but I still acted like I was a rock.

This was back when I was convinced Mom was trying to poison me after I saw this show where they tried to poison the Rifleman. He was all tied up and this bad guy shoved the poisoned food into his mouth, but the Rifleman just spit it out. I'd sit at the supper table and refuse to eat a thing she cooked. I just sat there with my teeth clenched, staring at what was on my plate wishing I had special powers to make it disappear into thin air. The old man hollered at me and said I had to sit there until I cleaned it up. I don't care if hell freezes over, you eat, he said. Once he chased me up the stairs smacking me but I still wouldn't talk or eat. In the middle of the night I'd sneak down and eat a handful of cereal or take a few hunks of baloney, but then once the old man caught me when he heard me open up the icebox and he said if I wasn't going to eat what my mother cooked for me I couldn't eat at all.

I didn't eat a thing for one whole weekend except for the slice of bread Abbie snuck me when nobody was looking. It was dried up by the time I got to eat it, but I ate it anyhow. I held each bite in my mouth, taking as long as I could, feeling like one of them prisoners that only gets bread and water. Nobody knew I had me a box of brown sugar hidden in the closet. I'd go in there and suck the lumps of sugar till I felt kind of sleepy and sick to my stomach.

After a while, I gave in. I figured if I was going to die anyhow, I might as well get it over with. But I still didn't talk for a long time. Mom said I was just trying to get attention. Leave her alone and she'll get over it, she said.

I'm still laying out back in the snow when Schertzie's car pulls up in the driveway. I wonder what it'd be like to just stay here till

I'm all buried in the snow but I finally get up. When I go back in the house, I'm so cold my teeth are chattering. Mom and Schertzie have already eaten up all the pizza and they're playing double solitaire. They don't even look up at me when I walk past they're so busy slapping the cards down trying to beat each other.

hope chest

T he Merchant got Abbie a hope chest for Valentine's Day and she started collecting stuff for the home her and The Merchant're going to have someday. She spent some of the money she had saved up from baby-sitting and sent away to this place in the back of one of her magazines. For only ten dollars, she got twenty pink towels and twenty washrags to match. The two of us made a stack of pot holders on our looms, and in Home Ec she made a white apron with two red pockets shaped like apples. She started reading recipes in magazines and writing them down on little white cards.

The Merchant took Abbie to the Giant Store and let her pick out this whole set of dishes. There's lime green and dark green ones. Orange ones and grey ones. You can mix or match depending on what you feel like. They come with teacups and juice glasses and even a salt and pepper shaker and a gravy boat. There's a mixing bowl and a salad bowl with the fork and spoon to toss your salad and even a bowl that's divided down the center so you could put your mashed potatoes on one side and your green beans on the other. They even come with forks and knives and spoons that have handles that match the colors of the plates. They've got enough to have company for supper with plates left over for having a piece of cake on. Abbie's happy because they're made out of Melmac. That means they can't ever break. If they're Melmac, they last a lifetime.

At night after she comes home from a date, Abbie opens up her hope chest—it's made out of cedar and has a key she wears on a chain around her neck—and she takes everything out. We unfold the towels and I count them and then she folds them back up. I tie the apron around her waist and tell her what I want her to fix me for supper, and she reads me the recipe for sloppy joes or devil's food cake.

"When I've got my very own house, you can come and stay with us," she says. "Me and The Merchant'll get one of them special davenports that has a bed inside of it and that'll be for you."

the stone angel

What happened is the old man went crazy. I don't know how else to say it. They ended up taking him over to Logansport. It all happened so fast. It was while he was at work. These guys found him all hunched over in a corner at the factory crying and saying stuff that nobody could make any sense out of. Abbie said it had something to do with how he thought he was Jesus. A bunch of guys all dressed in white jumped on him and tied him up in a straitjacket just the way they do in the movies.

"He wants to see you," Mom says. "The doctors claim it'll do him some good."

"All he's talking about is his Little Lana," Abbie says. She makes a face at me.

"Are you guys going?"

"Why should we? He didn't ask for neither one of us." The two of them are mad because Earl Schertz stopped coming over to visit after he heard the old man went nuts. Everybody all over town's talking about it. Schertzie didn't even call Mom or anything and when she went in to Molly's Bakery and bought an apple turnover, he acted like he'd never laid eyes on her before. She said he took the money from her without even trying to touch her hand.

They drive me over to Logansport and drop me off out in front of this big red brick building that looks like a schoolhouse except there's black iron gates on all the windows with icicles dangling down. The closer I get to it, the more that building seems to get bigger and bigger while I shrink way up till I'm sure I won't be able to reach the door handle to let myself in.

I have to sit in this room practically filled up with a big statue of an angel carved out of stone. She has gigantic wings and her hands are folded like she's praying. She has a smile on her face that gives me the creeps. I sit there and sit there, waiting and waiting while all these nurses swish by pushing their little carts. The old man doesn't even know who I am when the nurse finally takes me in.

"I've got a little girl named Lana," he says. "She's cute as a button. Loves more than anything to sit up on her daddy's lap.

"Tell me something," he says. "Ain't I the spitting image of Abe Lincoln?" He rubs the long prickly whiskers on his chin. "You know the Gettysburg Address?" He starts saying it himself before I even get a chance to begin.

He has on one of them white hospital gowns they give you, the kind that ties down the back. He's not tied up to his bed the way Abbie said he'd be. "See that one over there?" The old man points at the man in a plaid housecoat laying on the next bed watching the baseball game on TV. "He's a spy. A Russian. They're everywhere. Everywhere, I'm telling you. You can't get away from them."

He grabs my arm and leans over to whisper, "Do you know that Jesus Christ is on His way back? Any minute, when you least expect Him, there He'll be." His lips tickle my ear. His eyes have broken red veins in them and his skin looks grey like he's already dead.

solitaire

It's Easter Sunday and the old man is downstairs shuffling around in his black cardboard hospital slippers. Every once in a while he comes up and stands at the top of the stairs staring like he's about to say something then he turns and clomps back downstairs. I don't want to look at him with his red eyes and his hand like a chicken claw grabbing at the front of the stupid seersucker housecoat they gave him when he was in there. In the loony bin, Abbie keeps saying, like she just can't believe it's true. Mom says she thought they were going to lock him up and throw away the key, the way he was carrying on. Not just put him away for a measly three weeks. That's modern medicine for you, she says. They tie you up, plug you in, and zap. A few jolts of electricity and you're good as new. Whenever she talks about it she doesn't even lower her voice or anything. She acts like the old man forgot how to speak English.

We're not even celebrating Easter. Mom says I'm too old to be wanting to go on any egg hunts. I said she didn't have to hide the eggs or anything but it'd be fun to color them. She just gave me one of her looks so I shut up. Abbie's laying in bed acting like she's sick, waiting till The Merchant comes over and takes her out of here.

The old man turns the TV on full blast. This preacher's giving some kind of sermon about how we need to have peace in the world.

"Remember when Mom got us matching Easter outfits?" Abbie just groans and reaches under her pillow to turn up her transistor. Our hats had red wooden cherries on the brims and our dresses were made out of this see-through material that Mom starched so much the skirts stuck straight out all around. It felt kind of like being shoved in one of Schertzie's fancy cakes covered with swirly frosting.

I remember one Easter when I was a little kid I went downstairs early in the morning and Mom and the old man were in the kitchen drinking their coffee and acting like nothing was going on. Easter eggs were hiding all over the place. I could see them peeking out from under the leaves of Mom's plants and up on the shelf in the kitchen behind the black china teapot that used to be Mamaw Franklin's. I even found one in the icebox and another one on the rack in the oven. Mom and the old man laughed in a nice way and said what a good eye I had.

Now Mom's in the kitchen smoking her cigarettes and drinking her coffee and playing solitaire. She says we have to live with the old man now. The doctor says so and the lawyer says so. He's harmless now. He won't hurt a fly.

earthquake

M r. Ritter is pacing back and forth in front of this map he pulled down over the chalkboard, tapping his pointer on the floor the way he does, telling us about how come there's earthquakes. His voice goes up and down like he's singing us a song.

"See here? Right up here?" He traces the boot of Italy then points to a purple blob on the map across from it. "That's Yugoslavia. Two thousand people lost their lives in an earthquake disaster just this year." There's a smudge of chalk on his baggy grey pants.

"Now, there are earthquakes all the time. But not all of 'em lead to disasters like they had here in Yugoslavia. If it's a little bitty earthquake, you might not even know it. You might think you're hearing a semi rumbling through town. But if it's a big one, like the ones they get in Japan," he stabs at the map again. "Then you've got just ten seconds after you feel the first vibration. Just ten seconds to run for cover. Then everything trembles and shakes so hard bricks come loose and fall right out of the buildings."

Bobbie Andrews is sitting in the front row, waving her hand in the air so hard she practically falls out of her seat.

"Yes, Bobbie," Mr. Ritter says, like he's real tired and can't hardly hold back a yawn. Mr. Ritter is the only man teacher I've ever had. There's another one in high school that teaches English. But all the other teachers, not counting boys' Phys Ed, are ladies. Mom says a man that teaches school has got to be "that way." Why else would he want to spend the day with a bunch of snotty-nosed kids? I asked her what "that way" meant, but she just rolled her eyes and thrust her hip out to the side, flipping her hand around like a princess waiting for somebody to grab ahold of her fingers and kiss her hand. Mr. Ritter puts his hand on his hip the way Mom did and taps his pointer on the floor, waiting to see what old Bobbie'll say.

She sits up straight and pulls her skirt down around her knees. "The Bible tells us, for them that sin, the earth'll open right up," she says. "It'll open right up and swallow them sinners down alive. Houses and all." She looks around the room like she's sure any minute we'll all disappear.

Mr. Ritter yanks the map so hard it whirls up tight with a snap. He starts drawing what he calls seismic waves on the board. "Right underneath the earth's surface there's a bunch of rocks that're squeezing and stretching. Remember now, what I told you? How there's an enormous heat in the center of the earth? Put your thinking caps on, now. It's this heat that stretches the rocks till they break. Sometimes this makes the earth's surface crack. But the earth does *not*. I repeat. Does *not*. Open up and swallow anybody."

Fat Wendell Gilkey—the boy that sits behind me—a farmboy that comes in on the school bus with flecks of manure and yellow straw on the cuffs of his pants—leans forward and whispers. His Juicy Fruit breath is hot in my ear. "I got somethin' here 'at's ready to be swallered up." He jiggles his leg up and down, up and down. The back of my seat is hooked to his desktop, and him doing that makes me dizzy. The boys sitting near us snicker and laugh through their noses. I take tiny sips of air so nothing moves in my chest or my belly. I hold my elbows clenched against my sides, chewing on the inside of my cheeks. If I do that long enough, after a while I can almost disappear.

"Wendell?" Mr. Ritter says. "You got something to share with the rest of us?" Wendell grins, his big round face bright red. His striped jersey is pulled tight over his rolls of fat.

All of a sudden the classroom door opens wide and Gus Riley is standing there, holding his white cowboy hat, the badge on his jacket like an extra eye, staring us all down. "Could ya step out here with me in the corridor for a minute?" he asks Mr. Ritter.

As soon as the heavy door closes behind them, Bobbie Andrews turns around in her seat, her eyes like two green marbles darting over our faces. "You figure Mr. Ritter's getting sent to jail?" she asks. A spitball flies across the room and hits her right smack dab in the middle of the forehead. She looks stunned for a second, then turns and lifts her desktop, crouching underneath. She never gets it that the whole class hates her for being the preacher's kid.

Spitballs are flying across the room every which way and all the kids are ducking under their desks. "Bombs over Tokyo," Keith Rayle hollers. Then it seems like half the kids are out of their seats rushing around. Mike Cain's in front of the room, slapping his arm up and down, making loud fart sounds. Penny's sitting on her desktop, her legs crossed so you can see the hooks on her garter belt up under her skirt. She's looking into her compact, teasing her hair with a rat-tail comb. I stare at the book open in front of me and act like I'm all alone. At the top of the page, in bold letters, it says: PREDICTION OF EARTHQUAKES. The letters slide together and disappear in a blur. Wendell Gilkey taps me on the back. He taps me again and again, his fingertip sharp between my shoulders. Tap, tap, tap. I have seen his thick red hands with the split raggedy fingernails caked with dirt. I think of that finger of his jabbing me in the back of my white sweater. I turn around in my seat all ready to say *quit it* in my meanest voice. I turn around and there he is with his eyelids flipped up and stuck inside out. His eyelashes look like some kind of creepy bug legs crawling above his red, bloody-looking eyelids.

"Here he comes!" Mike Cain hollers.

Mr. Ritter's shadow is on the thick glass above the door. He stands turning the brass doorknob a tiny bit like he's giving us a signal. All the kids that've been cutting up rush to sit still with their hands folded on their desks before Mr. Ritter opens the door. He is a thin, bony man with hunched shoulders. If you saw him on *Alfred Hitchcock,* you'd know right away he was the one that did it. His pale eyes flick across the room and land on me. That's when I know the marshal is there because of me, like I'm the murderer on TV about to be taken off to prison. It feels like I'm whirling around on the Octopus at the carnival, spinning and turning, holding on for dear life, my belly dropping right out of me.

Mr. Ritter is leaning on my desk. His white shirt is so thin I can see the ribs on his undershirt right through it. There are yellow stains around the buttonholes. In his shirt pocket, the cigarettes are lined up in a pack of Lucky Strikes.

"Go get your things," he whispers. "Mr. Riley's here to take you on home." After he says that, he looks kind of embarrassed and he starts wiping at his face with his big white hanky. He walks up to the front of the room and slowly erases the drawing of seismic waves.

For a split second, I can't remember my combination. Then the numbers kind of flash in my mind. 22-16-43. I twirl the black dial around, but then I can't remember if I've passed 16 already or not. It feels like I've been standing there in front of my locker for hours. When I get to 43 it doesn't open so I have to do it again. Gus Riley doesn't say a thing. He leans on the grey lockers, staring up at the ceiling. Down the corridor, the janitor is wringing his mop, the bucket clanking, the grey stringy mop like an old lady's tangled head of hair sloshing across the floor. There are my books on the shelf: *Math in Everyday Life, The World Around Us, The Red Badge of Courage, Health and Safety.* My wrinkled gym suit and a damp towel shoved in the corner. A pile of papers all heaped up every which way on the bottom. There is my lunch sack, the brown paper stained with oil, the top folded down. Inside, the peanut-butter-and-jelly sandwich I wrapped in waxed paper that morning. A too-ripe red apple. I stand there looking at all my things, but I don't take anything. I stand there looking and looking like I'm in a dream. Gus Riley clears his throat and starts to whistle softly. I slip my red corduroy car coat on, buttoning the wooden buttons up slow.

I follow Gus Riley down the corridor. His silver handcuffs dangle down the side of his leg. His gun in the thick leather holster rocks from side to side. I wonder if it's loaded. If he ever has to use it on anybody the way the cops do on TV. I heard how he shot a mangy dog over behind the drugstore once, but I wasn't there to see it.

We go past the music room where the fifth-graders are lined up at the piano, their shoulders swaying as they sing "Joshua Fought the Battle of Jericho." Past the science room with the diagram of an earthworm pasted over the thick glass window, the parts labeled in red ink: *Brain. Hearts. Mouth. Intestine.* Down the polished wooden stairs, my hand on the smooth banister, dust motes swirling in the faint light coming through the window at the top of the stairs. Gus Riley presses his hat tight on his head. He shifts his pants like the gun and holster are weighing him down.

When we pass the principal's office, the floorboards creak and Miss Armstrong looks up from her typing, then down again real fast. The tap-tap-tap of her typing follows us down the hall to the front door. Gus Riley pushes it open and holds it for me to walk through under his arm. I think of how us kids used to play London Bridge, ducking under the outstretched arms, waiting for them to fall and lock us up.

Gus Riley stands at the top of the cement steps watching the flag furl and unfurl, flapping in the wind, the metal clanging on the flagpole. I look up at the sky. It's thick with clouds like wads of dirty cotton. The wind is so cold it feels like sharp teeth biting my bare legs. I shove my hands into my pockets. There is the nickel for my lunch milk. Soon, the other kids will be lined up in the cafeteria, pushing their orange trays along. In the corner of my pocket, with the bits of lint and sand, I touch the round circle of a Life Saver. I take it out. Wint-O-Green. I feel the way I do when I did something wrong but I can't figure out what it is and I'm standing on the back porch, the sound of hamburg frying and voices in the kitchen, and it's suppertime and I have to go in.

Gus Riley's car is parked at the curb behind the school bus. It looks like a big white icebox, the red light on top like a monkey hat. The gold letters on the door spell out WINDFALL POLICE. Gus Riley squinches his eyes up and turns to look back at the schoolhouse like he can see right through the bricks. Then he pulls his gloves on and opens his car door. He takes his hat off and tosses it on the seat. Everything he does is so slow it's like he's moving underwater. He opens the back door for me, and Abbie's in there blowing her nose on an old dirty Kleenex. She has on her wool plaid skirt with the big gold safety pin on the front and her yellow angora sweater. The car smells like her Jean Naté. She won't even look at me or anything. Her eyes are all red around the edges and her face is pale the way it gets when she's about to have a coughing fit. I have to climb over her legs, careful not to step on her toes since she won't scooch over. My bare leg brushes the scratchy hose on her knee. By accident, I jab her in the side with my elbow. I close my eyes, waiting for her to smack me on the side of my head, but nothing happens. "What's up?" I ask. Abbie stares at her fingernails. There is a chip in the pink nail polish on her thumbnail. She scrapes and scrapes at it, peeling the pink clear off.

The road stretches out ahead of us like we could drive and drive and never get home. I feel like I did that time me and Mom were driving home and a dark funnel cloud way across the cornfields was heading in our direction. Outside, the wind was whipping against the car so bad Mom couldn't hardly steer and the wind was whistling like when the train comes through town. Mom didn't know if we ought to pull over beside the road or keep going. She couldn't remember if it was safer to be in the car or in a house or out in the open in the middle of a field, so we kept driving really fast. It got pitch dark like it was the middle of the night. When we got home, the electricity was off. We ran around opening up all the windows so the house wouldn't explode. Then we huddled down cellar with a flashlight, waiting for the roof to blow off.

Mom's in the front room warming herself standing over the heater, one foot on each side of the floor grate. She doesn't even turn around. Me and Abbie go over and stand next to her. Heat is blowing up Mom's wool skirt. The air smells like hot cloth and warm skin.

"Can you believe this is all that's left?" Mom holds up the old man's billfold, the brown leather stained and wet, the edges black and peeling back like skin on the edge of a broken blister.

"What happened?" I say. "What?"

Mom and Abbie look at each other. Then Abbie starts crying and crying, not even trying to blow her nose. Her head bobs up and down. She makes a soft sound, like she's about to sneeze or hiccup. Her fingers dig into her cheeks, making bright red blotches. She rubs The Merchant's ring, fingering the stone like it's got some magic powers. Her whole face glistens with tears that smudge the black mascara, making black streaks. Seeing her cry like that makes the tears rush up to my eyes. I squeeze them tight. Tight. But the tears come anyway all salty on my lips, trickling down my neck, making my collar damp.

Mom's got these wet dollar bills that're stuck together. The paper is thin and raggedy, about to tear as she works at the edges, peeling one away from the other. Her thumbs smooth George Washington's face. "Ain't it something?" She shakes her head. "Ain't it something these here dollar bills made it? Through all that?" The dollars flutter in the heat. "One. Two. Three," she counts. "One for each of us. Ain't it something?"

She holds a damp dollar bill up so close to me I can almost taste the wet paper. There is the eye over the pyramid, just like I always pictured God's eye would be if you could see Him up in the sky.

"Take a good look," Mom says. "This here's a miracle if I ever did see one."

bean salad

The news spreads as quick as a grass fire at the end of summer. The phone wires slung from house to house hum and buzz all up and down the alley. Even before it hits the papers, everybody knows. All day long there's the murmur of "I'm so sorry" and "What a shame" coming through the front door.

Winona Flowers is sitting in the old man's chair, smoking, pinching a cigarette between her thumb and forefinger. "It's the do-gooder brigade," she says.

Marvella brings my favorite lemon cake and a baked ham. She stays, making coffee, combing my hair, cleaning up the kitchen for Mom. All these ladies from church come even though they've snubbed Mom for a million years. They bring potato salad. Macaroni and cheese. Meatloaf. Bean salad. Baked beans. Beans and franks.

Leota Tupper comes over with a plate of fried chicken. I have to run out and help her up the step. I take the plate from her and hold on to her elbow with my other hand to help her along. Her skin feels like tissue paper and she's so thin it seems like she could blow away if the wind took ahold of her. She stands at the front door telling Mom in her shaky voice about what a shame it is. "If there's anything I can do, you let me know," she says. Marvella comes out of the kitchen and helps her get back home. "What were you a thinking, getting up out of your bed like that?" I hear Marvella scolding her. "That poor little thing," Leota says.

Mom's laughing about how Leota brought us the same chicken the church ladies fixed her. "That old biddy didn't fry this up," she says. "Besides. Whoever heard of a plate of fried chicken without the breasts? She kept the best part for her own supper and brought us what was left when she was done picking it over."

"She'll probably send you a sympathy card somebody sent her clear back when Mr. Tupper croaked," Winona says. "She's been saving it for a special occasion."

All day long there's somebody at our front door. Even Mrs. Reeb, who never steps outside if she can help it, comes with a dried-beef-and-potato casserole. She stands just inside the front door, wringing her hands.

"Bob is all broke up about not finding Floyd sooner," she tells Mom. "He saw the smoke when he was headed over the bridge to deliver the Critneys' mail. It just didn't hit him till it was too late to do any good.

"Penny says to say hi to you," she tells me. She's wiping her eyes with the back of her hand.

Abbie is in the kitchen looking at all the food like she can't believe her eyes.

"It's better than Thanksgiving," she says.

"Better'n Fellowship Sunday," I tell her. The icebox is full, every shelf has something on it and the table is covered. Abbie gasps and holds on to her sides, singing, "Beans, beans, the musical fruit." She scoops a big spoonful of bean salad onto her plate. She takes a chicken leg. The Merchant has his plate full. Winona Flowers helps herself to some ham and cole slaw.

"Here comes Neila Grimes," Mom says. "About to bust her gut coming down the sidewalk. That old battle ax. She's such a nib nose, she probably wants to get her eye on what everybody else brought."

She's wearing white leather shoes and her white hose droops like cobwebs around her thin ankles. She hauls herself up on the porch and knocks, hollering, "Yoo-hoo!"

"You get this one," Mom says.

"Well. Least I could do in your time of trouble." Neila's all out of breath, handing me a heavy platter covered with wax paper. It's her famous lime Jell-O mold shaped like a cross. I rub the back of my leg with my toe.

"Your mother holding up all right?"

"Yeah."

"Well. Now." She sighs and pats her blue-grey hair, then

smooths her skirt. "It's a terrible thing. A tragedy. Just something awful. But I reckon it couldn't be helped. Your mother to home?" she asks, craning her neck to try to see around me at who all's in the front room. I tell her no and shut the door with my foot.

Abbie and The Merchant are sitting side by side on the davenport with their plates of food on the coffee table. He has one arm wrapped around Abbie's shoulders. He leans in close to her. She looks down at her lap. She's never looked so pretty. Her skin is pale like all the tears washed her down to new skin. She didn't spray and tease her hair so it's loose and spread down over her shoulders. The Merchant lifts it aside, tucking it carefully behind her ear, and whispers to her, trying to get her to have something to eat but she just stares down at the plate on her lap.

"The worst thing," she says, her voice full of tears, "is how everybody knows. Even folks that don't know us know."

Mom is at the door again. "Looky here. Can you believe it? Pain-in-the-Ass MacAbee with a lemon meringue pie. You know what I'd like to do with this!"

"I dare you!" Winona laughs like she's a hen that just laid an egg.

"Look who got down off her high horse to bake us this." Mom holds the pie up under my nose and I start to cry. This loud voice comes from inside of me asking *why why why* and I can't stop it. I feel like all the neighbors are standing in their backyards listening to me. Like my voice reaches clear uptown so that folks picking up their mail or stopping to have a jelly donut at Jack's can hear me. I don't even care. Mom stands there with her fists clenched like she's about to punch somebody. I grab her hands to pull her arms around me. Her fingers feel like ice cubes.

"Someone's at the door," Winona says. "You want me to get it?"

"No. I will." Mom acts like she can't wait to get away from me.

It's Shreida Huckaby with another bowl of bean salad. Mom dumps the whole thing into the trash, including the bowl. "I thought about handing it right back, telling her we already got enough bean salad to feed an army. Why don't you fix us something else? What d'ya figure she'd've done if I had?"

ain't it something?

I t'll do her good to get out of the house." Mom fishes around in her pocketbook for her car keys. "Don't'cha think?" She talks to Abbie about me like I'm not even there. I haven't gone anyplace except for the funeral parlor since the old man died. I haven't gone back to school even though I've missed over a week. I'm thinking maybe I'll never go back. It just doesn't seem right for me to start worrying about my homework or whether or not I'll pass the Earth Science test after what happened to the old man. I figure when somebody dies, you ought to just sit around a long time and think about it till it feels right to go on.

Mom and Abbie have been planning our future. Mom's going to sell the house to the first person that'll take it. Then she's going to take a bus back East and buy us a new house. Abbie's trying to decide whether or not to go with us. If she stays, she's going to quit high school and marry The Merchant. I don't have any choice about it.

"I won't know anybody there." Abbie lists the things wrong with going. She'll have to start all over. No one'll even know her name.

"But just think," Mom tells her. "There'll be dozens of opportunities to change that." By opportunities, she means dates. She acts like Massachusetts is filled with all these guys that're dying to take them out.

Mom hands me my car coat and I put it on. I don't even try to get out of going. I can tell she isn't about to budge on it. Abbie sits in the middle, fiddling with the radio. She listens to a station for a second, then flicks the dial till she finds the next one. As we drive out of town, songs and voices skitter through the car like the guys calling out at the carnival. ". . . Our Day Will Come . . .", ". . . rather fight than switch . . .", ". . . the fourth caller will . . .", "Doublemint, Doublemint, Doublemint . . .", "It's thirty-nine degrees in downtown Indianapolis. . . .", "There, I said it again."

"Here it is!" Abbie squeals and sits up tall, looking at herself in the rearview mirror, patting her hairdo. It's "I Will Follow Him," her latest favorite song. Abbie leans forward to turn the volume up high. She wiggles her shoulders like she's dancing. Her and Mom both sing along.

One thing Abbie can't stand is quiet. According to her, it's better to always have music on than it is to have to hear yourself think. When there's no radio around, she hums.

I stare out the window on my side. A mist, like clouds rising up from the ground, hangs around the silos and along the fences of the farmers' fields. The snow is all melted. In Indiana, in the springtime, the ground freezes and thaws and freezes and thaws till it turns to thick black mud. Then it starts raining like crazy. Our backyard is already filled up like a lake with the water halfway up the trunks of the cherry trees. The sump pump down cellar has been pumping water out all day and night.

When I was little, I used to always wade around the backyard with the water up to my knees, the thick mud oozing up through the mat of oak leaves covering the ground. I'd stay out there till I was blue with cold, wishing I'd catch polio. Afterwards, I'd limp around the house, dragging one of my legs behind me, hoping Danny Kaye would come down the alley to get me the way he did that kid in *The Five Pennies*.

"Here we are." Mom shifts the car into gear and pulls into this gas station across from the A&W in Tipton. The emergency brake clicks the way it does when she pushes it down with her toe. Abbie scoots across the seat after me. Her and Mom walk ahead, around the side of the gas station. I follow them past this stack of old black tires that looks like it's about to topple over. Some of them are from tractors and they have huge zigzag treads. There's a pile of silvery hubcaps next to a red air pump where a boy's putting air in his bicycle tires.

"You getting a hurry on spring?" Mom asks him.

"Yep." He bends over his bike to screw on the caps. I hear thunder, but when I look up there's a jet stream zipping across this tiny blue spot between the clouds. It lets out another sonic boom. Out in front, a car pulls up at the pump and the bell dings. "Fill 'er up?" some guy asks.

Mom's high heels scrape the pavement. As her and Abbie walk they lean towards each other, like their heads are about to touch. Any minute, I expect Mom to turn and whisper into Abbie's ear.

Out in back, surrounded by a chain-link fence, there's a bunch of old wrecked-up cars. Abbie calls it an auto graveyard. We pass a green car with the side caved in and the hood thrown up. Old dried-up weeds are sprouting out of where the engine used to be. There's a white convertible with the front end crinkled up, and a green station wagon crushed almost flat. "I hope nobody was in that thing when it got hit," Mom says. "Looks like a semi landed on it."

The doors have popped open. On the backseat, there's a dirty white baby blanket with circus clowns on it. Mom and Abbie walk ahead up the road to where it turns to gravel and dirt. There are car doors flung all over the place and the ground is so soggy with puddles I have to be careful to step where it's not too squishy. A pair of grey work gloves looks like twisted fingers reaching up out of the mud.

Mom and Abbie stop when they get to this one car. It doesn't hardly look like a car at all. It's really just a hunk of metal, orange with rust. You can see it was once a convertible but the top's completely gone. There's just the metal frame like the spokes of an umbrella. The tires are half burnt away with some wires poking out. All the windows are gone, even the front and back windshield.

"Here it is," Mom says. "This is it."

Abbie's leaning in on the passenger's side, trying to slam the glove compartment shut.

"Don't cut yourself," Mom says when I pick up a sheet of glass that's all cracked like the marbles we used to fry. We'd put them in the cast-iron pan with the lid on and turn the flame on high so we could hear them pop and see the cracked patterns inside. Abbie's humming but I can't figure out what the song is. Tiny square chunks of broken glass are sprinkled like teeth over the hood and dashboard and across the seats and floor. The rug is soggy and black. The seat cushions are bubbled and blistered with strips of the seat covers peeled back and curled tight like the bark on a cherry tree. Yellow foam rubber pokes through, looking like the burnt bottom of a sponge cake.

This guy in a blue uniform walks up. "This one's not going anywhere fast now, is it?" His teeth are large and shiny in his tanned leathery face. Across his shirt pocket, the name *Lud* is stitched in white.

Mom giggles the way she always does when some guy talks to her. It doesn't matter what kind of guy it is, she giggles and acts all bashful. "I reckon not." She takes her pack of cigarettes out of her pocketbook, tucking a cigarette into the V her fingers make.

Lud leans forward to light it for her, flicking his lighter open and cupping his hands around the blue flame. When he snaps it shut, I jump like I'm waking up from a dream. I notice the rearview mirror on the outside of the car looks brand new.

"Did ya hear about the fellow that was in it?" he asks.

"We sure did." Mom walks away and coughs a little. "Ain't it something?" She acts like she's real interested in this pickup truck that doesn't have any headlights, just holes like empty eye sockets.

"We've had more folks come to have a look at this one than we've ever had for anything else." Lud wipes his hands with a red rag, then he takes a comb out of his back pocket and runs it through his slicked-back hair. "It was in all the papers," he says. "Folks do like to have a look at a thing like 'at."

"I know what you mean." Mom has her arms wrapped around her waist like she's hugging herself.

"How long you figure he lasted? I mean, before he jumped?"

Mom's staring over at all the cars they have out in back. There's a white wooden fence and behind it there's the big white screen for the drive-in movie. I remember how when I was little, sometimes me and Mom would be out driving around and we'd pull over beside the road to watch the movie. It seemed like the big faces were coming right out of the sky. We couldn't hear what was going on but we'd sit and watch till I got tired. Now, the house where you buy your popcorn is poking up out of a huge puddle of water looking like a marshmallow floating on a cup of cocoa. There is this little river rushing by, and more wrecked cars—white and blue and green and red, tilted every which way—are half buried in the muddy water. With their hoods up, they look like some kind of fancy frogs in the *National Geographic*.

"You have to wonder about somebody that does a thing like 'at." Lud's smoking a pipe, fussing with his lighter trying to keep it going. "Have to be out of your right mind, wouldn't you say?"

"Look at this," Abbie's leaning in the car. She has one hand on the steering wheel, her thin white fingers wrapped around the twisted sunken circle of plastic. The horn is all caved in and the dashboard and the steering wheel look like the picture of cooling lava we have in our science book. Abbie pulls out a pair of glasses with the lenses gone and earpieces melted. She pinches them with the tips of her fingers like they're too hot to hold. They're exactly like the old man's.

Mom crushes her cigarette out with her toe, twisting it back and forth while Lud watches, like he has never seen a lady do that before.

We drive clear over to Dearborn to this place called Leo's Lounge where Mom says nobody'll know us. We can let our hair down, she says.

It's so dark inside after being outdoors, I have to stand still to let my eyes adjust. The air smells like spilled beer and sawdust, peanuts, and smoke. Over in the corner, up next to the plate-glass window, pool balls are knocking softly against each other. A guy with a hat pulled down almost to his nose leans across the green felt. I'm next to the cigarette machine reading the different brand names. Winston. Tarryton. Salem. Lucky Strike. I always read the names of things, even when I know what it's going to say. That's just the kind of person I am. Where Abbie's always got to have some music, I've got to have me something to read.

Guys in plaid flannel shirts are lined up at the dark polished wooden bar, perched on the edge of their stools listening to some kind of sports on the radio. A crowd cheers.

"What'd I tell ya? What'd I tell ya?" This one skinny, bald guy with his two front teeth missing slaps the guy next to him on his back. He slumps forward, staring at his mug of beer. "Don't be a spoilsport. Cough up."

Mom and Abbie are already sitting beside each other in a booth in back. I slide in across from them. Abbie's flipping through the songs on the jukebox. She has a quarter in front of her.

"All they've got here is oldies," she says, punching in the buttons. The waiter, a short guy bent half over with his head jutting forward, slinks across the room with a tray of drinks. "One highball." He places a glass in front of Mom. "And two cherry Cokes."

Mine and Abbie's have a green cherry floating on top of the crushed ice. Abbie picks hers up by the stem and pops it in her mouth. Mom stirs her drink with this little red stick that looks like a sword. She stirs it around and around, her eyes flicking towards the door, then over to the bar and back to her drink. She drinks it fast, like she's dying of thirst. I sip mine through the paper straw. On the side of my glass it says *Coke* in white letters. Mom pushes the sleeves of her white sweater up over her elbows and leans on the table. She lights another cigarette with the tip of the one she's finished with. She's drumming her red-painted fingernails on the tabletop.

"Compliments of the gents at the bar." The waiter sets three full glasses in front of us. He takes away me and Abbie's first ones even though we haven't had a chance to finish them. Mom looks over my head, grins, and lifts her glass. She clinks her glass against Abbie's. Then she reaches across the table to clink mine.

"Here's to the old man." She looks me right in the eye like she's never seen me before in her life. Her pupils are large and dark and I know if I was close enough I'd be able to see myself looking back.

"Here's to the old man," she says again. "That son of a gun. He's burnt to a crisp."

Abbie kind of gasps and claps her hand over her mouth. Mom tilts back and takes a big swallow. I watch the drink go down her throat. I have that floaty feeling I get like I'm up near the ceiling looking down at everything that's going on.

"Where'd you go? Planet Mars?" Mom's waving her hand in front of my face. People are always doing stuff like that to me, snapping their fingers sometimes or tweaking my cheek.

"Whatsa matter with her?" The skinny guy twirls around on

his stool and jerks his thumb at me. "We ain't so ugly she's got to bawl her eyes out over it, now are we?"

I hear somebody say, "It's the Franklin kid." Then nobody says anything.

On the way back home, Abbie leans back against the seat and acts like she's dozing. She leaves the radio on the same station. She doesn't even switch it when a commercial comes on. When we drive past the peat bogs, I roll my window down to let in the sweet, mossy smell. "You playing freeze-out?" Mom asks. "You off your rocker or something?"

"Mom!" Abbie says it like a warning. After what happened to the old man, with his going crazy and all, none of us is ever supposed to make a joke about it again.

"I'm a nutcase. I flipped my lid!" I want to scream. I wonder what will happen if I yank open the door and fling myself beside the road.

"Guess what?" Abbie turns to look at Mom.

"What?"

"I figured out what I'm going to do."

"You did, did you? So what'll it be? Adventure or the tried-and-true?"

"I'm getting married. You can call me Abigail Irene Merchant from now on."

the white river

H e planned it. As much as someone in his state of mind
could plan anything. A mind where every thought
echoed like footsteps in an empty warehouse. Planned
it, while feeling guilty of a crime he knows he committed. Even
though he can't remember what he did.

Images that have haunted him for years hover just out of his
reach, not quite gone, yet nothing he can get a good look at, just
a dimly lit room with a flimsy curtain over the window.

He planned it, in this state of mind, moving around the rooms
of his house in his hospital slippers, muttering, "My house. This
is my house. My household. I am the head of the household."
Wandering through the rooms up and down the stairs. There is
an image of a key left on a table tugging at him like a tiny child
at his sleeve. If only he could go back and pick that key up, he'd
know how to use it. Know where it fit. But he can't remember
what table he left it on and none of the tables in this house look
right. None of them have a thick black key nestled in the doilies
or beside the lamps. He does remember the day they brought him
home, how he had stood blinking in the bright sunlight, uncertain
which house was his. He can still feel the neighbors behind the
fluttering lace, all up and down the street, fingers lifting the venetian blinds. He feels them looking now while he's looking into the
mirror and trying to see beyond his eyes shining back at him.
While he's sitting in his chair in the front room watching the Viet-
nam War on television, talking to himself, saying, "I fought a
war. Yeah. Me and old Hairy Ass Truman. We showed the
Krauts. We got them Japs. Blew them off the face of the earth,
didn't we?"

253

He planned it as much as a thing like that is ever planned. Working on it as if he were two people. One going through the steps, planning, figuring, moving the pieces around. The other lying on his back in a field of grass watching a kite float off up into the clouds, the string broken forever, the red kite floating off forever while the other one planned.

Sometimes he gets a glimpse of himself cowering in the corner of his booth, under his workbench at the factory. Then comes the straitjacket. It's just like they say in all the jokes, he thinks, even as they strap his arms to his sides, pulling the flaps tight around him. Even as the electricity crackles through him.

On his first night home, he heard Ruth in the kitchen telling the girls she had no choice but to take him back. They had to live with him now. "The doctors say he's harmless. They took away his mean streak," she said.

He knew they didn't believe her. He pictured the mean streak that used to run through him like a thick dark river inside his bones. Now there was nothing running through him.

At first he thought God wanted him to take all of them. He'd stood with the matches in his hand, the yard around the edge of the house soaked with gasoline. Then he knew that wasn't it at all. After that, the emptiness inside gave way to the voice. God began to talk to him in earnest. To tell him the end was near and He needed Floyd's help.

Floyd decided to tell Lana about it, sure that if anyone could understand, she would. She was the most like him. Everybody said. He made her sit on the davenport and began.

"Didn't God talk to Moses from a burning bush? Now didn't he? And you know what that means, don't you? Fire. Even the waters'll burn. God says we know that all things work together for good to them that love God. By golly, I've loved God one way or another my whole life. Worked for the good of God even when the whole bunch of you laughed in my face. Didn't I let the word of God move me? Didn't I? And when God says all things work together, he means everything. Do you hear me? Are you listening to your old man? Sit up straight and act like it. I want you to know when God says all things, he means all things. Even the lowly little ants crawling on the ground. Them ones we all

254

step on and don't even notice. I'm telling you God's got all things working together. Everything loves God. But man doesn't know shit half the time even if he's standing right in it up to his gills. Man can hardly tell his ass from his elbow. But I know. I know what God's been saying all these years. I read the holy word. I've got the word of God whispering in my ear and don't you forget it. God's been talking louder and louder. Now He's telling me that the end is near. He's saying, Floyd, I'm calling you. You know all things work together for the good because all things love God. Most men are too busy fornicating and gambling and guzzling booze to pay any attention to loving God. Most of them won't even know I've been sent here to show them the way. It's women that get men off the track. If it wasn't for women, this world would be a better place. Men would ride a freight train right straight up to heaven. But women put a fire in men. They put a fire in men and men can't quench that fire. And the fire never goes out. Once it starts, it never goes out. Are you listening to what I'm saying, young lady? Stop fidgeting around and look me in the eye. What's so important up there on the ceiling you can't look your old man in the eye? I'm telling you. The end is near and God is calling us both. Let's praise the Lord. Get down on your knees with me and praise the Lord."

Floyd is kneeling in the front room, his head bowed, when the back door slams and Lana races down the alley toward town.

Floyd is up at the first light, dressing in the dark room, his fingers fumbling with the buttons down the front of his shirt. He stands at the kitchen sink slurping hot black coffee while out the window, the morning sun tries to break through the low-lying clouds at the edge of the frozen fields. He listens to his family sleeping, to the groan of the furnace kicking on, thinking how the house will warm up by the time they are awake.

He pushes the back door open and coughs as the cold air hits his lungs. At first he is afraid the car won't start, but then the engine kicks over easily. He lets it idle a few minutes, enjoying the sound of the motor, thinking how this car is a dream come true, the best move he ever made. As he drives, he waits for a sign from God. He knows God will tell him where to stop. His long pale fingers clench the steering wheel as he leans forward, his *breath freezing on the windshield. He scrapes a circle in the thin sheet of ice, praying, "I am in your hands, Lord. Be my guide."*

He drives slowly, the only one on the road at this hour. Too early even for Bob Reeb. Too early even for the milkman. Sparrows flutter down from phone lines to perch on fenceposts. Mourning doves, fat and top heavy, scratch in the bare dirt beside the road. Floyd rolls down his window, the freezing cold air hitting his face, making him feel wide awake. He smiles and takes a cigarette out of his shirt pocket, taps it against the dashboard, and punches in the lighter. How he loves this car. He draws in a long deep breath of smoke, feeling suddenly young again. He remembers dancing, his feet moving to the music, and flicks on the car radio. There is Perry Como singing, "Catch a falling star and put it in your pocket." He sings along, remembering when the four of them used to go for drives, the kids little, squirming in the backseat. He sings the words loudly, tapping his foot on the floor, just missing the beat.

He swerves around the sharp curve beside an old farm cemetery and heads on down the road that cuts across the flat farmland. A mist is rising up like steam as the sun gets higher. But it is still a grey day. A day that promises snow. A grey bone-chilling day with the window down, no hat on, singing along to Perry Como and waiting for God's word.

He is halfway across the White River Bridge when it comes to him. Halfway across, his tires singing on the metal floor of the bridge, when he knows God is telling him this is the place. He backs right up from the middle. Doesn't wait to finish crossing and turn around. Backs up, catching a glimpse of his own eyes in the rearview mirror, startled for a moment, as if he'd forgotten he was still there. He backs off the bridge and pulls on to the dirt road, the nose of his car pointing out over the embankment where a path leads down to the banks of the White River.

The White River. All those summer evenings fishing under the bridge. They called it the singing bridge from the high-pitched hum the tires made passing overhead. Floyd remembers Lana scrambling down the path, the weeds nearly high as her head, a can of worms in her tiny hands. He can taste the sweet white meat of the catfish they fried over the wood fire.

The river is dark and swollen, the water thick with mud. Chunks of yellow ice move downstream. In places the banks of the river are encrusted with ice. Broken branches and bits of newspaper and dried weeds are stuck in it. He turns off the ignition and waits. Sometimes God is like a wind rushing through his body, turning him upside down. Sometimes God is colors, beautiful colors like rainbows pulled from his eyes. This time, God comes to him in a blaze of golden light. Floyd can feel God touch his forehead. He can feel a warm spot where God's fingers land. He can hear God saying, "The time is now, Floyd. I've got my fiery ladder waiting to take you up to the other side."

Floyd gets out of the car and opens the trunk. The back of his car looks like an airplane to him, the tailfins like wings. He remembers how it felt when he first got it, how good it felt to ride fast down the long straight roads, the top down, the sun on his back. A Thunderbird. Just like driving a dream.

He takes the gas can out and begins to slosh gasoline over the car, the front and back seats, the floor. He stands beside the car, pouring the gasoline all over himself, from head to toe, the gasoline soaking his clothes, running on his bare skin like oil. The words from the Bible are singing inside of him. "Thou anointest my head with oil. He leadeth me beside the still waters. He restoreth my soul."

"Here I am, Lord!" he hollers up at the sky, seeing there the most beautiful light, golden with flecks of rose. He kneels on the bare ground, praying silently, trying to clear his mind, make it ready to receive God's instruction. When he becomes aware of his face on the cold ground, his wet body, his oily clothes sticking to his skin, he gets up and tries to brush himself off. Shivering, his shoulders hunched around his ears, he gets back into the car. He rolls up the window, turns the key in the ignition, and puts the heat on high. "Sure as hell is a cold one," he whispers. "A cold day in hell."

He can't remember now why he pulled off the road. He thinks he is on his way to work and sees by his watch he is going to be late. He punches in the cigarette lighter, taps a Lucky Strike against the dashboard, is taking a deep drag, staring into the coils of the lighter, when he hears the first crackle of fire. His lap is in flames. His clothes burning, the flames licking up his arms like the tongues of fire at Pentecost. The car seat is burning beneath him. He tries to sit still, to breathe, to wait like the monk on the evening news. How he'd stood in the village square, the crowd in a circle around him, letting his body be a prayer. And in the middle of the flames, in the center, there was the dark shadow everyone knew was a man.

Floyd waits for God to show him what to do next. He is certain any minute there will be a ladder falling from the sky so he can climb up. He opens the car door, the metal handle hot under his hand, the roar and smell of fire seeming to come from inside of him. He runs across the bridge, his arms raised up toward that cold grey sky, crying, "Take me, God. I'm ready. Take me."

Behind him, there is a huge explosion as the gas tank rips through the floor of the car. The windows shatter. He runs. Forgetting that running makes fire burn faster. Forgetting to roll on the ground. There is no one there to knock him down. No one to wrap him in a blanket and smother the flames. He is shocked by the sound of his own weeping. All at once he realizes that God is not there, that he has been forsaken. Wanting only to undo what he's already started, hungry to live, Floyd rushes toward the river, plunging into the icy water.

starter home

The old man is dead and gone now and we're supposed to act all happy. Just about the second the funeral was over, Mom took a bus to Massachusetts to find us a new place to live. She says she picked out a nice white house with green shutters. It's modern, practically brand new since only one other family has ever lived in it. She keeps going on and on about it. "It's like one of them dream houses you've had your eye on," she says.

She sold our house to these folks from Jackson County. She said she had to snap up their offer before they got wind of the old man and decided it was haunted. "They think they're getting themselves a bargain," she keeps saying. "Little do they know."

I pack up all my toys. My doll house and all the furniture. The stuffed bear I got for my first Christmas. The fifty-two Golden Books I've saved since I was a little kid. Mom says I'm too old to keep all this crap. What I ought to be thinking about now rhymes with toys, she says. "Hint hint," she goes. "It starts with a *b.*" I don't care what she says. I'm keeping my stuff anyhow even though there isn't any room for it in the car. The Merchant's going to bring it all over to store in his father's barn for me so someday I can come back and get it. The minute I get my license, that's the first thing I'm going to do.

When Abbie and The Merchant got married I cried so bad Mom said you'd think I was at another funeral. That just made me cry worse. They didn't even get a model home. They ended up buying an old trailer The Merchant calls their starter home. There isn't hardly enough room for the two of them to be in it at the same time and The Merchant had to build a special shed for

259

Abbie to put her hope chest in. When you go in the trailer, you have to walk sideways around their gigantic red davenport. The davenport's the kind you pull out to make into a bed, but it's the only bed they've got so I can never even stay over. The kitchen table folds up against the wall after you eat and the sink is so teensy you can't hardly squeeze the dishes in there.

They don't even have a regular bathroom door. If you want any privacy, what you have to do when you go to the bathroom is you have to use the closet door to make a door in front of the toilet. It unfolds like an accordion and there's these magnets on it. You have to yank on it good and slap it up against these other magnets that're stuck on the wall next to the toilet. You end up with just enough room to sit down. If you barely bump the door with your knee or elbow, it comes flying right open. The rest of the time, the toilet is sitting there right out in the open.

Mom's in the kitchen singing "Our Day Will Come." When I bring my boxes downstairs, she says, "We're getting what you call a clean slate. In Massachusetts, we can start life over again. Just remember what I told you. If anybody asks, you say your father was killed in a wreck." She's told me this a million times already. She keeps saying it over and over again like I'm some kind of parakeet that's learning the words. It makes me mad, especially when she says "your father." She never once called him that when he was alive.

Abbie and The Merchant come in the back door with a chocolate cake and some vanilla ice cream. "Surprise," Abbie says. "We thought we'd give you a little going-away party."

"My life is starting over," Mom says. "They say life begins at forty. Well, here I am. Raring to go! Ready to make a stab at it." She stabs at the air with the cake knife and says it again.

Abbie gets out another knife and cuts us all some cake. We sit around eating it.

"She still don't want to go," Mom says, meaning me.

"Well," Abbie says. "It won't be so bad once she gets used to it."

"I can't believe she wants to stay in this godforsaken place. You two neither. Whyn't you both come with us?"

"Ruthie, you know I've got my work here," The Merchant says.

"I'll tell you one thing," Mom says. "You won't find people in Massachusetts acting all hoity-toity like Hoosiers do. You don't have to wait for them to hand you an invitation on a silver platter. I'm happy to be leaving this hellhole once and for all. Cripes."

She gets up and starts looking in the cardboard boxes we've kept our dishes in since way back when the old man tore the cupboards out. The new guy that's moving in says he's a handyman. He already measured so he can make cupboards. Mom says she's leaving most of our stuff here since it's easier to just get new.

"You sure you don't need any of this crap?" Mom asks Abbie, rattling the silverware box under her nose.

"Me and Donnie don't have room for one more teaspoon."

I go out back and lie in the grass, looking up at the stars. I can hear Mom laughing from the kitchen. Gretchie is beside me, digging a hole and snorting. A light is on in Penny's room. I wonder what she'd do if I went over and scratched at her screen the way I used to do in the old days. Say, come out and look at the stars. I look up at the sky and remember all those times me and Penny laid out back watching for *Sputnik*. I can see the blinking light of an airplane and the Big Dipper's so clear I can count every star.

I remember that time me and Penny were sleeping out back in a blanket tent over the clothesline and we heard this funny rattling sound we were sure was an escaped convict. We grabbed each other screaming bloody murder and her daddy ran out the back door in his underwear with his shotgun in his hands. It turned out to be Little Red. He got loose from his doghouse and was dragging his chain behind him, running in circles all over the yard. He was so used to going around and around in circles the way he did he couldn't even figure out how to run away.

Abbie and The Merchant come out back to say good-bye to me.

"Sit up," Abbie says. She bends down and squeezes my arm. "Someday you'll look back at all this and be glad you left."

"Promise me something," I say.

"What?"

"Promise."

"But I have to know what I'm promising."

"Just promise. Please."

"Okay. I promise."

"Cross your heart."

"Just tell me."

"Cross your heart."

"OK. OK." She makes a big cross over her chest.

"Call me if Lonnie MacAbee wakes up."

"That's it?" She looks over at the MacAbees' house where the candle's burning in Lonnie's room. A candle's been burning there day and night since he went into the coma.

"And if he does, you'll go over and ask him what it was like."

"But we haven't talked to him or any of the MacAbees since I don't know when."

"Yeah. I know. But if I was here when he woke up, I'd go ask him. Being in a coma's like being dead. He's the only one that could say what it's like. And anyhow, you promised."

Abbie pushes my bangs up and kisses my forehead. I can feel the print of her lipstick on my skin. I can't remember her ever kissing me before.

"OK, I'll ask him. I really will."

"You be good now, squirt." The Merchant's voice sounds all funny like he's crying but I can't tell for sure.

After they drive off, Mom comes out to the trash barrel. She throws in a bunch of papers and stuff and sets it on fire. The other night I caught her trying to burn up all the old pictures, but I rescued some even though she about had a conniption. I saved two of the old man. One from when he was young, sitting in a rowboat, his hands on the oars. His face is almost pretty, all smooth like a girl's with his lips full and his cheeks glowing. The other one I took of him out in the backyard, laying in his swimming trunks in the lawn chair, clutching a bottle of beer. He's got his eyes shut and he's smiling like he's having a good dream. I watch now as big paper ashes float up and drift down the alley. Mom doesn't see me laying in the grass. She doesn't say my name or anything. She just goes back in the house and turns the radio on loud. I can see her dancing past the lighted windows. She's got one arm wrapped around her waist and the other up in the air

262

like she's dancing with a partner, twirling and dipping up and down.

The thing is, the whole thing about saying the old man was killed in a wreck seems funny to me. I don't mean funny in the ha-ha kind of way. I mean strange on account of the way me and Abbie spent practically our whole lives laying in our beds playing The Old Man's Gone for Good. We always liked him to die best in a wreck. He'd be driving home in a thunderstorm with the rain whipping against his windshield, the wipers slapping back and forth like crazy. Or he'd be out at midnight in a blizzard, the snow freezing to the windows. Or he'd be in a tornado, the air full of dust and the wind practically blowing the car off the road. Every time he'd be leaning forward, trying to make out the road in front of him, when all of a sudden, up ahead, there'd be these blinding headlights. He could never get out of the reckless driver's way in time.

leaving

I get up early and sneak downstairs. Mom's asleep in her room lying on her side with her blue hairnet wrapped around her curlers. The house feels creepy with all our stuff packed up and Mom's knickknack shelves hanging empty on the wall.

My flip flops sound so loud I take them off and walk barefoot in the wet grass. Mourning doves are cooing, making their sing-song sounds and scratching around the roots of the oak tree. The crickets are still singing, but quiet and slow like they're about to go to sleep. I swing in my swing one last time to see if I can touch the leaves yet. When I was a little kid I always figured someday I'd be big enough, my legs would be long enough, so I could push myself way up that high. Back then I figured I'd be able to touch the sky someday too. But no matter how hard I pump and stretch my legs out, the leaves are still out of reach.

The sky's starting to get wispy pink clouds where the sun is coming up over the cornfields. The earth really does look flat. I remember how Mrs. Zugel laughed till she got tears in her eyes that time I said I thought Columbus was wrong. "Anybody that's got eyes in their head can see it's flat," I'd said.

I start up the alley towards town. Gretchie runs ahead to sniff everything. There's Old Hoostie Dean coming down the alleyway poking through everybody's trash barrel. There is the good smell of last night's half-burnt trash. The grass is soft with dew and already my pants are wet nearly up to my knees.

"The old man's already gone to work now," I think. Then I remember the old man's dead. Whenever I think of that word, *dead,* I feel hollow inside like a rubber doll squeezed flat.

264

Butchie MacAbee's out back swatting the flowers off his mother's plants with his badminton racket. I stop and sniff the honeysuckle on the edge of the alley. I breathe in deep and think, "This is the last time I'll ever do this." When I think this, my whole chest aches like my heart is too big to fit inside of me. I sniff the flowers good and long.

Iggie Purtlebaugh's house looks haunted now, with the paint all peeling off the wood and a cat sunning itself on each and every windowsill. Since Iggie died in his sleep last winter, nobody's been living in his house. Marvella goes over every night and feeds the cats. She found homes for four of them, but they just ran back to Iggie's to live.

At the end of the alley, up under the pawpaw trees, I stop and put my flip flops back on and click the leash on Gretchie's collar. As I walk up the brick sidewalk towards town the rubber slapping my heels seems to say, "Leaving leaving leaving. Home home home." I stare hard at the marigolds in Neila Grimes's front yard. I'm trying not to cry, and at the same time I'm trying to keep ahold of everything so I won't forget.

All that's open this early is the post office and Jack's. When I go in to say good-bye to Mr. Connors, he comes and leans on the counter.

"No mail yet for Box Four-four-four. Ain't you kind of early?"

"We're moving today, Connie."

"Well. Things just won't be the same without you coming in asking for your letters." His eyes get all red and he looks at someplace above my head instead of at my face. Just about everybody in town now does the same thing. When they look at me, they're thinking about the old man. Connie blows his nose with a loud honk and then turns and starts sifting through this stack of envelopes. "You take care of your mom now, you hear?"

I look in the screen door of Jack's. Bacon is frying on the grill. The factory workers in their grey clothes are reading the newspaper, drinking coffee, and eating toast. Purtlebaugh's door is open and the fan on the ceiling whirls slowly, but the lights aren't on yet. It's not really Purtlebaugh's anymore since Iggie died. But we all still call it that and their name is still up on the sign. The water fountain is bubbling and the water's icy cold. I drink big gulps, tasting the sweet smell of wet copper pennies it has.

I go over the railroad tracks past the drugstore. A light is on in back where Mr. Applegate's probably packing up pills in white paper envelopes. I picture Mom at home making her coffee and taking one last look around the house. What if she leaves without me? I'll crouch behind the stack of boxes at the back of the drugstore, watch her drive up and down West Jackson Street, hanging her head out the window looking for me. Eventually she'll take off without me, and I'll go and live with Marvella.

The library's dark. I press my face up against the plate-glass window. There's the globe on Miss Fippin's desk where she stamps your books with her special pencil. From the day I got my library card, I was planning to read every single book in the whole place. I figured I'd start at one end and read and read till I got through them all. Then I'd know everything there is to know. But now I'll never get to do that. "There's libraries in Massachusetts," Mom says. "*Real* libraries. Fancy places. Not dumps with linoleum floors. Not a library the size of a beauty parlor."

I cross the street so I won't have to walk past Molly's Bakery, then I cross back so I can walk in front of the old bowling alley instead of Bisbee's Funeral Parlor.

Mr. Bisbee said the old man was in such bad shape he couldn't fix him up so we could have one last look at him. The casket had to be closed. He stuck a flag over it and that was that. Even sitting there at his funeral with Uncle Cleon bawling his eyes out and Mr. Bisbee talking about how God takes the weak, I couldn't picture the old man underneath that flag. I kept expecting him to come down the aisle and ask what was going on. And still, I keep expecting him to drive by in his red convertible. I'll be out walking uptown and he'll toot at me and pull over, saying how that wasn't him after all and how come we sold the house before he got a chance to finish fixing it up?

I go up past the Backlash to the cemetery at the end of town. The gate is unlocked so I go on in. Gretchie wants to chase a big robin hopping across the grass with a worm in its mouth but I won't let her go. My feet make crunching sounds as I walk up the gravel road to the hill in back. I look at the old graves first, the ones that're so worn down you can't read the names anymore. Some of them have fallen and broken in half. They lie flat and white on the silky grass. The caretaker hardly ever comes up here to cut the grass or anything since it's shady under the trees and the grass doesn't grow too tall. From where I sit I can look over the cemetery and beyond it to Windfall waking up. I watch the train pass through, then the Myrtles unlock the Feed and Seed and set the brooms and rakes out in front. Some guy is fishing in the reservoir from the bridge with a rod and reel, tossing his hook down into the water, then reeling it in again, empty. I start down the rows between the gravestones. Iggie and Maudie Purtlebaugh have a big grey polished one. Above their names, it says IN LOV- ING MEMORY and there's a white heart around it. A dried-up chrysanthemum plant wrapped in silver paper is tipped over beside it.

I walk and walk and I know I'm heading for the old man's grave but I take my time. I haven't been here since the funeral when we all stood by the hole in the ground. Mr. Bisbee, dressed in his black suit, read from the Bible. It was drizzling out and the air smelled like a freshly plowed field. Mr. Bisbee folded up the flag this special way and handed it to Mom. She tucked it under her arm. As they lowered the casket into the ground, Mom was supposed to toss some dirt onto it but she turned and walked away instead. Mr. Bisbee looked at me and Abbie like he was waiting for us to do it. The Merchant's face was bright pink. We all looked down at the polished wood casket at the bottom of the deep deep hole.

I'm crying and wiping my face with my arm and everything. I can't stop thinking about the last night. How the old man asked me to give him a kiss and I said no. I never once said no before. He was walking around the house, his skin all grey and hanging off of him like it belonged to somebody else. I was in the kitchen doing my homework and he put his hand on my shoulder. "How about a kiss for your old man?" he said. But I ran upstairs and he didn't come after me and now he's dead and I didn't even get to say good-bye.

I hear this toot and it's Marvella.

"I seen you out walking. I figured you might want a ride home." She pushes open the door and I climb into the car.

"It's all right," she says, pleating the cloth on her dress between her fingers, then smoothing it out. "It's all right, doll baby." She's crying too, I can tell by the sound of her voice. She

267

reaches down the front of her dress and pulls out a hanky. It's the one with violets embroidered on it that I made for her birthday.

"I called you up. Your mother said you wasn't to home. I said I'd come out and find you and here you are. I figured you'd end up here."

Marvella's got her arm around me and I breathe in her baby powder and sweat and fresh bread smells. I can see the old man's gravestone right in front of us through the windshield. It's small and grey and flat so if you want to see whose it is, you have to be standing looking down at it to read his name and his birthday and the day he died. There are these numbers that show he was in the army and a little flag shoved into the ground next to a cardboard vase of dried-up Easter lilies. The ground is a damp brown mound. Next to him, there's a grave that's only marked by a white wooden cross like the kind I made my cat Snowball when she got hit by the school bus when I was in first grade. She wasn't smashed up or anything. She only had a tiny drop of blood on her nose. But when I found her, her body was cold and stiff. I wrapped her around my neck the way she always let me carry her. I brushed her white fur and opened a can of cat food. I kept waiting, thinking she was going to wake up. Sometimes I think dying is like sleeping and sleeping forever and nobody can wake you up. It's like having dreams and all. You still feel like yourself, the way you do when you know you're having a dream. But the thing is, when you're dead you can't get back to the place where everybody you know is at.

"I'll plant some bulbs come fall and put in some violets. Those're your favorites still, right? When you come back you'll see them blooming all over. The violets'll spread. It'll seem like all this happened a long long time ago. Things'll get better. You wait and see." Marvella pats my hand. "It's just what the good Lord wanted, honey. There's no other explanation. His ways ain't for us to question."

"I figured you'd run off and left me." Mom smiles at me in this fake way like she's trying to show Marvella she'd be sad if I really did that.

Marvella's got a plate of homemade muffins so Mom boils water for coffee and we all sit at the table and eat. She's got cupcakes and cookies for me in a brown paper sack. Mom gets up the second she finishes. She goes in her room and starts combing and fussing with her hair in front of her mirror.

"I've got a little something for you." Marvella's chest is rising and falling fast the way it does when she's nervous. She goes out to her car and comes back in and puts this white box with no lid on the table. "I fixed this up for you. It'll fit there in the car behind your seat. Your mom said she'd leave room for it."

Marvella knows how much I hate looking at presents when the person that gave it to me is right there, so she goes to the sink and rinses out the coffee cups. At first I'm afraid to look. I don't know what I want it to be. It's this blue bowl filled with tiny plants. There's a girl made out of china. She's got a yellow dress on and she's sitting on a wooden bench under a streetlamp that's made out of china too. The dirt's covered with moss so it looks like grass, and the ferns look like trees. A tiny little vase of paper flowers is at her feet. I feel like I used to when I was a little kid and I'd stand on the open pages of my Golden Books hoping I'd end up inside the picture I was looking down at so hard.

"Let's get this show on the road." Mom comes out of her room and claps. "Up and at 'em."

"I want to be sure I didn't leave anything upstairs."

"I checked already."

"But *I* didn't."

"You know I want to get an early start."

"Oh, it can't hurt to let her have one last look," Marvella says. I run upstairs before Mom can stop me. The mattress on my bed is flipped up. All the drawers are empty and hanging open. The closet's empty, too, except for the hangers jumbled together in a knot on the clothes rod. In the corner, I see the pink rubber doll-house baby Abbie lost years ago, half hidden in a clump of dust. I wipe the dust off and put her in my pocket.

I look around me at my room. I feel kind of the way I do when I'm learning a long poem by heart, and I want to get every word just right, so when I stand up in front of class, I'll be able to say it like I know what it means.

"We haven't got all day," Mom hollers up the stairs. "Let's get a move on."

* * *

Marvella follows us out of town. I look out the back window until I can't see the house anymore, and then till I can't see the oak tree in our backyard. When there is nothing but cornfields and the hot smell of the green corn plants in the sun, I look at Marvella. She has her blue-rimmed glasses on the end of her nose, and she's staring ahead, like she's concentrating real hard. When we all drove to the cemetery, Marvella was behind us then too. She had her lights on then even though it was the middle of the day. Mom's chewing gum and snapping it between her front teeth. She has on her yellow chiffon scarf and the ends blow in the breeze.

We drive past the Seventh-Day Adventists' revival tents set up like a circus. REPENT. JESUS SAVES ALL SINNERS, says a big billboard beside the road. When we get to the White River, Mom drives over the bridge and pulls over. Marvella pulls up behind us.

"Ain't you getting out, Ruth?"

"No reason to."

Marvella crooks her finger at me. "C'mon," she says. "I think you oughta see what the town did for your dad."

We walk back over the bridge and stand in the middle. I never stood on the bridge before. We'd only drive over it and I'd been under it plenty of times fishing with the old man. I get this feeling, standing in the middle, that I could fall through the metal grates if I'm not careful. I could float right down into the water.

I wonder when it is God comes to get you. Is it while you're on your way to dying or after you go through the whole thing and you're gone? God sent an angel for Shadrach, Meshach, and Abednego to protect them from getting burnt up when they got sent to that fiery furnace to die for disobeying the king. But they didn't die. I wonder if they did if they would've ridden up to heaven on the angel's back.

"See, right there it is." Marvella has her palm between my shoulders. She points down at the river till I see what she's pointing at, a big wreath of red, white, and blue flowers floating on the muddy brown water.

"The whole town chipped in. It would've meant a lot to Floyd."

I try not to think of the old man jumping into that water. I don't turn my head, but out of the corner of my eye I can see where the fire burnt the bushes. They're black and charred the way the ground got that time me and Penny burnt up the back field. "Just don't you ever forget how much he loved you," Marvella says.

"We got a thousand miles to go!" Mom hollers.

take your last look

G retchie stands on my lap with her front paws on the dashboard, her ears flapping in the wind. I stare out my window while we drive. We pass a farmhouse with a red bicycle thrown on the front yard, the wheel still spinning. A boy with the whitest hair I have ever seen waves at us. Mom flicks on the radio. "Big Girls Don't Cry" comes on.

"This is your song," Mom says. The wind whips the ends of her scarf across her mouth. Soon, much sooner than I thought, we're on the highway. I close my eyes and Gretchie curls up and tucks her nose between her front paws.

"Don't cry," Mom says. "Whatever you do, don't start bawling. It just makes you look ugly."

I pretend I'm sleeping and then I am, dreaming I'm in a car that won't stay on the road. It's flying, rising up like an airplane and skimming over the road. I climb out the window and lie spread-eagled on the top, trying to hold it down.

Mom's shaking me. "Wake up," she says. "This is it. Take your last look."

WELCOME TO OHIO, a sign says. NEW HOPE 30 MILES.

Even though we're not in Indiana anymore, it doesn't look that different. There are still cornfields as far as I can see. The cornfields turn to slag heaps in Pennsylvania. My face gets gritty and my hair feels like straw. When we stop at a gas station, I get Gretchie water from a red rubber hose. The water is boiling hot from the hose sitting out in the sun. The sun is so bright the road shimmers the way I hear it does in the desert, making people think there's a lake up ahead.

Later on, we stop for hamburgs and eat them in the car to

save time. When Mom says she can't drive another mile, we pull over to the side of the road and lock the car doors. I lie down in the backseat trying to sleep while the semis rush by so fast the car shakes. Gretchie shivers and makes little moaning sounds. Mom is up front, leaning against her window, resting her elbow on the steering wheel. She's got her bare feet propped up on the dashboard. When the headlights from the cars and trucks flash across her face, I feel like we are still moving, like the seat under me is rushing forward and there is no way I can stop it.

That's when it dawns on me. Maybe God is just like the reckless driver. You never know when He's going to come along. You never know when you might turn a corner and there He'll be, coming right at you with His blinding headlights.

The typeface used in this book is a version of Sabon, originally designed in the 1960s by Jan Tschichold (1902–1974) at the behest of a consortium of manufacturers of metal type. As one who began as an outspoken design revolutionary—calling for the elimination of serifs, scorning revivals of historic typefaces—Tschichold seemed an odd choice, but he met the challenge brilliantly: The typeface was to be based on the fonts of the sixteenth-century French typefounder Claude Garamond but five percent narrower; it had to be identical for three different processes, working around the quirks of each, such as linotype's inability to "kern" (allow one character into the space of another, the way the top of a lowercase *f* overhangs other letters). Aside from Sabon, named for a sixteenth-century French punchcutter to avoid problems of attribution to Garamond, Tschichold is best remembered as the designer of the Penguin paperbacks of the late 1940s.